I0695149

Whisk Me Under the Mistletoe

Mistletoe Falls Series, Book #1

Tara Baisden

Sterling Ridge Press LLC

Copyright

Whisk Me Under the Mistletoe © 2025 by Tara Baisden

All rights reserved. No part of this book may be reproduced, distributed, or transmitted in any form or by any means, including photocopying, recording, or other electronic or mechanical methods, without the prior written permission of the author, except in the case of brief quotations embodied in critical reviews and certain other noncommercial uses permitted by copyright law.

This is a work of fiction. Names, characters, places, and incidents either are the product of the author's imagination or are used fictitiously. Any resemblance to actual persons, living or dead, events, or locales is entirely coincidental.

Cover designed by Sterling Ridge Press LLC

Published by: Sterling Ridge Press, LLC www.sterlingridgepress.com

ISBN: 978-1-966093-36-7 Printed in the United States of America

First Edition: September 2025

For permissions, contact: tara@tarabaisden.com or visit www.tarabaisden.com

Dedication

To everyone who believes in the magic of second chances, small-town dreams, and love that grows as naturally as Christmas trees in mountain soil.

To the bakers who rise before dawn to create comfort one pastry at a time, the farmers who nurture beauty through every season, and the community volunteers who prove that the best celebrations happen when we work together.

And to anyone who has ever stood at a crossroads between what looks good on paper and what makes your heart sing—may you always choose the path that leads you home.

With mistletoe and magic,
Tara

Contents

Chapter 1

Claire Whitfield hummed softly as she removed the baking sheet of cinnamon rolls from the oven, their golden tops glistening with buttery perfection. Steam rose in lazy spirals, carrying the delicious scent of brown sugar, vanilla, and butter—the essence of Saturday morning magic that had drawn customers to the Sugarplum Bakery for over fifty years.

Then the grinding sound started.

Claire's stomach clenched as the middle oven's mechanical complaint cut through her contentment like a rusty saw. She set the heavy pan on the stainless steel cooling rack, her flour-dusted hands steady despite the worry creeping up her spine. The ancient Blodgett oven had been making that sound for the past few days, as if clearing its throat before delivering bad news.

"Come on, old girl," Claire murmured to the temperamental machine, patting its warm side the way she might comfort a cranky friend. "Just give me through the weekend, okay? I promise I'll call Jerry on Monday to give you a little TLC."

The commercial kitchen stretched nearly the length of the historic brick building, with three veteran ovens lined against the wall like faithful soldiers. Stainless steel prep stations positioned for maximum efficiency and enough space for the choreographed ballet of morning baking that Claire had perfected over her ten months as owner. Through the tall windows at the front of the kitchen area facing Mistletoe Lane, the town square lay quiet under last night's fresh dusting of snow. Replica gas lamps cast pools of golden light on sidewalks that would soon bustle with Saturday morning foot traffic.

She'd been working in the kitchen since five that morning and had already made dozens of assorted muffins and apple and blueberry turnovers and several trays of cinnamon rolls. The familiar routine grounded her—industrial mixers whirring, ovens baking delectable baked goods, and the gradual transformation of simple ingredients into something that would make people smile and forget their troubles for a few precious moments.

The grinding sound returned, sharper this time, like metal teeth chewing on something they shouldn't. Claire winced as she opened the oven door to check on her latest creations, immediately greeted by a wave of fragrant heat that carried hints of butter and spice. The cinnamon rolls looked magnificent—perfect golden spirals with ribbons of cinnamon and brown sugar glistening between each tender layer. Below them, the apple turnovers had achieved that ideal shade of burnished gold, their flaky pastry shells crackling softly as they cooled, with sweet cinnamon-spiced filling peeking temptingly through the delicate slits she'd cut in each one.

"You sound like my dad's old pickup truck," she told the oven with a wry smile, the kind of one-sided conversation that kept her company during the quiet pre-dawn hours. "All growl and complaint, but you keep running when it matters."

The kitchen doors swung open with a familiar whoosh, bringing Joyce Dodson's cheerful voice.

"Morning, honey," Joyce called, already reaching for her apron hanging on the wooden peg beside the door. At fifty-four, she moved through the bakery with the confidence of someone who'd spent twenty years learning every corner of the operation—first as Grandma Mae Whitfield's right hand, now as Claire's invaluable partner in keeping Sugarplum Bakery running like clockwork. Her salt-and-pepper hair was pulled back in a practical bun, and her warm brown eyes immediately assessed the morning's progress with a practiced gaze that could spot trouble from across the room.

"That middle oven serenading you again?" Joyce asked, tying her apron strings with quick, efficient movements while the coffee maker hissed and gurgled in the background.

"It's got strong opinions this morning," Claire replied, closing the oven door with perhaps more force than necessary. The satisfying thunk echoed through the kitchen. "But look at these turnovers—absolutely gorgeous. I'm choosing to focus on the positives this morning."

Joyce's knowing look suggested she wasn't entirely buying Claire's determined optimism, but she'd worked with Whitfield women long enough to recognize their stubborn streak when she saw it. Instead of pushing, she poured herself a steaming mug of coffee.

"Smells like pure heaven in here," Joyce said, breathing deeply of the mingled scents of yeast, cinnamon, and vanilla.

The kitchen doors burst open again, bringing a whirlwind of infectious energy as Melanie Tate practically bounced through the entrance, followed by the steadier, more measured presence of Carol Fisher. At twenty-nine, Melanie vibrated with perpetual enthusiasm. Carol, steady and unflappable at thirty-nine, rolled up her sleeves and surveyed the day's tasks with the calm efficiency of someone who approached baking like a well-orchestrated military operation.

"Please tell me you made extra sugar cookies last night," Melanie said, bouncing on her toes while pulling her hair back more securely. "Mrs. Hillman called yesterday in full panic mode about her book club order, and you know how those ladies get when they can't have their absolute favorite sweets for their monthly meeting."

"Three dozen extras, ready for decorating," Claire confirmed, nodding toward the sheet pans nestled inside the glass-front holding cabinet like treasure waiting to be revealed. "I thought we could decorate them in autumn colors for the holiday season."

"Smart thinking," Carol said, washing her hands at the large prep sink. "Speaking of holiday seasons, the tree lighting ceremony is coming up fast. Hot chocolate booth again this year?"

The question made Claire pause; the Christmas season was coming soon. The bakery's busiest and most profitable time—loomed just around the corner like a wonderful, overwhelming storm. The tree-lighting ceremony took place the day after Thanksgiving and officially kicked off Mistletoe Falls' holiday tourism season. Sugarplum Bakery had traditionally provided warm beverages for the thousands of visitors who gathered in the town square to watch the massive tree burst into light.

"I'll call the town event coordinator later today," Claire said, mentally calculating both the opportunity and the logistics while adding another item to her already substantial to-do list. "This will be my first Christmas season as owner, so I want to make sure I understand all the expectations. But I'm thinking we could expand beyond just hot chocolate—maybe add coffee and a selection of holiday cookies."

"Ooh, ambitious and brilliant," Melanie said with approval, clapping her hands together like an excited child. "We could make those adorable Christmas tree sugar cookies that look like little works of art, and maybe some of your incredible snickerdoodles that practically melt in your mouth."

"Your grandma always kept it simple but special," Joyce offered gently, her tone carrying the wisdom of someone who'd watched Mae navigate countless holiday seasons. "Though she mentioned more than once that she wished she'd thought to add coffee to the mix."

Claire smiled. Grandma Mae had been full of ideas for improving the bakery, always planning the next seasonal display or menu addition with the enthusiasm of someone who genuinely loved what she did. It was one of the things Claire treasured most about running Sugarplum now—she could honor the traditions Mae had established while adding her own creative touches and innovations.

The middle oven interrupted her thoughts with another grinding complaint, like an old dog growling in its sleep.

"Maybe we should call Jerry," Melanie suggested, referring to the appliance repair specialist that serviced the area's restaurants. "He might be able to work some of his magic and—"

"It's fine for now," Claire interrupted, then immediately softened her tone when she saw the concerned looks from her staff. "I mean, it's still baking everything perfectly. These old Blodgetts just have personality, right?"

What she didn't say was that Jerry Peterson's last invoice had been nearly three thousand dollars—money the bakery could technically afford, but the kind of expense that made her chest tight with worry. She'd been carefully managing the books for months now, balancing ingredient costs with equipment maintenance while maintaining the quality and generous portions that kept customers coming back week after week.

Carol and Joyce exchanged one of their wordless glances.

"You know," Joyce said carefully, keeping her tone casual, "Mae used to say that sometimes the smartest business decision was spending money before you had to, not after."

Claire nodded, knowing Joyce was absolutely right but not quite ready to surrender to the inevitable expense. Every dollar spent on repairs was a dollar not available for the new ovens she'd been dreaming about or the kitchen renovation that was desperately needed.

"Let me get through this weekend," she said, "and then I'll make the call first thing Monday morning."

Needing to shift focus to something more pleasant, Claire retrieved a cooled tray of iced cinnamon rolls and pushed through the swinging doors that separated the bustling kitchen from the customer area. The transition always felt magical—stepping from the organized chaos of the commercial kitchen into the welcoming embrace of what she considered the bakery's living room.

The dining and customer area was her absolute favorite part of Sugarplum Bakery—a spacious, inviting room with soaring twelve-foot ceilings, exposed brick walls painted in warm ivory that glowed from the overhead lighting, and enormous windows that stretched nearly floor to ceiling along the Mistletoe Lane frontage. During the day, those windows flooded the space with natural light that made every pastry in the display cases look like it belonged in a magazine.

Vintage glass display cases lined the front counter like huge, elegant jewelry boxes. Each one designed to showcase the bakery's offerings at their most tempting, while the customer seating area spread throughout the rest of the space in an eclectic mix of comfort and charm.

Mae had collected the furniture over the years with an artist's eye for pieces that told stories—painted farmhouse tables that could seat families, intimate two-tops perfect for quiet conversations, vintage café chairs with character, and a few cozy armchairs clustered around a coffee table near the windows where customers could settle in with a book and a latte. Nothing matched, but everything harmonized to create an atmosphere of comfortable, cozy elegance that made people want to linger and make this place part of their routine.

Arranging the baked goods in the display cases was one of Claire's favorite rituals each morning—the artistic presentation that transformed simple baked goods into an irresistible showcase. She arranged the cinnamon rolls in a perfect spiral within the curved glass case, the glossy cream cheese icing catching the warm amber light from the pendant fixtures above like edible jewels.

Mae had taught her that presentation mattered as much as flavor, that the few extra minutes spent making things beautiful paid dividends in customer satisfaction, word-of-mouth marketing, and personal pride. Even on mornings when equipment struggled and expenses loomed, Claire could create something lovely in these display cases—something that would brighten someone's day.

"I'll get the coffee station ready," Melanie said, emerging from the kitchen with a tray of fresh mugs. She moved to the elaborate coffee setup at the far end of the customer area—a large, gleaming coffee machine that was Claire's pride and joy, flanked by thermal carafes for regular and decaf, plus the special hazelnut blend that had become unexpectedly popular.

Claire continued arranging pastries while watching Melanie work, both women moving through their routines in comfortable synchronization. The morning light was just beginning to filter through the large front windows, gradually illuminating the cozy seating area.

Regular customers had claimed their favorite spots over the years, and Claire could picture exactly how the Saturday morning would unfold—Tuck Fleming's corner table positioned for maximum conversation and people-watching, the book club's round table near the windows where natural light made reading a pleasure, and the small two-top where elderly Mrs. Phelps sat every Saturday morning with her late husband's photograph propped carefully against the sugar dispenser.

"I love Saturday mornings," Claire said, stepping back to admire her display work so far. "There's something absolutely magical about getting everything ready and knowing all our regulars will trickle in soon, each with their own little routines and preferences."

"Mrs. Phelps will arrive at eight-thirty on the dot," Melanie said. "Earl Grey tea with just a splash of honey, and one oatmeal cookie that she'll make last the entire hour while she tells Frank all about her week."

Claire smiled, thinking of the widow who maintained her Saturday morning tradition with touching dedication. Frank had passed away just two weeks before her Grandma Mae had, leaving Mrs. Phelps to maintain their ritual alone, still ordering tea for two out of habit.

Customers like Mrs. Phelps were exactly why Claire had left her sophisticated Atlanta café job to return home when she inherited Sugarplum Bakery ten months ago. Grandma Mae had built something precious here—not just a business, but a genuine gathering place where people felt welcomed, valued, and cared for. The bakery wasn't just about selling pastries; it was about creating moments of comfort and connection, whether that was a child's excitement over their decorated birthday cookie or a widow's quiet ritual that helped her remember love instead of dwelling on loss.

Claire had spent the past months learning to balance honoring Mae's legacy while adding her own innovations and personal touches. She'd introduced new seasonal flavors, upgraded the coffee program with the purchase of a new machine, and started a weekly cookie decorating class for children that had become wildly popular. She even began experimenting with gluten-free options that had surprised her with their popularity. The regulars had embraced her changes with enthusiasm, and business had grown steadily under her owner-ship—something that filled her with pride and gratitude every single day.

The morning prep continued with the efficient teamwork Claire had carefully fostered among her staff. In the kitchen, Melanie hummed Christmas carols while arranging sugar cookies for later dec-orating, her energy infectious even at this early hour. Carol method-ically worked on fresh muffin batches with the precise movements of someone who treated baking like an exact science, measuring in-gredients with mathematical precision. Joyce mixed the sweet bread dough that would bake throughout the morning, her experienced hands working the mixture with a rhythm born of years of practice.

The kitchen filled with comfortable chatter—discussions about weekend plans, gentle teasing about Melanie's latest dating adven-tures, and the kind of simple conversation that developed among peo-ple who genuinely enjoyed working together. The heavy-duty mixers hummed as they whirled ingredients together, oven timers chimed their warnings, and the whole kitchen space vibrated with productive, purposeful energy.

By seven forty-five, the display cases in the dining area were full and gleamed with perfectly arranged baked goods that looked like edible art. The coffee station was primed for the morning rush with every mug spotless. Claire surveyed her domain with a mixture of deep pride and excited anticipation.

She smoothed her apron with its cheerful pattern of dancing cup-cakes—a gift from her sister Rachel that made her smile every time she wore it—and tucked a wayward strand of chocolate-brown hair behind her ear. Her reflection in the chrome surface of the coffee machine showed a woman who looked confident and content, even if she occasionally worried about oven repairs and monthly expenses. This was her place, her calling, and despite the challenges, she couldn't imagine being anywhere else.

Saturday mornings brought a steady stream of early risers eager for fresh pastries and unhurried conversation, tourists visiting Mistletoe Falls to shop and enjoy its charm, and locals who treated Sugarplum as their weekend living room. She was ready to greet each customer with the genuine warmth that had become her trademark—the kind of authentic welcome that kept people coming back week after week.

Whatever challenges lay ahead—equipment repairs, holiday preparations, or the general adventures of running a small business in a Christmas-themed tourist town—she'd continue the Sugarplum Bakery tradition here in Mistletoe Falls, without fail. Grandma Mae would be proud of how far she'd come, but more importantly, Claire was proud of herself.

Squaring her shoulders and summoning her brightest smile, she flipped the wooden sign on the front door from "Closed" to "Open" and unlocked the deadbolt, then stepped back to welcome Mistletoe Falls to another perfect Saturday morning filled with the promise of warm pastries, good coffee, and the kind of small-town charm that made people feel like they'd found exactly what they didn't know they were looking for.

Chapter 2

Gabe Mills ran his hand along the Fraser fir's branches, checking for the perfect needle density that would make some family's Christmas morning magical, while Baxter sat beside him with the patient dignity of a farm dog who took his responsibilities seriously. The tree stood eight feet tall with symmetrical growth that spoke of careful attention—pruning at precisely the right moments, fertilizing when the soil demanded it, and the kind of daily observation that separated exceptional Christmas trees from merely adequate ones.

From this vantage point on the gentle rise of the farm, Gabe could survey the full scope of his 200-acre operation. Neat rows of Christmas trees marched across rolling hills in perfect formation, each section devoted to different varieties that would soon welcome thousands of families searching for their perfect holiday centerpiece. Fraser firs dominated the northern slopes with their classic Christmas tree silhouettes, while Noble firs claimed the southern exposure, their blue-green needles catching the morning light like scattered jewels. Beyond them, Virginia pines filled the lower meadows in cheerful abundance, their more affordable price point making Christmas magic accessible to young families and budget-conscious customers.

The November morning air carried winter's gentle bite, clean and cold enough to make every breath visible, while the Tennessee mountains that surrounded his property wore fresh caps of snow that caught the early sunlight like scattered diamonds.

"What do you think, Baxter?" Gabe asked, stepping back to survey the tree to his left with the critical eye he'd inherited from three generations of Christmas tree farmers. His breath created small clouds in the crisp air as he spoke. "Premium quality or just pretty good?"

Baxter tilted his head, those mismatched eyes—one warm amber, one bright blue—studying the tree with an expression that suggested he was genuinely considering the question. After a moment of deliberation, the Border Collie mix wagged his tail twice and sat straighter, which Gabe had come to interpret as wholehearted approval.

"Premium it is," Gabe agreed, pulling out his phone to add the tree's location to his digital inventory system—one of many technological improvements he'd implemented since taking over the farm four years ago.

He loved this time of year on the farm—the weeks before Thanksgiving when anticipation built like pressure in a kettle, when every tree needed final evaluation, and the property required countless preparations for the holiday rush that would transform his quiet sanctuary into Tennessee's busiest Christmas tree destination. The work satisfied him in ways his Nashville accounting career never had, engaging both his business mind and his hands in the kind of productive harmony that made ten-hour workdays feel like a good choice rather than an obligation.

Unlike his sterile corporate office life back in Nashville with its artificial lighting and recycled air, here he could feel the seasons changing in his bones and enjoy the outdoors daily. He could read weather patterns in cloud formations and measure success not just in profit margins but in the joy he witnessed on children's faces when they found their family's perfect tree. Every Fraser fir, Noble fir, and Virginia pine represented months of careful cultivation, but more importantly, each would become the centerpiece of someone's most treasured holiday memories.

Baxter suddenly stood, ears perked toward the main road, his whole body vibrating with alert attention. The dog's superior hearing had detected something Gabe's human ears hadn't yet caught, but a moment later, the distinctive rumble of Frank Whitman's ancient Ford pickup became audible as it made its way up the drive that curved through the property's entrance.

"We've got company, Baxter," Gabe murmured, automatically straightening his red flannel shirt and running a hand through his dark hair. At thirty, he had the lean build of someone who earned his living through physical work, his hands showing the calluses and small scars that came from daily interaction with tools, machinery, and occasionally uncooperative evergreen branches. Not that Frank Whitman would judge anyone's appearance—his seventy-two-year-old neighbor had been visiting the Mills family farm for as long as Gabe could remember, treating the property like an extension of his own backyard and Gabe like the grandson he'd never had.

The blue pickup truck appeared around the bend in the drive, its paint faded to the soft patina that came from decades of Tennessee weather. Frank parked near the main barn—a restored structure that housed equipment and served as the farm's operational headquarters—emerging from the cab with the careful movements of a man whose joints reminded him daily of seven decades of mountain living but whose smile remained as bright as summer sunshine.

"Morning, Gabe," Frank called, his voice carrying easily across the crisp air. "Rose sent me over with something she thought you might enjoy."

Baxter trotted forward to greet their visitor, tail wagging with genuine enthusiasm while Frank scratched behind the dog's ears. Gabe approached, curious about whatever thoughtful gift Rose Whitman had prepared.

"She didn't need to do that," Gabe said, though he was already anticipating whatever homemade delicacy she had sent. Rose Whitman's kitchen produced miracles on a regular basis—preserves that captured summer sunshine in glass jars, bread that made store-bought versions seem like cardboard in comparison, and spiced holiday cookies that had achieved legendary status throughout Mistletoe Falls.

"Try telling that woman she doesn't need to take care of everyone within a five-mile radius," Frank replied with the fond exasperation of a man who'd spent fifty-four years learning to appreciate his wife's generous nature. He reached into his truck to retrieve a small paper bag. "She made apple butter yesterday and somehow decided you looked too thin when she saw you at Fletcher's Hardware on Tuesday."

The bag contained two mason jars of apple butter that glowed like liquid amber in the morning light, the kind of rich, cinnamon-spiced perfection that transformed ordinary toast into a celebration. Rose had tied each jar with a cheerful red ribbon and attached a handwritten note in her careful cursive: "For Gabe—Because everyone needs something sweet in their life. Love, Rose."

"I appreciate this," Gabe said. "Please tell her I said thank you and that she absolutely didn't need to do this."

"Oh, I'll tell her," Frank said with a knowing chuckle. "But that won't stop her from worrying about you. It's what she does—take care of people whether they ask for it or not. Been that way since the day I met her, and I suspect she'll be fussing over folks until her last breath."

The two men stood in the crisp mountain air, their breath creating small clouds that dissipated quickly in the gentle breeze. Gabe had always admired Frank's contentment with the simple pleasures in life—good coffee, honest work, a well-maintained truck, and a wife who still laughed at his jokes after decades of marriage.

"How's the season shaping up?" Frank asked, nodding toward the neat rows of Christmas trees that stretched across rolling hills like living sculptures, their varying heights creating a natural rhythm across the landscape. "Looks like you've got another bumper crop this year."

"Best trees I've grown yet," Gabe replied with quiet pride, surveying his domain with the satisfaction of someone who understood exactly what his efforts had accomplished. His gaze moved systematically across the different sections. "The Fraser firs are absolutely magnificent this year. The Noble firs on the south slope are displaying that beautiful blue-green color that customers love, and even the Virginia pines are looking better than I expected after that dry spell in August."

"Your granddaddy would be proud. Old Thomas Mills always said this land was meant for growing Christmas trees, but I don't think even he imagined what could be accomplished here."

The compliment settled warmly in Gabe's chest, validation from someone whose opinion carried the authority of decades watching the Mills family farm evolve through multiple generations. Frank had been Thomas Mills' neighbor and best friend. He's watched Gabe's father, Rick, expand the tree operation when he took over and now served witness to Gabe's own innovations and improvements.

"Sometimes I wonder what Grandpa would say about the expansions I've made," Gabe mused, leaning against the split-rail fence that bordered the main growing area. His hands rested comfortably on the wood—fence posts he'd installed himself using lumber milled from trees cleared during the property's expansion. "Grandpa was pretty traditional in his approach—grow good trees, cut them fresh, and send families home happy. I wonder if he'd think I've overcomplicated things with the gift shop and all the activities we offer now."

"Your granddaddy was a practical man," Frank replied thoughtfully. "He'd probably say that if creating a destination experience brings more families to appreciate these Christmas trees, then you're doing exactly what needs to be done."

Baxter settled between the two men, his alert gaze scanning the property with the vigilance of a security professional. His increased attentiveness suggested he understood that busy times approached, and he was already preparing mentally for the influx of families, children, and excitement that would soon fill their peaceful sanctuary.

"The Barretts stopped by last week to pre-order their Christmas tree," Gabe said. "They've been coming here for three years running, and Mrs. Barrett told me our trees last longer and hold their needles better than anything she's found before. She said their tree from last year was still looking fresh when they took it down after New Year's. That's the kind of reputation you can't buy with advertising."

"Word of mouth," Frank agreed with a decisive nod. "Best marketing in the world, especially for something as personal as Christmas trees. Families make memories around their tree—you're not just selling timber, you're selling the centerpiece for their most precious celebrations."

The observation resonated with the deeper purpose that drove Gabe's perfectionist approach to tree cultivation. Every Christmas tree that left his property would become the focal point of Christmas morning joy, the backdrop for family photographs, and the gathering place for gift exchanges and holiday traditions that children would remember for decades.

"That's undoubtedly what I love about this work," Gabe said. "When I lived in Nashville, I spent my days staring at computer screens, managing numbers that represented other people's decisions and priorities. Here, I'm creating something tangible that becomes part of families' most treasured memories."

Frank studied him with the keen perception of someone who'd learned to read character through decades of observing human nature, noting the genuine satisfaction in Gabe's voice and the way his shoulders relaxed when he talked about his work. "No regrets about leaving the corporate world?"

"None," Gabe replied without hesitation. "I make a good living, the work I do feels important, and I sleep better at night knowing I've accomplished something meaningful. Four years of farming has proven that leaving Nashville was one of the best decisions I ever made."

The satisfaction in his voice reflected not just professional success but personal fulfillment that had been missing during his corporate years.

"Rose and I were talking about you just yesterday. She mentioned that you always seem content, but she wonders if you get lonely out here by yourself."

The comment landed with unexpected weight, touching something Gabe typically kept buried.

"I've got Baxter," Gabe said, attempting lightness while scratching behind his companion's ears, noting how the dog leaned into the affection with complete trust. "He's the best conversation partner. Never interrupts, always agrees with my decisions, and he's an excellent judge of character."

Frank chuckled. "Dogs make good companions, no argument there. But they're not much for sharing Sunday dinners or helping you celebrate good news or talking through problems that keep you awake at night."

The gentle observation settled into the space between them like a seed finding fertile ground. Gabe couldn't deny the accuracy of Frank's assessment—evenings on the farm could stretch long and quiet, filled with the satisfaction of work well done but lacking the warmth of shared conversation or companionship.

"I suppose I've gotten comfortable with solitude," Gabe admitted. "After my last relationship ended, I chose not to date for a while."

"Amanda, wasn't it?" Frank asked. "The gal who didn't appreciate country living?"

Gabe winced slightly at the memory, feeling the familiar tightness in his chest that accompanied thoughts of his former girlfriend's dismissive attitude toward everything he valued. "She made it clear that farming was beneath her ambitions. Called it 'quaint but impractical' and suggested I was wasting my education and potential for something that would never provide the lifestyle she expected. When I told her I was leaving Nashville to take over the family farm, she broke up with me that same evening."

"Sounds like she did you a favor," Frank said with blunt honesty.

"Yeah, you could look at it that way," Gabe replied. "But it made me realize how different my priorities are from most women my age. I'm not interested in climbing corporate ladders or impressing people with expensive restaurants and a city lifestyle. I like getting my hands dirty, working with tools and growing things, and going to bed knowing I've accomplished something good and put in a hard day of work."

"Nothing wrong with that. But don't let one woman's shallow judgment convince you that all women share her values. Rose fell in love with me when I was a broke eighteen-year-old mechanic with grease under my fingernails and big dreams about opening my own shop. She saw potential where others saw problems, and she chose to build something with me rather than trying to change me into someone else."

The story of Frank and Rose's courtship had become legendary in Mistletoe Falls—how the banker's daughter who'd been expected to marry someone "suitable," had chosen the young mechanic over more financially secure prospects, how they'd built their life together through determination and mutual support, and how their marriage had weathered decades of challenges and changes while growing stronger rather than weaker.

"Fifty-four years next month," Frank continued with obvious pride. "Best decision either of us ever made was to get married. We knew we wanted to spend our lives together, and everything else became details we could work out."

"I watch you and Rose together," Gabe said quietly, thinking of the countless times he'd observed their interactions at community events, church gatherings, and chance encounters around town. "The way you still laugh at each other's jokes, how you work together on projects, and the way she lights up when you walk into a room. That's what I want—a relationship with someone who chooses to build a life with me rather than trying to convince me to become someone else."

"Then you need to get off this farm occasionally," Frank replied with gentle firmness. "Good women don't typically wander onto Christmas tree farms looking for romance. They're at community events, church functions, local businesses, and social gatherings where they can meet eligible men who aren't hiding behind their work."

"I don't hide," Gabe protested, though the words lacked conviction even as he spoke them. "I participate in community events, I volunteer for town projects when they need help, and I shop at local businesses regularly."

"Do you really participate?" Frank challenged with a knowing smile. "Or do you just show up, go through the motions, and then leave as quickly as possible? There's a difference between being present and being available, son."

"Christmas season brings plenty of opportunities to get out and meet new people," he continued. "I know the town council is constantly searching for volunteers to help with decorating and organizing events. Might be a chance to meet new people while doing something good for Mistletoe Falls."

Baxter wagged his tail, then trotted toward the main barn with the purposeful stride of a dog who'd decided morning socializing had concluded and work needed to resume.

"One more thing," Frank said, reaching into his jacket pocket to retrieve a small envelope. "Rose asked me to give you this invitation. We're having a few friends over for Sunday dinner this week, and we'd love to have you join us. Nothing fancy—just good conversation and the chance to enjoy a home-cooked meal with neighbors who care about you."

"I'd love to come," Gabe replied, accepting the envelope with genuine gratitude. "It's been too long since I've experienced one of Rose's Sunday dinners. Fair warning though—I might monopolize the conversation asking about her recipes. She's one of the finest cooks I know."

"She'd be delighted," Frank assured him as he climbed back into his pickup truck. "Rose loves sharing her recipes with people who appreciate good food. Just don't be surprised if she spends the entire meal asking about your romantic prospects and offering unsolicited advice about eligible women in town. She's a determined matchmaker when she sets her mind to it."

"I'll consider myself warned and prepared," Gabe replied with a smile. "Thanks for the apple butter, the invitation, and the conversation."

"Welcome. See ya Sunday, Gabe," Frank said, starting the engine with a rumble that echoed across the quiet property and sent a few birds fluttering from nearby trees.

As the pickup truck disappeared around the bend in the drive, leaving only the sound of the gentle breeze through the trees, Baxter returned from his barn inspection and sat beside Gabe. The dog's steady presence provided comfort, but Frank's words had planted seeds of possibility that couldn't be ignored.

Chapter 3

The brass bell above Sugarplum Bakery's hunter green door chimed its familiar welcome as Gabe stepped inside, the rich scent of cinnamon, vanilla, and buttery pastry wrapping around him like a warm embrace. He'd been here every Saturday for the past ten months—coffee, a cinnamon roll, a half-dozen muffins to take home—but the best part of the ritual was the woman behind the counter.

Claire looked up from arranging an artful row of turnovers, a wayward strand of chocolate-brown hair catching the morning light. Her smile—warm, genuine, and entirely unguarded—hit him square in the chest, the way it always did, knocking loose the steady rhythm of his thoughts. For a man who could negotiate contracts without breaking a sweat, it was downright humbling how quickly she could undo him with one look.

"Morning, Gabe," she said. "Let me guess—coffee with a splash of cream, a cinnamon roll warmed up, and a half-dozen muffin variety pack?"

"You know me too well," he said, returning her smile, then cleared his throat. "Though... I might, uh, switch things up today."

Her eyes sparkled with mischief. "Oh no, a rebel in my bakery. What kind of switch are we talking about?"

This was it—the perfect opening for the business proposal he'd been rehearsing. Mention the North Pole Trading Post. Outline the customer traffic projections. Suggest daily baked-good deliveries. Easy.

Except his tongue seemed to have staged a mutiny.

"Well, I... uh..."

Claire tilted her head, bakery box in hand. "Gabe?"

His pulse gave an unhelpful kick. Before he could stop himself, he blurted, "Would you go into business with me?"

The question hung there—too loud, too direct, and nowhere near as casual as he'd planned. A shift in the room's hum told him the Saturday regulars had tuned in.

Great. Just great.

"I'm sorry... what?"

He raked a hand through his hair, feeling for all the world like a kid trying to work up the nerve to ask the prettiest girl in school to the dance. "That came out wrong. Or maybe it came out right, but not... the way I meant it."

Her lips curved, amusement dancing in her eyes. "Why don't you try again?"

He drew a breath, willing his voice to steady. "Right. Okay. So—I've built a gift shop on my farm. The North Pole Trading Post. It opens the day after Thanksgiving, and I'd like Sugarplum Bakery to supply the baked goods. Cookies, muffins, pastries... whatever you think will work best."

Behind him, customers had given up any pretense of pretending not to eavesdrop, their attention focused on what was shaping up to be prime small-town entertainment.

"A gift shop," Claire repeated, nodding encouragingly while beginning to arrange muffins in a bakery box.

"The idea is to create more of a destination experience on my farm—families select their trees, warm up with hot chocolate, browse for Christmas gifts, and maybe grab some fresh baked goods."

"And you'd like Sugarplum to supply those baked goods."

"Yes."

Claire moved to the coffee station, filling a ceramic mug with the dark roast blend he preferred, her movements thoughtful as she processed his proposal. "How many customers typically visit the farm?"

"Last year we had just over four thousand families between Thanksgiving and Christmas Eve. This year, with the gift shop and some additional marketing, I'm expecting even higher numbers."

Claire whistled softly. "Four thousand families? Gabe, that's incredible exposure. I'd be crazy not to seriously consider this."

"The thing is," Gabe said, his nervousness returning as he approached the more personal aspect of his proposal, "I was hoping for daily morning deliveries. I know that might be complicated with your schedule, but I could always arrange pickup if—"

"Daily deliveries wouldn't be a problem," Claire interrupted, setting his coffee down with a smile that made his morning feel suddenly brighter. "I actually love getting out of the kitchen occasionally and making deliveries. Besides, I haven't been to your family's farm since I was probably seventeen. I'd love to see how it's changed. I remember my Grandma Mae being incredibly particular about Christmas trees.

They had to smell exactly like Christmas, look perfectly symmetrical, and measure precisely eight feet tall."

The image of Mae Whitfield's tree-shopping expeditions made Gabe smile. "Grandpa Thomas used to say that Mae had the best eye for quality trees of any customer he'd ever served. She could spot a gap in the branches from fifty yards away."

"She absolutely could," Claire laughed, the sound bright and genuine and doing interesting things to his pulse rate. "And she'd make sure everyone within hearing distance understood exactly why that particular flaw disqualified the entire tree. But once she found the right one, she'd praise it like she'd discovered buried treasure and tip whoever helped load it like they'd performed a miracle."

The grinding noise that had been plaguing Claire's temperamental oven suddenly escalated to a mechanical shriek that suggested something far more serious than a mechanical complaint.

Claire's face went pale. "Excuse me," she said, already moving toward the kitchen with quick, purposeful strides. "I need to—"

The grinding stopped abruptly, replaced by an ominous silence that somehow felt worse than the noise. Then came a different sound—a low electrical hum that didn't belong in any properly functioning appliance, followed by the unmistakable acrid smell of burning wires.

"Oh, that's not good," Claire muttered, pushing through the swinging doors while Gabe followed on instinct.

The commercial kitchen spread before them in its usual organized chaos—sheet pans cooling on metal racks, mixing bowls soaking in sudsy water, and the morning's baking evidence scattered across stainless-steel surfaces. But the middle oven commanded attention like a mechanical emergency, its digital display flickering erratically between impossible temperature readings while thin wisps of smoke drifted from the ventilation panels.

"That looks bad," Gabe said.

Claire approached the malfunctioning oven with the careful respect someone might show an unpredictable animal, pressing buttons on the control panel while the display continued its chaotic dance of random numbers. "The entire temperature control system just failed," she said, her voice tight with controlled frustration. "Look at this—it's showing everything from 100 to 700 degrees."

"That can't be good."

"Absolutely not," Claire replied, stepping back and crossing her arms.

Dropping to one knee, Gabe searched for the electrical plug, his hands moving with the efficiency of someone used to troubleshooting on the fly. He found it, tugged it free, and the humming noise cut off instantly. Rising again, he brushed his palms on his jeans. "What about calling Jerry Peterson? Maybe he could squeeze you in this afternoon."

Claire's laugh held no humor. "Jerry's normally booked solid for at least a week, assuming he can even find replacement parts for equipment this old. These Blodgetts were built in the eighties, and they're not exactly making new parts for them anymore."

"Equipment rental?" he suggested. "Something temporary until Jerry can evaluate the situation?"

"Expensive," Claire said, then seemed to shake herself out of her worry spiral. Her shoulders squared with visible determination, and when she looked at him, her expression had shifted to something approaching excitement. "Actually, you know what? This might be the perfect time for your business proposal. Additional revenue from your gift shop could help offset whatever this repair is going to cost me."

"Are you sure? This feels like a lot of pressure to add to an already stressful situation."

"Honestly, business decisions under pressure seem to be my specialty lately," Claire replied with a wry smile that didn't quite reach her eyes. "Besides, your idea sounds exactly like something Grandma Mae would have told me to grab with both hands and run with it."

"If you're sure, then let's talk specifics," Gabe said, leaning against one of the prep counters. "The gift shop has a great display space for your products, including refrigeration for anything that needs it. I'm thinking cookies available for sampling, with muffins, pastries, and other specialty items for purchase."

"Free samples are brilliant marketing," Claire said, her business mind fully engaged despite the crisis literally smoking behind them. "Once people taste the quality, they'll want to buy more and maybe visit the bakery in town."

They spent several minutes discussing simple logistics while the disabled oven cooled in the background.

"This is an exciting opportunity," she said finally, genuine excitement replacing the worry that had clouded her features. "You get amazing baked goods that enhance your customers' experience, and I get access to thousands of potential new customers."

"Plus, it gives me a legitimate excuse to see you every day during the Christmas season instead of just Saturday mornings."

The words slipped out before he could stop them, revealing more personal interest than he'd intended. Claire's cheeks flushed pink, but her smile suggested the admission wasn't unwelcome.

"Well," she said, busying herself with wiping an already-clean counter, "daily business meetings would certainly be more... efficient than weekly social visits."

The gentle teasing in her voice gave him hope that his slip hadn't derailed their professional discussion. "Should we make this official? I could come back this afternoon with a simple partnership agreement."

"I'd like that," Claire replied, glancing once more at the dark display screen of her defeated oven. "And Gabe? Thank you. The timing really couldn't be more perfect, even if your delivery method was a little unconventional."

"I promise to practice my business presentations before our next meeting," he said, earning a smile that made his morning feel suddenly brighter.

"Don't practice too much," Claire replied, her eyes sparkling with amusement. "There was something charming about your nervous honesty."

"I'll see you this afternoon," Gabe replied, pausing to meet her eyes directly. "And Claire? That oven situation will work out. Problems always seem impossible until they're solved, and then they just become stories about obstacles you overcame."

Her grateful smile followed him back into the customer area, where several regulars made no attempt to hide their interest in the proceedings. Gabe nodded politely to his unwitting audience, collected his baked goods and coffee, left payment on the counter, and headed for the door with considerably more spring in his step than when he'd arrived.

Chapter 4

Claire balanced a tray carefully as she maneuvered between the tables, gathering the afternoon's collection of ceramic mugs and crumb-scattered plates. The Saturday crowd had thinned to a comfortable handful of regulars—Mrs. Abbott working on her weekly word search puzzle with the determination of someone convinced that "seven-letter word for contentment" was definitely hiding in there somewhere, the Carter twins sharing a chocolate chip cookie with the careful precision that came from years of negotiating equal portions, and Mr. Jameson nursing his third cup of coffee while reading every word of the Mistletoe Falls Gazette for what had to be the second time.

The familiar rhythm of cleaning up the dining area soothed her nerves after the morning's oven crisis. Each table told the story of the day—sticky rings from children's hot chocolate that spoke of Saturday family traditions, scattered sugar packets from customers who preferred their coffee sweeter than standard, and the occasional forgotten reading glasses she'd learned to collect in a small wicker basket behind the counter labeled "Lost & Found."

The brass bell above the front door chimed its familiar welcome, and Claire looked up to see Gabe stepping inside, a manila folder tucked under one arm and an expression that hinted of the morning's endearing nervousness. He'd changed from his flannel work shirt into a clean button-down in soft blue that brought out the green flecks in his eyes.

"Perfect timing," Claire said, setting down her tray and smoothing her apron. "I just finished my table rounds. Coffee? I have a feeling we're going to need caffeine to get through all the details."

"Coffee sounds great," Gabe replied, his shoulders relaxing as he took in the cozy afternoon atmosphere. "I brought some ideas, but nothing carved in stone. Figured we should talk through what actually makes sense before putting anything official on paper."

Claire appreciated his approach immediately—collaborative instead of dictatorial, flexible instead of rigid. Too many business discussions from her Atlanta restaurant days had felt like negotiations between enemy forces.

"Dark roast, still okay?" she asked, moving toward the coffee station while Gabe selected a table near the windows where the late afternoon light would make document review easier and cast everything in the kind of golden glow that made even mundane business conversations feel special.

"Yes, that's fine. Your memory's impressive."

"It's not as hard as you'd think," Claire replied, filling two ceramic mugs. "Most people are creatures of habit, especially with comfort foods or beverages. Plus, remembering what makes someone happy feels like a small way to show I actually care about them as people, not just walking wallets."

She carried the mugs to their table, and Gabe automatically stood to pull out her chair.

"So," Claire said, settling across from him, "tell me about this North Pole Trading Post. The whole concept sounds fascinating."

Gabe opened his folder, revealing several pages covered with his neat handwriting and what appeared to be carefully sketched floor plans. "The building's about twelve hundred square feet, positioned right where families naturally flow from picking out their tree. The idea is they can warm up, browse for gifts, and hopefully grab some amazing baked goods without feeling like they're being pushed through a sales funnel."

He turned one sketch toward her, pointing to different sections with the kind of enthusiasm that made his whole posture shift forward. "This area's for Christmas ornaments and decorations, this section features locally made crafts, and this entire wall is designed specifically for food and beverage displays. I had commercial-grade refrigerated cases and warming units installed to keep everything at a perfect temperature."

Claire studied the drawings with growing excitement, impressed by the thoughtful layout and attention to customer flow. "Gabe, this is incredibly well planned. You've obviously put serious thought into creating a real experience, not just slapping up a gift counter as an afterthought."

"My business background is finally proving useful for something fun," Gabe said with a self-deprecating grin. "I spent enough years analyzing customer behavior and retail efficiency to understand what makes people want to linger and spend money. But the goal isn't manipulation—it's creating an environment where families genuinely enjoy being."

"And my baked goods would fit into this vision how?"

Gabe leaned forward, his enthusiasm clear in every gesture. "Here's what I'm picturing—we make it an experience. A plate of small cookie samples near the entrance. No pressure, no sales pitch—just an open invitation to taste the quality. They get a free treat, maybe linger a little longer, and before they know it, they're shopping."

"Free samples. I agree it would absolutely be needed in your shop. They taste, they linger, and they shop for gifts and baked goods. Plus, they'll probably end up visiting the bakery in town."

"Exactly! And it creates this welcoming atmosphere that says, 'We're not here to separate you from your money; we're here to make your day a little sweeter.' Literally."

"Did you just make a baking joke?"

"Oh, I've got plenty more where that came from. Fair warning—I might be a little half-baked when it comes to humor."

"Okay, that one was terrible," Claire said, still laughing. "But I'll give you points for commitment to the theme."

Their easy banter felt natural, comfortable in a way that surprised her. Business discussions didn't usually involve this much genuine laughter, but somehow Gabe had managed to make contract negotiations feel like hanging out with a friend who happened to have really good ideas.

"So realistically, how many people are we talking about on a busy day?" Claire asked, pulling her mind back to practical matters.

"Last year we averaged about two hundred families per day—lighter on weekdays, absolute chaos on weekends," Gabe explained, consulting one of his printed sheets. "So maybe ten dozen small cookies daily for samples, plus whatever makes sense for actual sales—muffins, pastries, seasonal specialties, whatever you're excited about making."

"Ten dozen small cookies," Claire repeated, her baker's brain automatically running through ingredient calculations and prep time.

"Totally manageable, especially if I batch-prepare and freeze extras. For sales items, I could rotate based on what I'm already making for the bakery, maybe test some new seasonal things."

"That's where I was hoping you'd use complete creative freedom."

"Complete creative freedom?"

"I want you to make whatever excites you," he explained, meeting her gaze directly with an earnestness that made her stomach flutter unexpectedly. "New recipe you want to test? Bring it. Seasonal ingredients inspire something special? Go for it. Think my customers would love something unique? Then do it. I trust your judgment completely."

Claire stared at him momentarily speechless. Every supplier relationship from her Atlanta days had involved detailed contracts, predetermined specifications, and approval processes for any deviation from the plan. The idea of a business partner actually encouraging experimentation and trusting her professional judgment felt almost too good to be true.

"You're serious about the creative freedom part?" she asked carefully. "No predetermined menus, no approval committees, no 'let's run this by management' nonsense?"

"Completely serious. Look, you're the expert here, not me. You understand flavors, seasonal preferences, and what makes people happy through food—why would I want to limit your expertise with my ignorance?"

The simple logic of his statement hit Claire with unexpected force. She'd spent years working for people who micromanaged every aspect of kitchen operations despite having no culinary training themselves, enduring endless meetings where bean counters made menu decisions based on cost analysis rather than whether something actually tasted good.

"That's... refreshing. Most partnerships I've experienced involved a lot more control and a lot less trust."

"Then you've been working with fools," Gabe replied bluntly. "Good partnerships should be about playing to everyone's strengths. You're brilliant at creating things that make people happy through food. I'm decent at creating spaces where people want to spend time and money. Seems like we'd make a pretty good team."

Claire lifted her coffee mug to hide the pleased smile that threatened to take over her entire face. He'd just called her brilliant, which was doing interesting things to her pulse rate.

"Okay, so pricing," she said, steering toward safer practical territory. "What kind of structure were you thinking?"

"I was hoping you'd tell me what's fair," Gabe said, pulling out another sheet covered with neat columns of numbers. "I researched what similar operations pay for baked goods, but I'd rather base our deal on what's actually reasonable for the quality and quantity you're willing to provide."

He slid the paper across the table, his fingers briefly brushing hers as she reached for it—a contact so fleeting she might have imagined it, except for the little spark of awareness that shot up her arm.

"These are wholesale prices for mass-produced stuff; these are retail prices at tourist traps; and these are my estimates for what premium, locally made items should actually cost."

Claire studied the numbers, impressed with his thoroughness. The wholesale prices reflected rock-bottom costs for items made with cheap ingredients and shipped from industrial facilities. The retail prices showed what tourists typically paid for convenience rather than quality. But his estimates for premium local goods showed a real understanding of value that went beyond simple math.

"Your research is spot-on," she said. "These premium estimates match exactly what I'd charge for the same items at the bakery."

"Perfect. Then let's use those as our baseline—you price everything at your normal retail rates, I handle all the customer transactions, and we split revenue seventy-thirty in your favor."

"Seventy-thirty?" Claire repeated, certain she'd misheard. "That seems incredibly generous for someone providing the location, equipment, and sales service."

"You're providing a product people want that takes time to create," Gabe pointed out reasonably. "Plus daily delivery, plus creative expertise, plus the reputation and quality that'll make customers excited to buy. If anything, I should probably offer you eighty-twenty."

"Absolutely not," Claire said quickly. "Seventy-thirty is more than fair—assuming you're really sincere and comfortable with those numbers business-wise."

"More than comfortable. I'm hoping this partnership brings new families to the farm who might not have visited otherwise, and I'm betting your baked goods will make people stay longer and browse more and also visit your bakery. I suggest that we both place advertising materials in each other's businesses as well... it's just good marketing."

Claire leaned back in her chair, studying the man across from her with growing appreciation and, if she was honest, attraction. Every aspect of their discussion had revealed character traits she found professionally impressive and personally compelling—fairness, intelligence, trust in others' expertise, and collaborative problem-solving that prioritized mutual success.

"Daily delivery logistics," she said, consulting her mental schedule. "I assume early morning before you open?"

"That would be ideal. We usually open at ten during the week and at nine on the weekends during the season, so anytime before then works. Though I don't want to create an impossible burden on your schedule."

"No worries. Morning deliveries sound perfect. I'd love an excuse to get out and take a scheduled break every day."

Something shifted in Gabe's expression—a subtle intensification that made Claire suddenly hyperaware of him.

"The farm's beautiful that time of morning, especially during the Christmas season when everything's decorated and magical. Peaceful, but in the best possible way."

"Peaceful sounds amazing after the chaos of morning baking," Claire replied, then felt heat rise in her cheeks. "I mean, from a business perspective. Getting out of the kitchen will be a nice change of routine."

They spent the next twenty minutes working through practical details—seasonal product variations, payment schedules, weather contingencies, and backup plans for equipment failures. Throughout the discussion, Claire found herself increasingly impressed with Gabe's thoughtful questions and responses.

"I think we've covered everything major," she said finally, reviewing the notes she'd scribbled on her notepad. "This feels like the start of something really good for both of us business-wise."

"I hope it's the start of something good in other ways too."

Claire nodded. The possibilities sent a little thrill through her that she tried to dismiss.

"So when do we make this official?" She asked, focusing on safer practical matters.

"How about Monday morning?" Gabe suggested, gathering his papers. "You could come out to the farm, see the Trading Post setup in person, and get a feel for how your products might work in the space.

Then if everything looks good, we can sign a simple contract and start planning for opening day."

"Monday morning sounds perfect," Claire agreed, already anticipating the visit with more excitement than seemed strictly professional. "What time works for your schedule?"

"How about ten-thirty?" Gabe proposed.

"Ten-thirty's perfect," Claire confirmed, mentally rearranging her Monday routine. "I'll bring some sample items so you can see how they look in your displays."

"That sounds great," Gabe said, standing and extending his hand. "I'm really looking forward to working with you, Claire."

His hand enveloped hers with warmth and gentle strength. What should have been a brief professional handshake lingered just a moment longer than strictly necessary, long enough for Claire to notice the way his thumb brushed across her knuckles, long enough for her to feel the flutter of awareness that suggested this partnership might develop in directions that had nothing to do with baked goods.

"I'm looking forward to it too," she replied, meaning the words more completely than she'd expected. "I haven't seen your family's farm in years, and I remember it being magical. I can't wait to see how it's evolved."

"It's definitely grown in the last few years since I've taken over the farm. I think you'll be impressed with what we've built. At least, I really hope you will be."

"I'm sure I will be," Claire assured him, touched by the hint of uncertainty in his voice that suggested her opinion mattered to him beyond simple business considerations.

After Gabe left, Claire watched through the window as his pickup truck disappeared down Mistletoe Lane. The partnership they'd just negotiated felt like considerably more than a simple business arrangement.

For the first time since returning to Mistletoe Falls, Claire found herself genuinely excited about something that had nothing to do with honoring Mae's memory or proving her worthiness as the bakery's successor.

Monday morning couldn't arrive soon enough.

Chapter 5

Claire guided her SUV around another gentle curve of the mountain road, humming along with the radio as the familiar landscape of her childhood slowly transformed before her eyes. The sample boxes on the passenger seat—carefully packed with an assortment of her best cookies, muffins, and seasonal pastries—shifted slightly with each turn, their contents secured with tissue paper and tied with Sugarplum's signature ribbon.

The wooden sign for Mistletoe Christmas Tree Farm appeared ahead, far more elaborate than she remembered from childhood visits. Carved evergreen branches framed elegant script lettering, while small spotlights waited to illuminate the entrance after dark. But nothing—absolutely nothing—had prepared her for the view that unfolded as she turned onto the property's main drive.

"Holy cow," Claire breathed, pressing the brake pedal as she took in the transformation before her.

Professional wooden signage welcomed visitors with hand-carved lettering that announced "Mistletoe Christmas Tree Farm - Creating

Magical Memories Since 1924," surrounded by carefully maintained landscaping that showcased native mountain plants. Stone pillars flanked the entrance, their surfaces incorporating natural fieldstone that complemented the mountain setting while establishing an immediate sense of quality and permanence that belonged on a magazine spread.

The Christmas tree farm of her childhood memories—a charming but modest operation with neat rows of trees and a simple checkout shed—had grown into something that belonged on the cover of a magazine. The drive curved gracefully through meticulously landscaped grounds, where mature evergreens created natural boundaries between different areas of activity.

To her left, thousands of Christmas trees marched across gently rolling hills in perfect formation, their varying heights creating a natural rhythm across the landscape that spoke of careful planning and years of patient cultivation. Fraser firs dominated the nearer slopes with their classic Christmas tree silhouettes, while Noble firs and Virginia pines extended toward the tree line in neat sections that suggested serious agricultural expertise and attention to customer preferences.

But it was the infrastructure that truly made her jaw drop. Multiple barn structures, painted in deep barn red or forest green with cream trim, dotted the property at strategic locations like pieces of a perfectly planned puzzle. A covered pavilion near a pond reflected the morning sunlight off its metal roof, while paved pathways meandered between different activity areas.

Claire parked near the main barn, a beautifully restored structure that had been expanded significantly since her childhood visits. The building maintained its agricultural authenticity while clearly housing sophisticated modern operations, complete with loading docks and professional signage. She sat in her car for a moment, genuinely awed by the scale and beauty of what surrounded her.

"Okay, Mistletoe Falls," she said aloud to no one, "when did we get a Christmas tree resort in our backyard?"

A sharp bark echoed across the morning air, and Claire looked over to see a medium-sized dog bounding toward her car with the enthusiasm of a one-dog welcoming committee. The Border Collie mix sported a gorgeous coat of golden-brown and white markings, mismatched eyes—one warm amber, one bright blue—that gave him a distinctly roguish appearance, and a tail that wagged with such vigor his entire back end wiggled in harmony.

She opened her car door cautiously, unsure of the dog's temperament despite his friendly appearance. The dog immediately planted himself directly near her door with the kind of focused attention that suggested she'd just become the most fascinating thing in his universe.

"Well, hello there, handsome," Claire said, extending her hand for the customary sniff inspection.

Instead of the cautious investigation she'd expected, the dog gently rested his head on her palm, those mismatched eyes gazing up at her with what could only be described as absolute adoration. When she scratched behind his ear with her free hand, he leaned into the attention with a soft sigh of contentment that seemed to show she'd passed some crucial test she hadn't known she was taking.

"Baxter! What's gotten into you, boy?"

Claire looked up to see Gabe approaching, his expression shifting from mild concern to something approaching amazement as he took in the scene before him. He wore dark jeans that showed honest wear, a forest green flannel shirt, and work boots that bore evidence of farm labor. His dark hair caught the morning light, and his sleeves were rolled up, revealing muscular forearms that spoke of physical work.

"I honestly don't understand this," Gabe said, stopping several feet away with the air of someone witnessing a minor miracle. "Baxter's friendly with people, sure, but he's never... he doesn't usually..."

"What?" Claire asked, continuing to pet the dog, who seemed determined to maintain constant physical contact with her hand. "Is something wrong? Should I not be petting him?"

"No, no, it's fine. It's just—he rarely chooses people like this," Gabe explained, his voice carrying genuine wonder. "Baxter's polite with strangers, tolerates customers well, and loves attention from kids. But he's never just... claimed someone as his person before except for me. That's what he's doing right now—officially claiming you."

As if to emphasize Gabe's point, Baxter shifted position to sit directly beside Claire's legs, leaning his considerable weight against her while maintaining that steady, adoring gaze upward. The gesture felt both protective and possessive, as if the dog had decided she belonged in his pack and intended to make that relationship permanent.

"Maybe he just likes the smell of the bakery that probably follows me everywhere," Claire suggested with a laugh.

"Trust me, Baxter encounters plenty of food smells around here. Several of my employees always carry treats in their pockets for him. This is entirely different."

"Well, I've always had a way with animals. Maybe he just recognizes a kindred spirit."

"If that's the case, you should feel very honored," Gabe said, his smile transforming his entire face. "Baxter's got notoriously high standards when it comes to people."

Claire gestured toward the impressive landscape surrounding them. "Gabe, this place is absolutely incredible. This is like a Christmas theme park. In the best possible way."

"Four years of constant improvements and probably too much caffeine," he replied with the kind of self-deprecating humor she was beginning to recognize as characteristic. "Though I'll admit, I might have gotten a little carried away with the whole 'destination experience' concept."

"Carried away? This looks like something from a tourism brochure. 'Come experience the magic of Tennessee Christmas traditions.' How many acres are we talking about here?"

"Just over two hundred now," Gabe said, beginning to walk toward the barn entrance while Baxter trotted beside Claire with obvious contentment, occasionally looking up at her as if making sure she wasn't planning to disappear. "Granddad started with about sixty acres back in the day. Dad expanded to around one-fifty. I've added bits and pieces since I took over."

"Bits and pieces," Claire repeated with obvious amusement, pausing to take in the full scope of his achievement. Her gaze traveled across rolling hills covered with Christmas trees in various stages of growth, from saplings only a few feet tall to magnificent specimens that had to be twelve feet tall. "Gabe, how do you manage all of this without losing your mind?"

"Very carefully, with lots of help from good employees, and a detailed spreadsheet for everything," he replied with a grin that made her chest flutter. "Also, Baxter here is an excellent supervisor. He keeps me honest about taking breaks and not working twelve-hour days continually."

As if understanding the compliment, Baxter wagged his tail but remained firmly positioned beside Claire.

"Come on, let me show you a few things," Gabe said, walking through the barn's wide doors into a spacious interior that managed to combine rustic charm with modern efficiency in a way that made Claire's organizational heart sing.

Professional-grade equipment lined one wall—chainsaws, tree-netting machines, and specialized transportation tools that spoke to serious agricultural operations. But the space also featured comfortable seating areas where families could wait during busy times, along with educational displays that taught visitors about tree varieties and sustainable farming practices without being preachy or boring.

"We process thousands of trees each season," Gabe explained, running his hand along a specialized machine that wrapped trees in protective netting with mechanical precision. "Each one's hand-selected either by my crew or the customer themselves, freshly cut, and properly prepared for transport."

"Thousands of trees," Claire repeated, her respect for his operation growing with each new detail she absorbed. "This isn't just a family farm anymore—it's a major agricultural business."

"It's still family at heart," Gabe said. "Come on, let me show you the parts that are pure fun."

They walked toward another barn, this one alive with the sounds of various animal noises—gentle lowing, soft bleating, and what sounded suspiciously like the contented grunting of very happy pigs.

"Let me guess," Claire said with a grin, "a petting zoo?"

"Yep, I added it two years ago when I realized how many families were bringing small children. Just one of those extra things I added to create a whole memorable experience for those that shop with us."

The interior of the animal barn revealed a carefully designed space that accommodated both animal welfare and family entertainment without feeling chaotic or overwhelming. Miniature horses, goats, sheep, miniature pigs, and rabbits occupied spacious, spotlessly clean enclosures that allowed children to interact safely with friendly animals. The professional-quality fencing and gates suggested serious attention to safety regulations, while the animals themselves appeared healthy, well-socialized, and accustomed to gentle human contact.

"This is absolutely adorable," Claire said as a particularly friendly goat poked its head between the fence railings and gazed at her with hopeful brown eyes. "These animals are clearly loved and incredibly well-cared for."

"Jim Parker manages all our livestock—he's got thirty years of experience with farm animals and infinite patience with excited children," Gabe explained.

"Gabe, is this the famous Claire from Sugarplum Bakery?"

They turned to see a young woman approaching from the far end of the barn, her bright smile and confident stride suggesting she belonged to the operation. She had blonde hair pulled back in a practical ponytail, paint-stained jeans that spoke of recent creative projects, and an energy that seemed to vibrate with enthusiasm.

"Claire, meet Brianna Kelly," Gabe said. "She's the creative genius behind our social media presence and the organizational mastermind behind the North Pole Trading Post. I'd be completely lost without her."

"And I'd be unemployed without his willingness to let me turn his gorgeous farm into Instagram gold," Brianna replied. "I am so thrilled to finally meet you! I've been stalking Sugarplum's Instagram account over the weekend, and its seasonal items look absolutely amazing. I have to come visit you soon."

"Please come by anytime," Claire said, warming immediately to Brianna's enthusiastic personality. "Though I have to say, what Gabe's created here on this farm is pretty Instagram-worthy itself."

"Right?" Brianna practically bounced with excitement. "Wait until you see the Trading Post."

The walk to the gift shop took them past additional areas Claire hadn't initially noticed—several fire pits surrounded by rustic log seating where families could gather, wagons for hayride tours around the property, and what appeared to be a small outdoor stage.

"Entertainment?" Claire asked, gesturing toward the stage area.

"Friday and Saturday nights during the month of December. Local musicians, storytellers, carolers, and sometimes even a magician or puppet show for the kids. Families can make an entire evening out of their tree selection—dinner in town first, then come here for live entertainment, tree selection under the stars with help from our additional lighting, and hot chocolate around the fire pit."

"You've literally thought of everything," Claire said, genuinely impressed. "Some families probably end up staying here for hours."

"That's the idea," Gabe replied with a grin. "I figured some people want efficiency—quick in and out with a perfect tree. Others want to make selecting their Christmas tree into a special family tradition and memory-making experience. We try to accommodate both preferences without making anyone feel rushed or bored."

The North Pole Trading Post sat at the natural convergence point where families would flow after completing their tree selection, positioned to catch customers when they were relaxed, happy, and in the mood to extend their magical farm experience. The building itself maintained the rustic aesthetic of the rest of the farm, deep barn red with cream trim and natural stone accents.

"Ready for the big reveal?" Brianna asked, her hand on the door handle and practically vibrating with anticipation. "Because I'm pretty sure this is going to blow your mind."

Claire nodded.

The interior of the Trading Post exceeded every assumption she'd had and then kept going. Professional retail design guided customers through carefully arranged displays of Christmas ornaments, locally made crafts, holiday decorations, and gift items that ranged from affordable children's souvenirs to high-end artisan pieces that probably cost more than her monthly grocery budget. The space felt warm and inviting despite its impressive scale, with lighting that showed merchandise to the best advantage and comfortable seating areas that encouraged customers to stay awhile rather than hurried transactions.

But it was the food service area that made Claire's breath catch in her throat.

"Gabe," she said, approaching the gleaming display cases and professional warming equipment positioned along one entire wall, "this is a mini commercial setup. You could run a legitimate café out of here."

"That's sort of the idea, just on a smaller, more specialized scale," he replied, and she could hear both pride and slight nervousness in his voice.

"We've got refrigerated cases for items that need to stay cool, warming displays for fresh pastries or other types of food, a premium coffee and hot cocoa station with all the bells and whistles, and a point-of-sale system that integrates with our main inventory management software," Brianna added, clearly proud of their technological sophistication. "Plus enough counter space for customer service without feeling cramped or rushed."

"The coffee and hot cocoa station alone probably cost a small fortune," Claire murmured, taking in the professional-grade machines and carefully arranged beverage service area that looked like it belonged in an upscale urban café.

"We wanted to offer something genuinely special," Gabe said, then paused and turned to face her directly. "But honestly, the real centerpiece of this whole area is going to be your baked goods. Everything else is just supporting players."

The sincerity in his voice, combined with the way he was looking at her—like her opinion was the most important thing in his world right now—made something warm and fluttery unfold in her chest.

"Fresh pastries here in the warming cases, cookies and grab-and-go items in the main refrigerated displays, and we're planning to put your business cards, bakery information, and any promotional materials you want right here where people can easily take them home," Brianna said.

"So what's the verdict?" Gabe asked. "Think this partnership is going to work?"

Claire looked around the impressive operation once more. "I think this partnership is going to exceed both our wildest expectations."

Gabe found himself standing straighter at her enthusiastic response, the last of his nervous tension finally easing.

"I can picture it all clearly in my mind; the social media opportunities will be absolutely amazing. Families sharing photos of their beautiful baked goods alongside their Christmas trees and posts about the complete magical experience they had here—that's the kind of authentic marketing you literally cannot buy," Brianna said.

They spent the next twenty minutes working through minor practical details. Throughout the discussion, Claire found herself increasingly impressed not just with the scale of what Gabe had built but with his thoughtful attention to customer experience and his genuine concern for making sure their partnership succeeded for both businesses.

Baxter, who had been patiently maintaining his self-appointed position as Claire's personal escort throughout the entire tour, suddenly perked up and trotted toward the front windows. A moment later, the rumble of a large vehicle approaching became audible to human ears.

"Expecting company?" Claire asked.

"Delivery truck," Brianna replied, checking her watch. "More Christmas inventory arriving right on schedule. You're about to witness how seriously we take logistics and organization around here."

Through the windows, Claire watched a substantial truck navigate the property's internal road system.

"We schedule deliveries year-round to avoid the absolute chaos of trying to stock everything during the busy season itself. Advance planning and organization make everything manageable instead of completely overwhelming," Gabe said.

"Smart business approach," Claire observed, thinking of her own occasional struggles with managing inventory during peak times. "Preparation really does make all the difference between smooth operations and crisis management."

"That's Gabe's corporate background showing through," Brianna said. "Most agricultural operations just wing it and hope for the best, but Gabe treats this like the sophisticated business it actually is."

Claire found herself studying Gabe, realizing that the man who seemed so comfortable with physical farm labor and straightforward conversation had obviously brought considerable analytical and planning skills to creating this operation.

"I should probably head back to the bakery," she said with genuine reluctance. "Jerry is supposed to look at my temperamental oven this afternoon, and I need to be there when he arrives."

"Of course," Gabe said. "But we're officially partners now? You're completely comfortable with everything we've discussed?"

"More than comfortable—I'm excited," Claire assured him, meaning the words more completely than simple business enthusiasm could explain. "Gabe, what you've built here is extraordinary, and I'm honestly honored to be part of it."

"The honor's entirely mine," Gabe replied with sincerity that made her cheeks warm.

They began walking back toward the parking area, Baxter maintaining his position beside Claire like a devoted escort who took his responsibilities seriously. The morning had transformed her understanding not just of the farm's scale and sophistication but of Gabe himself—the quiet Saturday morning customer had revealed depths of business acumen, creative vision, and genuine thoughtfulness she hadn't suspected before.

"Claire," Gabe said as they reached her SUV, "I want you to know how much I appreciate you taking a chance on this partnership. Having Sugarplum represented here means more to me than I can probably express—both personally and professionally."

"The feeling is absolutely mutual. I have a really good feeling about this whole venture."

Baxter chose that moment to lean into Claire's leg with such obvious affection that both humans had to laugh at his shameless attention-seeking behavior.

"I think someone's going to miss you," Gabe observed with amusement.

"Well, he won't have to wait long, just a few weeks," Claire said, giving the dog a final scratch behind the ears that made his tail wag with contentment. "I'll be back the day after Thanksgiving with fresh baked goods, ready to officially launch our partnership."

"We'll both be looking forward to it," Gabe said, opening the driver's side door of the SUV for her.

As she started the engine, her gaze fell on the sample boxes still sitting in her passenger seat.

"Oh, my gosh!" she gasped as she pushed the button to lower the driver's side window. "Gabe, I'm so sorry! I completely forgot—I brought samples!"

Gabe's eyebrows rose in surprise.

"I spent extra time this morning packing examples of cookies, muffins, and seasonal pastries—just a random assortment for you and your employees to taste test. I was so blown away when I pulled up by what you've built here that I completely forgot about these!"

"You brought samples?" Gabe asked, his face lighting up with genuine delight. "That's incredibly thoughtful of you."

"I can't believe I got so distracted by your amazing operation that I forgot that I brought them!"

Gabe's warm laugh made her embarrassment ease slightly. "We'll call it even because I forgot all about reviewing the contract with you."

"No worries, we have time between now and opening day for that."

"I agree... no worries. I'll make sure I share these samples with Brianna and the others that are working today," Gabe promised, his hands briefly brushing hers as he accepted the boxes. "Professional quality assessment, of course."

"Of course," Claire agreed.

Baxter sat at attention beside Gabe, both of them watching her with expressions that made leaving feel surprisingly difficult. She pushed the button to raise the lowered window and waved goodbye, noting how Gabe's genuine smile transformed his entire face.

The drive back down the mountain road provided time to process everything she'd experienced, though her thoughts kept circling back to details that had nothing to do with business logistics. The scope of Gabe's achievement impressed her professionally, but it was his obvious passion for creating meaningful experiences for families that appealed to her personally. He'd built something that honored tradition while embracing innovation, something that prioritized customer satisfaction over pure profit margins.

She'd been so focused on running her bakery that she'd missed really seeing the quietly accomplished man who'd been coming to her establishment every Saturday morning without fail.

This partnership he'd suggested would bring them together every single day during the Christmas season, creating opportunities for conversation and connection. The thought should have felt purely professional, but the flutter of anticipation in her chest suggested her interest in daily farm visits had very little to do with baked goods. It had everything to do with spending time with the man who'd created something truly magical in the Tennessee mountains.

By the time she reached the bakery, one thing had become obvious: daily visits to Mistletoe Christmas Tree Farm were going to be the highlight of her upcoming holiday season, and not just for business reasons.

Chapter 6

Claire secured the white bakery box with Sugarplum's signature ribbon, finishing it with a neat bow while Mrs. Hillman counted exact change from her coin purse with the deliberate pace of someone who treated each transaction as a social event worth savoring.

"Now, those blueberry muffins won't be too tart, will they?" Mrs. Hillman asked. "You know Mildred Patterson—that woman could find fault with chocolate cake at the pearly gates. Last week she told me those grocery store muffins she bought made her face pucker up like she'd been kissing a pickle for an hour."

Claire bit back a smile. "These are perfectly sweet, Mrs. Hillman. I use only the plumpest berries, and I add just enough sugar to make them sing. Mildred's going to love them so much she might actually smile."

"Well, that would be a Christmas miracle worth witnessing," Mrs. Hillman chuckled, then leaned closer conspiratorially. "Speaking of Christmas, I heard through the grapevine that you're partnering with

Gabe Mills out at the tree farm. Smart business move, honey. That boy's built something special out there."

Before Claire could respond, the brass bell above the door announced Jerry Peterson's arrival. He carried his weathered toolbox like a doctor making house calls. His patient expression had been earned through thirty years of coaxing life from reluctant appliances that preferred retirement to continued service.

"Afternoon, ladies," Jerry said, nodding politely while setting his toolbox beside the counter with a gentle thud. "Claire, that middle oven... again... my goodness. From what you described over the phone, it sounds like the temperature control board's finally decided to throw in the towel."

Claire's stomach performed a little flip. "How bad are we talking, Jerry? Scale of one to financial disaster?"

"Won't know for sure until I take a look, but those old units are like my ex-wife—temperamental, expensive, and they make a lot of noise when they're upset."

Mrs. Hillman snorted with laughter. "Jerry Peterson, you shouldn't speak ill of your ex-wife."

"You're right, Mrs. Hillman. That was unfair to the oven."

After Mrs. Hillman departed with her muffins and a final encouraging pat on Claire's arm—along with promises to report back on Mildred's reaction—Jerry hefted his toolbox with the resigned sigh of a man preparing for battle.

"Lead the way to the patient," he said. "Let's see what we're dealing with."

"Sadie," Claire called to her youngest employee, who was arranging napkin dispensers with the kind of attention to detail that suggested either perfectionism or procrastination from actual work, "could you handle the front while I'm in the kitchen with Jerry?"

Sadie Kirk looked up from her task, her dark hair escaping its ponytail in wispy tendrils that gave her a slightly disheveled charm. "Absolutely. Take your time—I've got everything under control out here. If anyone needs anything complicated, I'll just smile sweetly and come find you."

Claire pushed through the swinging doors into the commercial kitchen, immediately wrapped in the afternoon symphony of productive chaos. Joyce stood at the main prep station, portioning cookie dough while humming a holiday tune. Melanie worked at the decorating table with the focused intensity of an artist, applying delicate icing designs to sugar cookies while occasionally muttering things like, "Come on, you silly cookie, cooperate." Carol managed three different mixing bowls simultaneously, her movements so economical and precise she could have been conducting an orchestra.

"Ladies, our mechanical savior has arrived," Claire announced with theatrical flair.

"Thank the baking gods," Joyce said, looking up from her cookie dough with obvious relief.

Jerry approached the silent appliance with the careful assessment of a doctor examining a patient who'd been complaining of mysterious symptoms. He opened the oven door, peered inside with a small flashlight, and then began removing the front control panel with efficient movements.

"While Jerry performs surgery," Claire said, pulling a notepad from her apron pocket, "I wanted to talk about something exciting. I've officially partnered with Mistletoe Christmas Tree Farm to provide baked goods for their new gift shop."

"The Mills farm?" Melanie asked, pausing mid-decoration to look up with obvious excitement. "Oh my gosh, that place is absolutely magical! My whole family goes there every year, and each season it gets more amazing. Last year they had actual reindeer!"

"They were just regular deer with jingle bells," Carol corrected with deadpan precision.

"Don't ruin the magic, Carol," Melanie protested. "They looked like reindeer to me."

"Really?" Claire settled at the small desk where she kept recipe development notes. "I haven't been there since I was a teenager. I was honestly shocked at how much that farm has grown. It's like Gabe has built a Christmas wonderland right here in Mistletoe Falls."

"Gabe Mills," Joyce said with obvious approval, wiping her hands on her apron and moving closer to Claire's desk. "Now there's a man who knows what he's doing. I took my grandkids out there last year, and it was wonderful."

"Plus he's easy on the eyes," Melanie added with a grin, earning a sharp look from Joyce.

"Melanie Anne Tate," Joyce scolded in her best maternal voice.

"What? I'm just saying the man's attractive. It's an objective observation. Like saying the sky is blue or chocolate is delicious."

"He's a good man," Carol said simply, still mixing but clearly following the conversation. "Helps out folks who need it, doesn't make a big show of it. That counts for more than looks."

"He does seem really thoughtful. We spent quite a while this morning discussing our partnership, and he kept asking for my input instead of just telling me what he wanted," Claire said.

"Smart man knows when he's found an expert," Joyce said with satisfaction. "So what kinds of goodies are you planning to tempt his customers with?"

"That's what I wanted all of you to have input on," Claire replied, opening her notepad to a fresh page. "They have professional display cases and warming equipment, so we've got lots of options. I'm thinking bite-sized cookies for free sampling—"

"Free samples!" Melanie interrupted with the enthusiasm of someone who'd just discovered buried treasure. "That's brilliant!"

"So what varieties do you all think would work best for samples?" Claire asked.

"Sugar cookies!" Joyce and Melanie said simultaneously, then pointed at each other.

"Jinx!" Melanie declared. "But seriously, decorated Christmas ones. Kids go crazy for them."

"Gingerbread," Carol added, not looking up from her mixing. "Classic holiday flavor that makes people think of family traditions and spending money."

"Ooh, and our snickerdoodles," Melanie chimed in. "They're like cinnamon sugar hugs for your mouth."

Claire made notes, her enthusiasm building as they discussed possibilities. "What about grab-and-go items? Muffins that families can eat while they're walking around looking at trees?"

"Cranberry orange," Joyce said immediately.

"Apple cinnamon," Carol suggested.

From his position half-inside the oven's control panel, Jerry's voice emerged muffled but authoritative. "Chocolate chip muffins. My grandkids would stage a revolution if they went somewhere with treats and couldn't find anything that contained chocolate."

The women laughed, and Claire dutifully added Jerry's suggestion to her growing list.

"Jerry, does your family buy their Christmas tree at the Mills farm?" Claire asked.

"Every year for the past decade. Started when my daughter moved back to town with her kids. Now it's this whole big family production—three generations arguing about which tree is perfect while the littlest grandkids wear themselves out running between the trees."

"I'm starting to think I may need to upgrade my normal Christmas tree this year," Claire said with a self-deprecating laugh.

"What do you normally do for your tree?" Melanie asked, pausing in her icing work to look at Claire with genuine curiosity.

Claire felt heat creep up her neck as four expectant faces stared at her. "Well, when I lived in Atlanta, I had a small artificial tree. Nothing fancy."

"An artificial tree?" Joyce's voice pitched higher with each word. "Claire Elisabeth Whitfield, please tell me you're joking."

"It's practical!" Claire protested weakly. "No needles to vacuum, no watering to remember, and I can use the same one every year—"

"Your grandma Mae would rise from her grave if she knew about this artificial tree business," Joyce declared with dramatic flair. "That woman believed a proper Christmas tree should smell like Christmas and make her entire house feel magical."

"I know, I know," Claire replied. "Grandma used to spend forever at the tree farm, examining every tree like she was selecting a crown jewel. Her standards of Christmas tree perfection were legendary."

"Well, now that your partners with the best tree farm in Tennessee, you have no excuse," Melanie pointed out with satisfaction.

"After seeing what Gabe's created out there, I'm seriously considering a real tree this year."

"Plus, a real tree in your apartment would smell wonderful," Joyce added. "There's nothing like the fresh smell of a real tree to make a home feel like Christmas."

Jerry wiped his hands on a shop rag while wearing the expression of someone delivering mixed news. "Alright, ladies, I've got good news and not-so-good news. The immediate problem is fixable—a bad temperature sensor that I can replace today. Should have you back in business within a couple of hours."

"Perfect!" Claire said, relief flooding through her. "What's the not-so-good news?"

"This oven is from the eighties, and the parts are getting harder to find. Today's repair will keep you running because I have a spare part on hand, but I'd strongly recommend starting to think about replacement options soon."

Claire's stomach performed another uncomfortable flip. "Replacement as in... a whole new oven?"

"Commercial ovens this age are like old pickup trucks," Jerry explained gently. "You can keep fixing them with duct tape and prayers, but eventually the repair costs start exceeding the value. These Blodgetts were built to last, but this one's already outlived several presidents and most of my hairline."

"How much are we talking about for a new commercial oven that's the best in your opinion? I've priced a few already, and I experienced sticker shock."

"Good quality unit that'll serve your needs and last twenty years or longer? Probably fifteen to twenty thousand, depending on features and whether you want all the bells and whistles."

Just hearing that dollar estimate spoken out loud had Claire feeling like she'd stepped into a cold shower. Twenty thousand dollars would put a significant dent in her savings account.

"Today's repair should buy you time," Jerry continued, clearly recognizing her expression. "No need to make any immediate decisions. Just something to keep in mind when you're planning next year's budget and wondering whether to take that vacation to Hawaii."

"I'll take functioning ovens over Hawaiian vacations any day," Claire said, forcing a smile.

As Jerry returned to his work, Claire tried to refocus on partnership planning. But the financial implications of oven replacement kept creeping into her thoughts like uninvited guests at a party.

"The tree farm partnership sounds like perfect timing," Joyce said. "Additional revenue stream right when you might need it most."

"My thoughts exactly," Claire admitted. "Sometimes I think Grandma's still looking out for me, sending opportunities just when I need them most."

"Your grandma always said that successful business was about building relationships with good people," Joyce said, settling into the chair beside Claire's desk. "Sounds like Gabe Mills is exactly the kind of partner Mae would have encouraged you to work with."

Melanie looked up from her cookie decorating, curiosity bright in her eyes. "What's he like? I mean, I've seen him around town, but I've never really talked to him. He always seemed quiet. Reserved, maybe?"

Claire considered the question, remembering the morning's conversation and Gabe's careful attention to her opinions. "I thought he was just quiet too at first, but he opened up quite a bit while I was at his farm. He's really thoughtful—he actually listens when you talk instead of just waiting for his turn to speak. And he genuinely seems to care about creating something special for families, not just making money."

"Plus, his dog has excellent taste in people," she added with a smile.

"His dog?" Carol asked with amusement.

"Baxter. Border collie mix who apparently decided I was his new favorite person within about thirty seconds of meeting me. Gabe said he'd never seen Baxter warm up to a stranger so quickly."

"Animals are exceptional judges of character," Joyce said.

Eventually, through continued conversation, Claire had a comprehensive list of products that would work well for daily deliveries to the Christmas tree farm.

By three-thirty, Jerry had successfully installed the new temperature sensor and was running calibration tests that filled the kitchen with the familiar hum of a properly functioning oven.

"Temperature's holding steady at exactly what you set it for," Jerry announced, closing the oven door with satisfaction. "Should be good as new for the foreseeable future."

"Jerry, you're a lifesaver," Claire said, meaning every word. "What do I owe you?"

"Parts and labor come to six hundred and forty-seven dollars. Not too painful for emergency services."

Claire retrieved her checkbook from the desk drawer, grateful that today's crisis had proven manageable both mechanically and financially. "Worth every penny to have that oven back in working order."

"Remember what I said about long-term planning," Jerry added as he packed his tools. "No rush, but something to keep in mind as you think about next year's budget. I'll keep my ears open for any restaurants going out of business in the area, and if I hear of anything I'll let you know."

After Jerry departed with payment and promises to respond quickly to any future equipment emergencies, Claire found herself looking at the successfully repaired oven with mixed emotions. Relief at today's resolution battled with anxiety about future expenses she couldn't predict or control.

"You okay?" Joyce asked, noting Claire's thoughtful expression.

"Just thinking about everything Jerry said. Equipment replacement costs and long-term planning. I hope I can keep this place running exactly the way Mae would have wanted."

"Mae dealt with the same challenges," Joyce reminded her gently. "Equipment breaks down, expenses arise, and occasionally you have to make decisions based on a wing and a prayer. But she always said that building something worthwhile required both courage and community support."

"Community support like business partnerships with handsome local farmers," Melanie added with a grin.

"Exactly," Claire agreed, feeling her optimism return. "Today's repair bought us time, and the partnership with Gabe will provide additional income. Things will work out."

Joyce glanced at the clock above the prep station, her expression shifting. "Please tell me you haven't forgotten about tonight's Christmas event planning meeting at the community center."

Claire's stomach dropped as the completely forgotten obligation crashed back into her consciousness. "I did. What time?"

"Six o'clock," Joyce replied with the patient tone of someone who'd expected exactly this reaction. "Mayor Hayes is expecting you to be there."

"I can't believe I nearly forgot," Claire said, mentally reshuffling her evening plans. "I should probably text Hannah to see if she wants to ride together."

She pulled out her phone, scrolling to find the contact information for Hannah Billings, her closest friend since childhood and current owner of Holly Belle Boutique. Hannah had been her anchor during the transition of taking over the bakery, providing both emotional support and practical advice about small business management from someone who understood the challenges firsthand.

"Hannah's going to laugh at me for being scattered," Claire muttered, typing quickly. "She's been reminding me about community involvement for months."

The response came back almost immediately: *Pick you up at 5:45? Don't forget. 5:45 on the dot. I have so much to tell you!*

Perfect, Claire texted back.

Claire glanced once more at her successfully repaired oven, then at the notes she'd compiled about products for the tree farm partnership. Everything seemed to be falling into place with the kind of fortunate timing that felt almost too good to be coincidental.

"I should probably box up some cookies for tonight's meeting," she said, already mentally selecting items that would travel well and represent the bakery's range.

"Excellent idea," Carol agreed. "Nothing says 'Sugarplum Bakery wants to participate' like showing up with refreshments."

"And maybe some of those mini muffins," Joyce suggested. "They're perfect for meetings—no mess, easy to eat while talking."

As her staff began the closing tasks for shutting the bakery down for the day, Claire found herself smiling.

Everything seemed to be falling into place with the kind of fortunate timing that felt almost too good to be coincidental. As Mae used to say, sometimes the universe provided exactly what you needed, exactly when you needed it most—as long as you remained open to recognizing opportunities when they presented themselves.

Chapter 7

Claire adjusted her grip on the bakery box balanced in her lap as Hannah pulled into the parking lot of the Mistletoe Falls Community Center. The converted railroad depot practically hummed with energy.

"Wow, look at this turnout," Hannah said, checking her lipstick in the rearview mirror before gathering her oversized purse and leather portfolio. "Either Christmas planning is more popular than I thought, or someone spread rumors about free food."

"Probably both," Claire replied, watching Mayor Hayes greet arrivals at the door with his trademark enthusiasm.

They approached the entrance together, Hannah's heels clicking confidently on the wet pavement while Claire navigated more cautiously in her practical flats. The winter air carried a delicious mixture of wood smoke from nearby chimneys and the promising aroma of coffee drifting from the community center.

"Please tell me you brought snickerdoodles," Hannah said, eyeing the bakery box. "I may have skipped dinner in favor of reorganizing my fall inventory, and if I have to listen to two hours of committee assignments on an empty stomach, someone's going to get hurt."

"Snickerdoodles, mini apple cinnamon muffins, and chocolate chip cookies," Claire confirmed, pulling open the heavy wooden door.

The community center wrapped them in its familiar warmth, a blend of holiday coziness and the lively hum of small-town democracy at work. Folding chairs, arranged in an easy semicircle, faced a modest raised platform where Mayor Roger Hayes shuffled through a stack of papers. Beside him, Raquel Davis—Mistletoe Falls' event coordinator and a woman who could probably broker world peace armed with nothing more than a few clipboards and a reasonable budget—was already orchestrating the evening with effortless command.

"I love this building," Hannah said, taking in the soaring ceiling with its original exposed beams and restored hardwood floors. "It's like the perfect backdrop for a Norman Rockwell painting about civic engagement."

They drifted toward the refreshment table, where Claire lifted the lid on her bakery box and began arranging cookies and muffins on paper plates with the practiced care of someone who had spent years turning food into invitations. The sweet scent of cinnamon and sugar beckoned nearby residents, who gathered with grateful smiles and murmured thanks, turning the simple spread into a shared moment of comfort.

"Claire Whitfield, bless your heart," said Mrs. Abbott, reaching for a snickerdoodle. "These look absolutely divine. I was hoping someone would bring real food instead of store-bought cookies that taste like cardboard."

"I heard that, Meredith," called Tom Morrison from across the room. "My wife brought those store-bought cookies last month."

"Then your wife has excellent taste in husbands and questionable taste in desserts," Mrs. Abbott shot back with a grin.

Claire and Hannah exchanged amused glances as they turned to find seats among the growing crowd.

"Claire! Hannah!" Joyce Dodson's voice carried across the room as she waved them toward two empty chairs she'd apparently been guarding like precious territory.

They navigated through clusters of familiar faces—business owners comparing holiday marketing strategies, longtime residents sharing opinions about everything from weather to politics, and younger families who'd moved to Mistletoe Falls seeking the kind of community involvement that larger cities couldn't provide. Claire found herself stopped every few steps by customers who wanted to chat about recent bakery additions, ask about holiday specialties, or simply express appreciation for her family's continued contribution to the town.

"You're becoming quite the local celebrity," Hannah murmured as they finally settled into their chairs. "I counted at least four people who specifically mentioned visiting Sugarplum this week just to see what new deliciousness you've created."

"Word travels fast in small towns," Claire replied, as she noticed a familiar figure across the room.

Gabe stood near the coffee station, engaged in what looked like a serious conversation with Jerry Peterson and two other men she recognized as local contractors. He'd traded his usual work clothes for dark jeans and a deep blue pullover. When he laughed at something Jerry said, the sound carried across the room in a way that made Claire's pulse skip unexpectedly.

"Earth to Claire," Hannah said with obvious amusement, following her friend's gaze. "You're staring."

"I'm not staring," Claire protested, forcing herself to look away. "I was just... observing the crowd."

"Uh-huh. And Gabe Mills just happened to be the most fascinating part of your crowd observation?"

"Hannah—"

"I'm just saying."

Mayor Hayes stepped to the microphone with the kind of theatrical flair that suggested he'd missed his calling as a game show host.

"Good evening, everyone, and thank you for braving this chilly November night to help us plan the most magical Christmas season Mistletoe Falls has ever seen!" His warm voice carried easily through the restored space, immediately capturing attention and gradually quieting the scattered conversations. "I know Monday evenings are precious family time, so we'll try to keep things moving efficiently while making sure everyone gets their say."

"Translation: we'll be here until nine-thirty arguing about table placement at the community potluck and what color tablecloths for the Mistletoe Ball this year," Hannah whispered, earning a gentle elbow from Claire.

"Before we dive into the fun stuff," Mayor Hayes continued, "I want to share some exciting news. This year's holiday celebrations are already generating more buzz than we've ever seen. Tourism numbers are up thirty percent from last year, and early reservations at our lodges, hotels, and inns suggest we'll have visitors from as far away as Florida and Michigan."

Excited murmurs rippled through the crowd, punctuated by the satisfied expressions of business owners who understood exactly what increased tourism meant for their bottom lines and their community's reputation.

"Now, our brilliant event coordinator Raquel Davis has been working her organizational magic to turn our Christmas dreams for the town into reality," Mayor Hayes said, gesturing toward the woman beside him who looked like she could successfully coordinate a moon landing if given proper notice and enough volunteers. "Raquel, would you like to walk us through this year's spectacular lineup?"

Raquel stepped forward with the confidence of someone who'd learned that managing community events required equal parts military precision and kindergarten teacher patience. Her neat blazer and perfectly organized clipboard suggested the systematic approach that turned potential chaos into smoothly orchestrated celebrations.

"Thank you, Roger," she said. "This year's Christmas celebration will span from the tree lighting ceremony on the Friday after Thanksgiving through New Year's Day, with major events every weekend and smaller activities throughout each week."

She began outlining an ambitious schedule that made Claire wonder if Raquel ever slept—holiday markets featuring local artisans, caroling competitions, Santa's workshop events, a gingerbread house building competition, and several other activities.

"Each event requires volunteer coordination," Raquel continued, "and we're hoping to match people with activities that align with their interests and expertise. For example, our local business owners often contribute their time and services or products that enhance the community celebration while showcasing what makes Mistletoe Falls genuinely special."

"Meaning: we need free labor and donated goods," Tom Morrison called out good-naturedly, earning chuckles from around the room.

"Exactly, Tom, but we prefer to call it 'community investment,'" Raquel replied with a grin. "It sounds much more dignified than begging."

Claire found herself genuinely impressed by the scope of planning required to create a holiday experience that would satisfy both residents and thousands of visitors. The coordination involved seemed almost overwhelming, yet Raquel presented it with the calm assurance of someone who thrived on transforming complex challenges into memorable experiences.

"Let's start with our crown jewel—the Christmas tree lighting ceremony," Raquel said, flipping to a new page on her clipboard. "This year we're adding extra activities before the actual tree lighting, plus some special touches that will make the evening even more memorable."

She paused to scan the crowd; her gaze settling on Claire with obvious intention. "Claire Whitfield, you'll be continuing the beautiful tradition Mae established by providing hot cocoa for the ceremony, correct?"

Claire stood suddenly conscious of the attention focused on her. "Yes, I will. In fact, I'd love to expand the refreshment offerings this year—add coffee and a selection of holiday cookies if that would be helpful."

Approving nods and murmurs of appreciation rippled through the crowd.

"That would be wonderful, Claire. Thank you so much," Raquel said, making notes on her clipboard. "Now, for our centerpiece—the tree itself. Gabe Mills has generously provided our community Christmas tree for the past four years, creating what I'm pretty sure is the most photographed tree in Tennessee. Gabe, are you willing to continue that tradition?"

Across the room, Gabe stood with the same quiet confidence Claire had observed during their business discussions.

"Of course," he said. "I've already got my eye on a twelve-foot Fraser fir that should create exactly the kind of centerpiece this town deserves."

"Excellent," Raquel replied, then paused with the expression of someone whose mental gears were clicking into place. "Which brings us to coordination. Given that both Claire and Gabe are contributing essential elements to the tree lighting ceremony, it makes perfect logical sense to assign them as our Tree Setup, Decoration, and Refreshment Team."

Claire nearly choked on the sip of water she'd just taken. She looked across the room to meet Gabe's equally startled gaze. The logical pairing hit her with unexpected force—she hadn't expected being officially partnered with him for what sounded like extensive collaboration, let alone assigned to leading a team of volunteers for the community's most important holiday event.

Hannah leaned closer to Claire. "Did you know about this?"

"Absolutely not," Claire whispered back, still processing the implications of being assigned as Gabe's partner. "Raquel asked if I'd volunteer for something when I spoke with her last week, but she certainly didn't mention turning me into half of a coordination team!"

"Oh, this is delicious," Hannah murmured, her eyes practically sparkling with glee.

Raquel continued outlining the coordination requirements with the thoroughness of someone who'd learned from years of holiday event management experience—some of it undoubtedly gained through trial and error that had become legendary community stories.

"You'll need to schedule tree delivery and installation, coordinate decoration timing, plan refreshment station placement, and work with our sound system volunteers and the town electrician to ensure everything functions smoothly," she explained, making it sound both manageable and completely terrifying.

The list of responsibilities felt simultaneously exciting and overwhelming. Claire had envisioned contributing refreshments as a relatively straightforward commitment—show up with hot cocoa, coffee, and cookies, serve them during the ceremony, clean up afterward, and go home satisfied with her community contribution. But coordinating with Gabe on tree installation, decoration logistics, and crowd management for what could be thousands of attendees sounded considerably more involved.

"We'll provide you with contact information for all the volunteers," Raquel added, "plus a detailed binder from previous years' ceremonies. You'll have complete creative freedom to make this year's event special. The only requirement is that everything reflect the quality, warmth, and holiday magic that make Mistletoe Falls' Christmas celebrations truly unique."

As the meeting continued, Claire found her attention drifting between Raquel's presentation and the coordination requirements she and Gabe would need to manage.

The responsibility felt significant but also oddly exciting.

"Earth to Claire again," Hannah murmured during a lull in Raquel's presentation about the holiday market. "You're doing that thing where you stare into space while your brain processes information at light speed and probably creates seventeen different contingency plans."

"I'm just thinking about logistics," Claire replied quietly.

"And thinking about spending lots of quality time with a certain handsome tree farmer," Hannah added with barely concealed amusement.

"Gabe... Claire, do either of you have any questions?" Raquel asked.

Gabe stood. "How much planning time are we talking about? I want to make sure Claire and I have adequate time to coordinate all the details you've outlined without feeling rushed."

The consideration in his voice—making sure they had adequate time, referring to them as a team—made something warm flutter in Claire's chest.

"You have just over two weeks," Raquel replied. "I know that sounds tight, but most of the infrastructure is already established from previous years. You'll primarily be coordinating timing, making sure all the elements work together smoothly, and managing your volunteer teams. The binder I mentioned will be invaluable—it's practically a step-by-step guide."

Claire stood. "Will we have access to the community center's kitchen facilities for refreshment preparation, or should I plan on using the bakery exclusively?"

"You'll have full access to everything here," Raquel assured her. "Kitchen, storage space, setup areas, plus plenty of volunteer help for both preparation and cleanup. We want this to be as manageable as possible for both of you."

"What about weather contingencies?" Gabe asked, demonstrating the kind of practical thinking that impressed Claire. "December weather can be unpredictable."

"The ceremony happens regardless," Mayor Hayes chimed in. "Snow just makes it more magical."

As the meeting progressed through the remaining agenda items, Claire stole occasional glances across the room at Gabe. He listened attentively during each discussion, occasionally asking thoughtful questions. When he laughed at Mayor Hayes' joke about tourism marketing budgets, she noticed how the expression transformed his entire face.

The meeting concluded just after eight o'clock. Residents began gathering their belongings and clustering into small groups for continued conversations about specific projects and coordination details.

"Well, that was certainly interesting," Hannah said. "You and Gabe, official community partners. How absolutely delightful!"

"It's a practical pairing," Claire replied. "We both have essential contributions to the ceremony, so coordination makes perfect sense."

"Practical," Hannah repeated with obvious skepticism, her tone suggesting she found that explanation about as convincing as claiming the sky was green. "Is that what we're calling it? Because from where I was sitting, watching you two exchange glances across the room was more entertaining than cable television."

"Hannah—"

"Listen, I've told you this before. You need to have a life outside the bakery. Mae never intended for you to become a hermit who only emerges for grocery shopping and picking up the latest novel at the bookstore. You need to get out and meet more people, enjoy life... maybe even start dating again. And Gabe Mills is available and attractive. You and Gabe working together on the tree lighting ceremony is perfection. I'm just saying."

Before Claire could formulate a response that would discourage Hannah's increasingly obvious matchmaking enthusiasm, she noticed Gabe approaching them, weaving through clusters of lingering residents with a purposeful stride.

"Claire," he said, nodding politely to Hannah before focusing his attention on her with an intensity that made her pulse quicken slightly. "I hope you don't mind being paired up for the ceremony. I had no idea Raquel was planning to turn us into an official coordination team."

"I didn't either," Claire admitted, standing and smoothing her coat while trying to appear more composed than she felt. "But I think we can make it work well."

Hannah cleared her throat pointedly, reminding Claire of her presence. "Hannah Billings, I don't think we've properly met before," she introduced herself with the bright smile that had made her successful in retail sales. "I own the Holly Belle Boutique downtown."

"Gabe Mills," he replied, accepting Hannah's handshake. "It's a pleasure to meet you. I've heard good things about your boutique from my sister Brooke and several of my employees."

"Small-town networks," Hannah said with obvious pleasure at the recognition. "Everyone eventually connects to everyone else through business, family, or community involvement. It's one of the things I love most about Mistletoe Falls."

"I was thinking," Gabe said, turning his attention back to Claire. "Would you be available to meet sometime tomorrow? We should probably start planning sooner rather than later. I have a feeling these two weeks will disappear faster than we expect."

The suggestion made perfect sense, though Claire noticed her pulse quickening at the prospect of their first official planning session. "Tomorrow afternoon would work for me. Why don't you come to the bakery around three?"

"Three o'clock at the bakery sounds perfect. I'll stop by the Chamber of Commerce beforehand and pick up that binder Raquel mentioned."

"And I'll call her first thing in the morning and ask her to email the volunteer contact information she promised," Claire replied.

Hannah watched this exchange with barely concealed delight, her expression suggesting she found the entire scenario far more entertaining than tonight's official meeting proceedings.

"I should let you both get home," Gabe said. "I have a feeling we're going to create something special for the community this year, Claire."

"I'm looking forward to it."

After Gabe left, Hannah turned to Claire with obvious satisfaction.

"So," she said with an exaggerated innocence that fooled absolutely no one, "a meeting tomorrow afternoon."

"Mm-hmm," Claire said. "It's just an opportunity to plan for an important community event."

"Whatever you need to tell yourself, honey," Hannah replied cheerfully, linking arms with Claire as they headed toward the exit. "Though I will say, there were definitely some serious sparks flying between the two of you this evening."

"You're impossible."

"I'm observant. There's a difference."

Chapter 8

Gabe sat in his truck outside Sugarplum Bakery, wondering how a simple meeting with Claire could make his pulse quicken like a teenager preparing for his first date. The manila folder beside the binder on his passenger seat contained his notes about tree installation logistics from previous years. Preparations for today's meeting had kept him awake until nearly midnight. Though if he was honest, the real reason for his restlessness had less to do with event planning and more to do with the prospect of spending time working closely with Claire.

He'd told himself this was just practical planning between two adults for a community event. He'd even rehearsed casual conversation topics during the drive into town. But as he pushed through the familiar bakery door and caught sight of Claire at a table near the front windows, all his careful mental preparation scattered like leaves in a windstorm.

She'd spread what looked like enough organizational materials to coordinate a small military operation across the vintage painted table surface—laptop open beside printed email pages, multiple notepads in different colors, and enough pens to supply a college classroom. But it was Claire herself who made him forget about planning binders and volunteer lists. She'd traded her usual flour-dusted apron for a soft burgundy sweater that brought out the warm highlights in her chocolate-brown hair. When she looked up at his approach, her smile hit him with the kind of impact that stopped him in his tracks for a few seconds.

"Well, look who came prepared," she said, gesturing at the binder and folder under his arm.

"Great minds think alike," Gabe replied, gesturing toward the table. "This looks like mission control for a space launch."

"Hey, I have a reputation to maintain," Claire said with mock seriousness, closing her laptop. "Proper planning prevents problems, and I'm not about to let my first major Mistletoe Falls event turn into a disaster."

"Smart," Gabe said.

"Alright, you two planning mavens," Joyce's voice interrupted as she approached their table carrying a wooden tray laden with steaming ceramic mugs and a plate of cookies. "I figured you might need proper fuel for all this serious planning. Nothing helps tackle big projects like good coffee and fresh cookies."

"Joyce, you're an angel," Claire said, reaching immediately for a coffee mug. "We've got two weeks to pull this whole thing together without causing a community disaster. Caffeine might be the only thing standing between success and my having a complete organizational meltdown."

"Excellent coffee plus great cookies," Gabe added. "These might actually be the most important strategic planning tools in Mistletoe Falls."

"Flatterer," Joyce replied, though she looked pleased. "I'll leave you two to your work. Holler if you need refills or moral support."

As Joyce returned to her duties behind the counter, Gabe opened the planning binder and spread it beside Claire's materials, immediately impressed by the thoroughness of documentation from previous years. Detailed schedules, volunteer assignments, equipment lists, weather contingency plans, and photographs from past ceremonies created a comprehensive guide that made their task seem simultaneously more manageable and more complex.

"My goodness," Claire said. "Raquel wasn't kidding about this being a step-by-step guide. This is like having a manual for organizing the Olympics."

"Look at this volunteer list from last year," Gabe said, pointing to a section that contained nearly forty names divided into categories with military precision. "Stage setup, sound system, decorating committee, crowd management, cleanup crew..."

"And we're supposed to manage all of this while keeping our regular businesses running during what happens to be the busiest season of the year. No pressure at all."

They spent the next half hour working through the binder systematically, and Gabe found himself genuinely impressed by how naturally their collaboration developed. Claire approached everything with the same meticulous attention to detail she brought to baking, while he contributed the kind of practical problem-solving that came from years of managing complex agricultural operations. When they divided responsibilities, the process felt less like negotiation and more like two people who understood each other's strengths working toward a common goal.

"So you'll handle everything tree-related—transportation, installation, coordination with the town electrician for lighting," Claire summarized, making neat notes in her color-coded system that somehow managed to be both organized and artistic. "I'll take refreshment planning, volunteer coordination, and liaison work with the community center kitchen."

"What about the volunteer assignments?" Gabe asked, consulting the intimidating list of names Raquel had provided.

Claire considered this while unconsciously twirling her pen—a gesture that Gabe was beginning to recognize as her thinking process and found unexpectedly endearing.

"Let's divide the volunteers list by personal connection," she said. "I'd rather call everyone I know who's volunteering their time and ask them what they would like to help with. It seems more respectful than treating people like names on an organizational chart, you know?"

"Great idea."

"I know about half of these people personally," Claire said, reviewing the list with careful attention while occasionally making notes beside specific entries.

They worked through the volunteer list methodically, with Claire claiming names like Hannah, her parents Rob and Linda, her sister Rachel, and several regular bakery customers who'd volunteered for refreshment duties. Gabe took responsibility for contacting his parents, his sister Brooke and brother-in-law Shane, plus several business contacts and farming neighbors who'd offered to help.

"Your whole family volunteered," Claire said. "That's incredibly generous of them."

"Mom's been looking for ways to get more involved in the community since she and Dad retired. She's convinced that staying active is the secret to aging gracefully and a happy retirement lifestyle."

"And your sister?"

"Brooke volunteers for everything whether she has time or not," Gabe said. "She claims that community involvement keeps her connected to neighbors and sets a good example for the kids. Plus, Shane loves any project that lets him use his organizational skills outside of work." He grinned. "And he's learned that saying yes to whatever Brooke wants makes for a much more peaceful marriage."

Claire laughed, the sound bright and genuine in the cozy bakery atmosphere. "That sounds like a smart strategy."

"What about your family?" he asked.

"Dad's in heaven when he has projects that involve building or fixing things," she replied. "He's helped with the tree lighting setup for years—says it gives him an excuse to use power tools for community service instead of just honey-do lists. Mom brings her teacher superpowers to organizing people and making sure everyone feels included and valued." She paused, pen tapping gently against her notepad. "And Rachel volunteers for everything because she genuinely enjoys helping people have amazing experiences. She's the one who always remembers the little details that make events feel special instead of just functional."

"Sounds like we both come from families who believe showing up matters," Gabe said. "What do you think about walking over to the town square? Maybe think through crowd flow and setup requirements."

"Excellent idea," Claire agreed, getting up to retrieve her coat. "I'm much better at problem-solving when I can actually see what I'm working with."

They left the warmth of the bakery together, crossed Mistletoe Lane, and stepped onto the snow-covered town square. Its well-maintained paths winding between mature oak trees whose remaining leaves clung stubbornly against the season's advance. Snow had dusted the gazebo's Victorian gingerbread trim and settled in gentle accumulations around the base of trees, creating the kind of picture-perfect winter scene that belonged on Christmas cards.

"So the tree goes here," Gabe said, walking to an area beside the gazebo where previous ceremonies had positioned the community centerpiece. "Twelve feet of Fraser fir, positioned so people can gather naturally in a circle around it."

Claire studied the designated area with the same systematic attention she'd brought to their planning session, walking around the perimeter while considering angles and practical requirements. "How many people are expected to attend?"

"Last year's estimate was around a thousand, though that includes families who arrive and leave throughout the evening rather than everyone staying for the entire program," Gabe explained, consulting the planning binder. "The challenge is accommodating peak attendance while allowing people to move around without disrupting the ceremony for others."

"And the refreshment stations go where?"

"In previous years they were positioned along the perimeter," he said, pointing to several locations. "Far enough from the main ceremony to avoid disruption, close enough for easy access."

Claire walked to each suggested refreshment location, testing sightlines and considering practical details like electrical access for coffee and hot cocoa dispensers, proximity to the community center for supply runs, and crowd flow patterns that would prevent bottlenecks.

"This is actually going to work beautifully," she said finally, returning to where he stood near the gazebo with obvious satisfaction in her voice. "Plenty of space for circulation, multiple entry and exit points, and the square's natural shape will help everyone see and hear even if they're not standing right in front. I suggest leaving everything the way it's been set up in the past."

Working through logistical details together felt surprisingly natural, their different areas of expertise complementing rather than conflicting with each other. Gabe found himself genuinely impressed by Claire's systematic thinking and practical problem-solving approach, but more than that, he was struck by how easy it felt to collaborate with her—how their conversation flowed without awkwardness and how they seemed to anticipate each other's concerns and considerations.

"There's one more thing I wanted to run by you," he said as they completed their circuit of the square, suddenly feeling nervous about his next suggestion. "The tree selection itself. I've got my eye on a certain tree that should be perfect for the ceremony, but I'd appreciate having a second opinion."

Claire turned to face him directly. "You want my input on tree selection? I wouldn't know the first thing about choosing a Christmas tree, especially not one for the whole community."

"But you've got an eye for quality and beauty. I want to make sure this year's community tree is absolutely spectacular, and your opinion matters to me."

The admission came out more personal than he'd intended, and he felt heat creep up his neck as Claire's expression shifted to something that looked like pleased surprise.

"I'm not sure how much help I'd actually be."

"Come on, it'll be fun," he said, trying to recapture casual friendliness while his pulse hammered at the thought of spending more time with her. "How about Thursday? Say around three?"

"Thursday at three," Claire repeated. "I'll be there... but I make no promises that I'll be any help in finding the perfect tree."

As they walked back across Mistletoe Lane toward the bakery, Gabe found himself looking forward to Thursday's tree selection with enthusiasm that had nothing to do with community responsibilities. It had everything to do with the prospect of sharing something important to him with someone whose opinion had begun to matter in ways that went well beyond professional courtesy.

"I have a really good feeling about this entire event," Claire said as they paused outside Sugarplum's entrance, her cheeks pink from the cold air and her eyes bright with the kind of excitement that made his chest tighten. "We're going to create something amazing for the community."

"I think you're right."

"Well, I should get inside and start making those volunteer calls."

"I'll tackle my list tonight," Gabe promised. "And Claire? Thanks for working through all of this with me. I couldn't ask for a better partner."

"See you Thursday," she replied, meeting his gaze with an expression that made his pulse skip before disappearing through the bakery door.

Chapter 9

Claire pushed her car door shut with her hip while holding a bakery box. Before she could take two steps, Baxter bounded toward her like a furry missile launched from a happiness cannon, his mismatched eyes bright with what could only be described as pure, unadulterated joy.

"Well, hello there, handsome," Claire laughed, crouching carefully while trying not to drop everything. Baxter immediately pressed his entire body against her with blissful contentment.

"I see my dog has officially transferred his loyalty," Gabe called out, approaching from the direction of the main barn with a grin that made something flutter unexpectedly in Claire's chest. His cheeks were slightly flushed from the cold air, and snowflakes caught in his dark hair like tiny Christmas decorations. "Should I be offended or impressed by your powers of canine persuasion?"

"Don't blame me," Claire replied, standing and holding up the white bakery box with its cheerful red ribbon. "I brought peanut butter cookies. I'm not above bribing my way into a dog's good graces."

Gabe's eyebrows rose with obvious interest. "Peanut butter cookies and tree consultation services? This might officially be the best day I've had since... well, since you agreed to partner with me and deliver baked goods to the gift shop."

"Are you saying my baking is more exciting than your social life?" Claire teased.

"I'm saying your baking is more exciting than most people's social lives," Gabe replied with the kind of easy humor that made her realize how much she'd been eagerly awaiting this afternoon. "Fair warning for today's adventure... I take tree selection seriously. We might trudge through snow for a while."

"Good thing I came prepared," Claire said, lifting one boot to show off her practical hiking footwear. "These babies have survived my sister's idea of casual hiking. I think they can handle your tree farm."

Baxter chose that moment to plop his entire weight onto her left foot, gazing up at her with an expression that somehow conveyed both complete adoration and a firm refusal to let her escape his vicinity.

"Baxter, you're being ridiculous," Gabe said. "She's not going to disappear into thin air if you stop using her as a footstool."

"I don't mind," Claire assured him, reaching down to scratch behind Baxter's ears. The dog immediately leaned into her touch with a contented sigh that sounded almost human. "Besides, I appreciate someone who appreciates my company this much."

Gabe cleared his throat and gestured toward the gift shop. "Should we drop off the cookies before we head out?"

"Sure," Claire said, falling into step beside him while Baxter trotted along like a self-appointed chaperone.

After depositing the box of cookies inside the North Pole Trading Post, they ventured into the tree fields. The afternoon sun created diamonds out of snow crystals clinging to evergreen branches, and their breath made small clouds in the crisp air that spoke of winter's serious arrival.

"Okay, so the community tree has to be absolutely spectacular," Gabe explained as they approached a tall grove of Fraser firs. "We're talking about a tree that hundreds of people will scrutinize, photograph, and judge for the entire holiday season."

"No pressure at all. Just find one perfect tree out of thousands that will satisfy everyone's collective vision of Christmas magic," Claire said with mock seriousness. "Piece of cake."

"Exactly. Glad we're on the same page."

The first section featured trees in the ten-to-twelve-foot range, their branches thick and symmetrical with the kind of classic Christmas tree shape that belonged on greeting cards and in childhood dreams.

"What am I supposed to be looking for?" Claire asked, approaching a particularly full specimen that looked perfect to her completely untrained eye. "I mean, they're all gorgeous. How do you even begin to choose?"

"Here, let me show you," Gabe said, moving to stand beside her in front of the tree she'd been admiring. As he reached toward a branch to demonstrate, his shoulder brushed against hers, and Claire caught the clean scent of his cologne. "This one's beautiful, but see how the spacing between these branch layers isn't quite even? And look here—the trunk has a slight curve that would make it tricky to position properly in the town square."

He guided her attention to details she would never have noticed, his voice patient and genuinely enthusiastic as he explained what separated merely good trees from the spectacular ones.

"How long does it take for a tree to grow to this size?"

"These Fraser firs are a little over nine years old," Gabe replied, moving to examine another nearby tree while she continued analyzing the first one like she was judging a baking competition. "Nine years of pruning, fertilizing, protecting them from weather and pests, making sure they develop exactly the right shape and needle density that'll make families fall in love at first sight."

The genuine pride and craftsmanship in his voice reminded Claire of her own feelings about creating the perfect pastry or wedding cake—the satisfaction that came from producing something that would create joy for others. "That's a long-term investment in other people's happiness."

"Pretty much." Gabe glanced at her. "Though I have to admit, seeing families find their perfect tree makes all those years of work worth it."

They moved through several more sections, with Gabe explaining the differences between Fraser firs, Noble firs, and Virginia pines while Claire found herself asking increasingly detailed questions that revealed her natural curiosity and appreciation for expertise. More than the technical knowledge, though, she enjoyed watching him in his element—confident without being arrogant, knowledgeable without being condescending, and completely at ease in this world he'd created through years of dedicated effort.

"Tell me something," Gabe said as they walked toward a more mature section of trees, their boots crunching through snow while Baxter explored interesting scents. "What were Christmas mornings like when you were growing up? I'm curious what kind of holiday memories you're drawing from when you picture the perfect Christmas tree."

The question caught Claire off guard with its personal nature.

"Oh, Christmas morning in the Whitfield house was wonderful," she said, warming to the subject as childhood memories bubbled up with surprising vividness. "Dad would get up at some ungodly hour to start coffee, then wake everyone up by playing Christmas carols loud enough to register complaints from three blocks away. Mom would have been up since five making these elaborate Christmas breakfast productions—pancakes shaped like snowmen, hot chocolate loaded with enough marshmallows to qualify as a structural hazard."

"Sounds like your mom takes Christmas morning as seriously as you take baking," Gabe observed with amusement.

"The apple doesn't fall far from the perfectionist tree," Claire acknowledged.

"What about Christmas trees? You mentioned before your family shopped here."

Claire's face lit up with obvious delight. "Oh, the annual Whitfield tree expeditions were legendary. Dad gathered enough winter gear to outfit a polar expedition, and Mom would make a thermos of hot chocolate. Once we got here, Grandma Mae would spend approximately forever debating the merits of various trees. Rachel and I would argue over which tree was perfect and why, and my parents just stood there patiently, letting us work through our entire decision-making process without rushing us."

Claire laughed, remembering those intense childhood tree debates with sudden clarity. "Rachel always wanted the tallest tree possible—she was convinced bigger automatically meant better. I was obsessed with fullness and branch spacing because I'd calculated exactly how many ornaments we needed to hang."

"And who usually won these epic tree negotiations?"

"We actually developed a pretty sophisticated compromise system. We'd find trees that met Rachel's height requirements but passed my rigorous density inspection. Then Grandma Mae would chime in and make the final decision."

"What about you?" Claire asked as they approached another section of impressive specimens. "What were Christmas mornings like in the Mills household?"

"Mom would start cooking Christmas breakfast around dawn—the smell of bacon and cinnamon rolls would eventually wake everyone up whether we wanted to be conscious or not. Dad would build this enormous fire in the fireplace, and we'd all gather in the living room still wearing pajamas to open presents."

"Sounds perfect."

"It was, except for the great Christmas morning philosophy divide," Gabe continued with a grin. "Brooke wanted to tear through everything at maximum speed, while I preferred to take my time with each gift individually."

Claire found herself completely charmed by the image of young Gabe methodically unwrapping presents while his sister vibrated with impatience nearby. "How did your parents handle the conflict?"

"Mom instituted a rotation system—one person opened a gift while everyone else watched, then we moved to the next person. It forced Brooke to slow down and gave me permission to take my time without holding up the entire Christmas morning production."

"Brilliant parenting."

"Mom was always good at managing family dynamics," Gabe said. "Still is, actually. These days she spends most of her energy trying to manage my social life with the same efficiency."

"How's that working out for her?"

"Not well. Turns out adult social lives are more complicated than Christmas morning present rotation."

Something in his tone suggested layers of meaning that Claire wasn't quite ready to explore, though she found herself curious.

"What about now?" Gabe asked as they crested a small rise that revealed yet another section of magnificent trees stretching toward the mountain horizon. "Do you have Christmas traditions of your own, or are you trying to recreate those childhood celebrations?"

The question touched something tender in Claire's chest, reminding her how dramatically her life had shifted over the past year and how much she was still figuring out about her new reality.

"The last few years have been pretty different," she admitted, stepping carefully through deeper snow while considering how much honesty this conversation could handle. "When I was in Atlanta, Christmas was fairly low-key. Small apartment, artificial tree, nothing too elaborate. I came home when I could, but working in restaurants made holiday scheduling... challenging."

"So you're an artificial tree convert?" Gabe asked with obvious horror that was so exaggerated it made her laugh.

"I was an artificial tree pragmatist," Claire corrected. "Though I'll admit, I'm seriously reconsidering my position on the live tree debate."

"Good, because I was about to question everything I thought I knew about your character," Gabe replied with mock seriousness. "Artificial trees in the apartment of a woman who creates edible magic for a living? That's like... I don't know, a musician who only listens to elevator music."

"That's a terrible analogy."

"But accurate?"

"Possibly accurate," Claire conceded with a grin. "Though in my defense, living in a small apartment doesn't exactly encourage elaborate Christmas decorating. Besides, what if I choose the wrong tree? I can't even remember how to care for a live tree."

Gabe slowed, then stopped, turning toward her with a look that sent a warm flutter through her chest. "Claire, you can't pick the wrong one. Christmas trees are like people—each one's unique. You just choose the one that feels right."

She arched a brow, letting her gaze linger on him a beat longer than necessary. "Well... in that case, I guess I'll have to consult the expert when I'm ready to upgrade from artificial to authentic."

His answering grin was slow, knowing. "I'll even throw in free delivery."

They wandered on, weaving through different sections as they compared trees and traded thoughts, until Gabe guided them toward a secluded grove perched on higher ground. From there, the entire farm unfolded in a sweeping panorama—orderly rows of evergreens marching toward the mountain horizon, the cluster of barns and outbuildings nestled at the center, and every detail of an operation clearly shaped by years of vision, careful planning, and tireless dedication.

"These are premium trees," Gabe explained as they approached a section that immediately struck Claire as different from the others. These trees were larger, more mature, and had a full, luxurious growth that suggested they'd received special attention and care.

Claire moved among the magnificent trees with growing awe. Each one seemed more impressive than the last, but when she rounded a particularly full Noble fir and caught sight of what stood beyond it, her breath caught in her throat with genuine wonder.

The tree commanded attention like a natural monument—at least fourteen feet tall, its branches perfectly layered in decreasing circles that created flawless symmetry from every angle. The fullness was extraordinary, dense enough to support countless ornaments while maintaining the classic Christmas tree silhouette that existed more often in imagination than reality. But it wasn't just the technical perfection that stopped Claire in her tracks; it was the way the tree seemed to embody every childhood dream of Christmas magic, standing there in its snowy grove like it had been waiting specifically for this moment of discovery.

"Oh my word," Claire breathed, approaching the magnificent tree with something approaching reverence. "Gabe, this is…"

"Something special?" he supplied, watching her reaction with close attention.

"This is the one." Claire walked slowly around the tree's perimeter again, taking in its beauty from every conceivable angle while her mind automatically calculated the visual impact this tree would create in the town square. "This is absolutely, definitely, without question the one."

Gabe watched her with an expression that seemed pleased by her enthusiasm.

Baxter had positioned himself beside the tree's base, tail wagging as if he understood the significance of this moment and offered his complete approval of Claire's selection.

"It's definitely taller than the twelve feet we discussed," Gabe pointed out. "Probably closer to fourteen, maybe fifteen feet. It would definitely dominate the town square."

"It would be spectacular in the town square. People would see this tree from blocks away, and every photograph would look like something from a Christmas movie. Children would remember this tree for the rest of their lives."

"Then this is our community tree," he said. "Though I should warn you, getting a tree this size positioned and decorated is going to require some serious coordination."

"Worth it," Claire replied without hesitation, finally turning away from the tree to meet his gaze directly. "Completely worth whatever extra effort it requires. This tree is pure Christmas magic, and everyone who sees it is going to know we didn't settle for good enough when we could have extraordinary."

They stood together beside the magnificent Fraser fir, both imagining how it would look positioned in the town square, decorated with thousands of lights and ornaments and surrounded by families creating memories that would last a lifetime. The moment felt significant in ways that had nothing to do with community event planning and everything to do with two people discovering they shared the same vision of what made something truly special.

"We should probably head back," Gabe said eventually.

"Of course," Claire agreed, taking one last look at their selection. "This has been one of my favorite afternoons in a very long time. I had no idea tree selection could be so... educational."

"Educational?" Gabe repeated with amusement.

"Among other things. It's nice spending time with someone who cares about creating something special as much as I do."

The walk back provided an opportunity for comfortable conversation about logistics and practical details, but underneath their planning discussion, Claire felt the warmth of genuine connection that went beyond community service. Gabe's easy humor, his obvious expertise balanced with genuine humility, and his thoughtful attention to what she thought and felt created the kind of afternoon that made her realize how much she'd been missing meaningful adult companionship outside the bakery.

"Thanks for coming out today," Gabe said as they reached her car, automatically opening the door for her. "I honestly couldn't have made a better choice without your input."

"I think you probably could have," Claire said, settling into her driver's seat, "but I'm really glad you asked me to be part of it."

"See you Saturday morning?" Gabe asked, stepping back from her car while Baxter reluctantly moved aside to allow her departure.

"I'll be there," Claire replied, starting her engine and thinking that Saturday morning couldn't arrive soon enough.

Chapter 10

Claire finished ringing up Mrs. Palmer's order of apple turnovers when Tommy Moore from Mancino's Pizza entered the bakery balancing two large pizza boxes. He had the excitement of someone who'd learned that Friday afternoon deliveries meant hungry people and decent tips.

"Two large pizzas, Clair," Tommy said as he set the boxes on the counter while the rich aroma of melted cheese and pepperoni began competing with the bakery's signature scents of cinnamon and vanilla.

"Perfect," Claire said, pulling cash from the register. "Thanks for the quick delivery, Tommy. I know Friday afternoons get crazy for you guys."

"No problem at all," he replied, accepting payment plus a generous tip with obvious appreciation. "Enjoy your lunch, and tell Ms. Joyce I said hello."

After Tommy departed, Claire gathered the warm pizza boxes and pushed through the swinging doors to the kitchen with her hip, where Joyce, Melanie, and Carol were finishing their afternoon prep work.

"Lunchtime, courtesy of your boss," Claire announced, while three faces turned toward her with expressions of surprised delight. "And planning time. We've got refreshment booth logistics to figure out for the tree lighting ceremony."

"A pizza lunch?" Melanie asked, abandoning her cookie decorating. "Claire, you didn't need to do that, but I'm definitely not complaining."

"Good teamwork deserves good food," Claire replied, already moving back toward the customer area to rearrange seating. "We need to tackle some serious planning, and everything goes better with carbohydrates."

Joyce wiped her hands on her apron, following Claire. "Either we're in trouble or you're in an exceptionally good mood."

"Definitely the good mood option," Claire confirmed, pushing two of the vintage tables together near the front windows where afternoon sunlight would make their impromptu meeting feel less like work and more like hanging out with friends.

Carol emerged from the kitchen carrying plates and napkins, while Melanie bounced along behind her with an armload of drinks from the bakery's refrigerator.

"So what's got you feeding us pizza and calling planning meetings?" Carol asked. "Not that I'm complaining—just curious about what's inspired this burst of generous management style."

Claire opened the first pizza box, releasing a cloud of aromatic steam. "The tree lighting ceremony refreshment booth. We've got less than two weeks to coordinate everything, and I want to make sure we're completely prepared instead of scrambling at the last minute."

"Tree lighting ceremony," Joyce repeated, accepting a slice of pepperoni pizza while studying Claire with the kind of maternal attention that missed very little. "How's the planning working out with Gabe?"

"Really well, actually," she replied. "Yesterday we walked around his farm and selected the tree. Everything's falling into place better than I expected."

"Yesterday you went tree hunting with Gabe Mills," Melanie said, pausing mid-bite to look at Claire with obvious interest. "That sounds... fun."

"It was fun," Claire confirmed. "Plus, I learned a lot. I had no idea how much science and artistry go into growing the perfect Christmas tree. Now, about our refreshments for the ceremony—"

"You're practically glowing today," Joyce interrupted, setting down her pizza to study Claire with maternal scrutiny. "I haven't seen you this energetic and happy since... well, since you came back to town. What's changed?"

"I don't know," she admitted honestly, considering the question while taking another bite of pizza. "Maybe it's getting more involved in community events, or having the oven working properly again, or the excitement of the business partnership with the farm. Everything just feels... lighter lately. More manageable and fun instead of constantly overwhelming. It's probably just the Christmas vibes hitting me... I feel like a kid again."

"Could be all those things," Carol agreed diplomatically.

"Or could it be that you're actually spending time outside the bakery?" Joyce added.

Melanie nodded enthusiastically. "When was the last time you did something fun that wasn't work- or volunteer-related? I mean really fun, not just productive activities that happen to be enjoyable."

The question made Claire pause, slice of pizza halfway to her mouth, as she tried to remember recreational activities that didn't somehow connect to bakery operations.

"See?" Joyce said gently, noting Claire's thoughtful silence. "You've been working so much that you can't even recall."

"Point taken," Claire conceded, reaching for her drink. "Maybe I have been a little too focused on work lately."

"A little too focused," Carol said. "Claire, you work seven days a week, arrive before dawn, and work all day. That's not focus—that's using work to avoid having a personal life."

The frank assessment hit closer to the truth than Claire preferred to acknowledge.

"Okay... let's focus, girls," she said, pulling out the notepad from her apron pocket, "refreshment booth. We're expecting potentially a thousand families throughout the evening, with peak crowds during the actual tree lighting ceremony."

"A thousand families," Melanie repeated, setting down her pizza to stare at Claire with wide eyes.

"Which is why we need to plan this carefully instead of winging it and hoping for the best," Claire replied. "We'll have three refreshment stations positioned around the square's perimeter—far enough from the main ceremony to avoid disruption, close enough for easy access."

Joyce leaned forward with obvious interest. "We're still serving hot chocolate, coffee, and cookies, right?"

"Yes, though I want your input on specifics," Claire said. "Hot chocolate and coffee are easy, no worries or planning needed for those. But for cookies, I want to offer something special that represents Sugarplum at its best."

"Holiday cookies," Melanie said immediately, her eyes lighting up with obvious excitement. "Decorated Christmas trees, stars, snowflakes—something beautiful that photographs well and tastes amazing."

"Practical considerations though," Carol added with her characteristic attention to logistical details. "Decorated cookies are gorgeous, but they're also delicate and time-consuming. We're talking about making hundreds of cookies, plus regular bakery operations, plus preparation time, plus the fact that we also have our first delivery to Gabe's farm the same day as the tree lighting ceremony."

Claire nodded, appreciating Carol's realistic assessment of production requirements. "That's precisely why I want to delegate the cookie planning to Melanie. You're our decoration specialist, and you understand both artistic presentation and practical execution better than anyone."

Melanie's face lit up with obvious pleasure at the recognition and responsibility. "Really? You want me to plan the whole cookie situation?"

"Yep. Production scheduling, decoration timeline, packaging for easy serving—all of it," Claire confirmed. "I trust your judgment completely, and I know you'll create something that makes us all proud."

"This is going to be so fun," Melanie said, pulling out her own notepad from her apron pocket with the enthusiasm of someone who'd just been handed creative control over a project she genuinely loved. "I'm thinking elegant but not overly complicated—maybe three different shapes with coordinated color schemes that look beautiful together."

"Perfect approach," Joyce agreed with approval. "Traditional enough to feel like Christmas, distinctive enough to show our quality and creativity."

They spent the next twenty minutes working through practical details—quantities based on expected attendance, preparation schedules that wouldn't interfere with regular bakery operations, and delivery to the community center kitchen facilities for volunteers to create trays the day of the event.

"What about serving logistics?" Carol asked, consulting the notes she'd been taking throughout their discussion. "Cups, napkins, serving stations, volunteer coordination?"

"The town provides basic supplies, and all of those are stored at the community center. I have 2 volunteers who will be here Friday afternoon to help us load and transport all the cookies and coffee and hot chocolate supplies to the community center. Then I have 6 volunteers lined up to make hot chocolate, get coffee brewing, and help us create cookie trays as well," Claire explained, referring to her notes. "I've decided we'll close the bakery early that day, I'm thinking around noonish, that way we have all hands on deck to help in the afternoon, plus that should give each of us plenty of time to go home and change before the ceremony begins. I've already lined up volunteers to help at each refreshment station, two per booth, but if each of you could volunteer in a booth, that would be great. I'll float between booths and help where needed."

Claire found herself smiling at how naturally the planning was coming together, each potential challenge accompanied by practical solutions that felt both manageable and exciting rather than overwhelming and stressful.

"I have a really good feeling about this whole event," she said, reaching for another slice of pizza. "It feels like everything's falling into place perfectly."

"That's because you're working with good people who share your standards and values," Joyce observed. "Mae always said the secret to successful events was choosing collaborators who cared about excellence as much as you do."

"Gabe definitely cares about excellence," Claire said, then caught the knowing look that passed between Joyce and Melanie.

"Among other admirable qualities, I'm sure," Joyce said with barely concealed amusement.

Claire grinned before looking down at her notes.

"This is all going to be amazing," Melanie said with obvious excitement, closing her notepad with satisfaction. "I can already picture how beautiful everything's going to look—the decorated cookies, the hot chocolate and coffee stations, families gathering around a gorgeous Christmas tree."

"Speaking of the Christmas tree," Joyce said, "tell us about it."

Claire's face lit up with enthusiasm. "We found the perfect tree," she said, leaning forward as excitement crept into her voice. "Fourteen feet of absolute Christmas perfection—full and gorgeous, exactly the kind of tree that becomes legendary. People are going to remember this tree for years."

"Sounds like the tree selection was successful," Carol observed with amusement.

"Very successful," Claire confirmed. "Gabe knows everything about growing beautiful trees, and walking through his farm was like getting a private tour of Christmas magic in progress. I had no idea how much work goes into a farm like his."

"Well... I can't wait to see this tree," Joyce said. "I'm glad you went and helped Gabe select one."

They finished their planning session, clearing away pizza boxes and returning tables to their original positions while discussing details for the baked goods they would be providing soon to Gabe's farm. The combination of good food, collaborative problem-solving, and supportive friendship had created exactly the kind of afternoon that made Claire remember why she'd fallen in love with the idea of owning Sugarplum Bakery in the first place.

"Thanks for lunch and for trusting me with the cookie planning," Melanie said, gathering her notes with obvious pride. "I promise I'll create something that makes everyone proud to be associated with Sugarplum."

"I know you will," Claire assured her, meaning every word. "I can't wait to see what you come up with. I've allowed extra in the budget for you to be creative."

As her employees returned to their afternoon tasks with renewed energy and obvious satisfaction, Claire found herself looking forward to the tree lighting ceremony with excitement that went beyond professional pride or community service obligations. The collaborative planning, supportive teamwork, and growing anticipation for the event itself had reminded her how much she enjoyed being part of something meaningful that brought people together.

Standing in her beautifully organized bakery, surrounded by the evidence of successful planning and supported by people who genuinely cared about her wellbeing, Claire felt a contentment and excitement about the future that she hadn't experienced since returning to Mistletoe Falls. Everything seemed to be falling into place with the kind of fortunate timing that suggested sometimes the universe provided exactly what you needed, exactly when you were finally ready to recognize and appreciate it.

Chapter 11

G abe pushed open the Sugarplum Bakery's front door with Derrick Monroe right behind him. The familiar Saturday morning atmosphere greeted them—animated conversations, the hiss of the espresso machine, and the kind of comfortable bustle that made the place feel more like a community gathering place than a business.

"Man, it smells incredible in here," Derrick said, unwinding his scarf while scanning the packed tables with appreciation. At thirty-one, Gabe's assistant manager and best friend had the weathered hands of someone who knew his way around farm equipment and the easy confidence of a man who'd never met a stranger he couldn't win over.

Gabe automatically searched for Claire. She was arranging pastries in one of the display cases behind the counter.

They made their way to the counter, weaving between tables where locals lingered over coffee and gossip with the unhurried satisfaction of people who understood Saturday mornings weren't made for rushing.

"Morning, Gabe," Claire said, looking up with a smile that did something to his chest he was still trying to figure out. Her brown eyes sparkled with what looked like genuine pleasure at seeing him.

"Morning," he replied. "Brought back up today. This is Derrick Monroe—he keeps my farm from falling apart."

"Nice to meet you, Derrick," Claire said, extending her hand. "First time at Sugarplum?"

"Nah, I've been in a few times," Derrick said, accepting her handshake while eyeing the display cases. "But Gabe won't quit talking about your cinnamon rolls, so I figured I'd see what all the fuss was about."

Claire laughed—a genuine sound that Gabe loved to hear. "He's developed quite a Saturday morning routine. Let me guess, Gabe," she continued, already moving toward the coffee station, "black coffee, cinnamon roll, and a mixed six-pack of muffins for the week."

"You know me too well," Gabe said, pulling out his wallet. "Plus whatever Derrick wants, since I dragged him away from his normal Saturday morning routine."

"Very generous boss behavior," Derrick said, studying the display cases with the focused attention of someone who took food decisions seriously. "Claire, any recommendations, or should I just follow Gabe's lead and get a cinnamon roll?"

"Well," Claire said thoughtfully, filling a ceramic mug with dark roast while considering Derrick's question, "if you like cinnamon and want something that'll spoil you for grocery store pastries forever, I'd suggest a cinnamon roll. They're Mae's original recipe, and I honestly believe they're the best in Tennessee."

"Sold," Derrick replied immediately. "Coffee and a cinnamon roll that'll ruin my standards for life."

As Claire warmed their cinnamon rolls and assembled Gabe's muffin selection, she glanced up at them. "How long have the two of you been working together?"

"Four years," Derrick replied. "Started seasonal, but this guy convinced me to stick around when he realized I actually knew a Fraser fir from a Noble fir."

"Plus, he's the only person I've found who can handle equipment repairs, customer complaints, and December chaos without losing his mind and still have a sense of humor," Gabe added.

"Speaking of December chaos," Claire said, setting steaming cinnamon rolls in front of them, "how are opening day preparations going?"

"Chaos describes it perfectly," Derrick said. "Gabe's got everything planned down to the last detail, but there's always something unexpected that keeps us on our toes."

"This year we're adding evening tours," Gabe explained. "Twilight wagon rides, fire pits, hot chocolate under the stars. Trying to give couples something special."

Claire paused, her hands stilling on the counter. "That sounds interesting. Like something from a Christmas movie."

"Yeah, well, we'll see if it actually works or if we end up with frozen customers and cranky horses," Derrick said with a grin.

"Romantic Christmas tree farm dates," Claire mused.

Gabe watched color creep up her neck as she seemed to wrestle with something. She glanced at him, then away, then back again.

"Actually," she blurted, her words coming faster, "speaking of... I mean, I wanted to ask..." She took a breath, straightening her shoulders. "Would you go out for dinner with me tonight? Mancino's Pizza Place, maybe..."

"Dinner?"

"Yeah. Just to go over ceremony stuff. A business dinner... a partnership celebration." The words tumbled over each other like she was trying to convince herself as much as him.

"Pizza sounds good," he managed, setting down his mug before he dropped it. "What time?"

"Six? If that works for you?"

"It's a date," Gabe said, then immediately felt his face grow warm. "I mean—"

"Right," Claire said with a smile that suggested she wasn't fooled by his correction. "Business meeting date. With pizza."

"And probably some tree discussion," Derrick added helpfully, earning a sharp look from Gabe.

"Definitely tree discussion," Claire agreed, her eyes dancing with amusement. "So... six at Mancino's?"

"Six at Mancino's," Gabe said, while trying not to grin like an idiot.

They walked to a table by the windows, and Derrick immediately bit into his cinnamon roll with the focus of a man conducting serious research.

"Wow," he said after a moment, looking down at the pastry with something approaching reverence. "Okay, you weren't kidding."

"Told you."

"This is dangerous. I might have to start coming to town every Saturday just for these." Derrick took another bite, then looked up at Gabe with a knowing expression. "So. Claire seems nice."

"She is."

"Pretty, too."

"Derrick—"

"And she just asked you out."

"It's a business dinner."

Derrick snorted. "Right. Pizza at six on Saturday night. That's totally a business meeting." He leaned back in his chair, studying Gabe with the expression of someone who was enjoying watching his friend dance around the obvious. "When's the last time you were invited to a business meeting that made you look like you'd been hit by lightning?"

Gabe considered this while drinking his coffee and watching Claire interact with other customers. She moved through the bakery with natural grace, remembering people's preferences and asking about family members.

"She could probably have her pick of available men in Mistletoe Falls," Gabe said.

"Maybe," Derrick agreed, "but she asked you. Not some other available man—you. That should tell you something about what she sees when she looks at you."

"What do you think she sees?"

"A good man who works hard and is stable. Someone who treats people well and cares about his community. Someone with a sense of humor..." Derrick grinned. "Plus, you're not terrible to look at, you smell better than most farmers, and your dog clearly adores her, which is basically a character reference from the most honest judge on the planet."

"Baxter is unusually attached to her," Gabe admitted.

"Animals know things we're too stubborn to admit. Baxter's trying to tell you something important, and you should probably listen."

They finished their breakfast while talking through farm preparations—staff schedules, equipment checks, the usual pre-season logistics. But Gabe found himself stealing glances at Claire.

"So... are you ready for tonight?" Derrick asked as they gathered their things.

"Ready for what?"

"Ready to have dinner with someone you're obviously thunderstruck by?" Derrick clarified.

The question made Gabe pause. "I think so. It's just pizza."

"Right," Derrick said with obvious skepticism. "Just remember—she asked you. That means she already decided you're worth her time. Try not to overthink it big guy."

They approached the counter to return their dishes, and Claire looked up with that same warm smile, though Gabe caught something that might have been nervous anticipation in her eyes.

"Thanks for breakfast," Derrick said. "That cinnamon roll lived up to the hype. I'll definitely be back."

"You're always welcome," Claire replied, then her gaze shifted to Gabe. "I'm looking forward to tonight."

"Me too," Gabe said, and meant it more than he realized.

As they headed toward the door, Gabe glanced back toward the counter where Claire was already helping the next customer but caught his backward look and waved.

"That woman is definitely into you," Derrick observed as they stepped back into the crisp November air.

"Hope so," Gabe admitted.

"Nervous?"

"Terrified."

"Good," Derrick said with satisfaction, clapping his friend on the shoulder as they walked toward Gabe's truck.

Chapter 12

Claire checked her reflection one last time in the rearview mirror before stepping into the crisp evening air. Mancino's Pizza buzzed with Saturday night energy, warm light spilling from windows onto snow-dusted sidewalks. The rich aroma of garlic and melting cheese welcomed her as she opened the door.

She spotted Gabe immediately in a corner booth, and her stomach did a small flip. He'd traded his usual flannel for a white button-down that made his shoulders look broader. When he caught sight of her, his face lit up with a smile that sent warmth flooding through her chest.

"Hey," she said, sliding into the booth while trying to look more composed than she felt.

"Hey yourself." His eyes crinkled at the corners. "You look... wow."

Claire felt her cheeks warm. She'd changed clothes three times before settling on dark jeans and the emerald sweater Hannah swore brought out her eye color. "Thanks. You clean up pretty well yourself."

"So," he said, drumming his fingers on the red Formica table. "How long has it been since you've been on a—" He paused. "Am I allowed to call this a date, or are we still pretending it's a business meeting?"

Claire laughed, surprised by his directness. "I vote for a date."

"Good. I have to admit I've been nervous all day." He leaned forward slightly. "How nervous are we talking on your end?"

"I may have sat in the parking lot for ten minutes giving myself a pep talk."

"Really? You seem fine now."

"Pure adrenaline. My panic set in around sweater change number three earlier this evening."

"Three sweaters?" Gabe grinned. "What were the other options?"

"That's classified information."

"Well, well, what do we have here?"

They both looked up to see Rosetta Mancino approaching with menus and a knowing smile. Her steel-gray hair was pulled back in its usual bun, her apron bearing the evidence of forty years of pizza battles.

"Evening, Mrs. Mancino," Gabe said, color creeping up his neck.

"Rosetta, please. I've known you since you were knee-high to a grasshopper." Her dark eyes sparkled as she looked between them. "And Claire Whitfield! Haven't seen you in here since you were a teenager. Heard you took over Mae's place—God rest her soul. That woman made apple turnovers that could make angels weep."

"I'm doing my best to live up to her reputation," Claire said.

"From what I hear, you're succeeding beautifully." Rosetta turned back to Gabe. "I remember when your mama used to drag you in here after Little League, covered head to toe in dirt and demanding extra cheese on everything."

"Some things never change," Gabe replied with good humor.

"Well, I should hope you stay cleaner these days." Rosetta chuckled. "Now, can I get you two something to drink?"

After Rosetta bustled away with their orders—Coke for Gabe, sweet tea for Claire—they sat looking at each other across the table.

"So," Gabe said, "should I be worried this is where you bring all your dates?"

"What dates?" The words slipped out before Claire could stop them, and she immediately looked embarrassed. "I mean—"

"Hey." Gabe's voice was gentle. "I wasn't trying to make you uncomfortable. This is a big deal for me too."

Their eyes met, and something shifted in the air between them. The pretense that this was casual fell away, replaced by the acknowledgment that whatever was happening between them felt important.

"Can I ask you something?" Gabe said.

"Go for it."

"What really made you come back to Mistletoe Falls? I know about Mae and the bakery, but you had a whole life in Atlanta. That couldn't have been easy to walk away from."

Claire traced the rim of her water glass, considering. "You want the polite answer or the honest one?"

"Always honest."

"I'll give you both. The polite answer is I came home to honor Mae's legacy and keep the family business alive." She looked up at him. "The honest answer is I was miserable in Atlanta. I had this picture of what success was supposed to look like—trendy restaurant, sophisticated clientele, being part of something important. But I woke up every morning feeling empty and alone."

Gabe nodded slowly. "Like you were sleepwalking through life."

"Exactly. Coming home felt like finally being able to breathe again. Does that make sense?"

"Perfect sense."

Rosetta returned with their drinks and an expectant expression. "So, what'll it be tonight? The Supreme's popular, or if you're feeling adventurous, there's Buffalo Chicken."

Claire glanced at Gabe. "What do you usually order on a pizza?"

"I'm easy. Whatever you want."

"Come on, you must have a preference."

"Seriously, I like just about everything. I can't stand anchovies, but I can pick them off if you want them. You pick... honest."

Claire felt a moment of panic. What if she chose something he hated? What if he was just being polite? She stared at the menu, suddenly overwhelmed.

"Okay," she said finally after a few moments. "A large Supreme, but can you add banana peppers?"

Gabe's face lit up as if she'd just solved world hunger. "You like banana peppers on pizza?"

"Love them. I know it's weird—"

"Weird? Claire, banana peppers are the most underrated pizza topping in existence. A pizza without banana peppers is just bread with sauce."

She stared at him. "Really?"

"Really. I've been trying to convert people for years. Most people look at me like I'm crazy."

"Most people are wrong."

"Exactly." Gabe leaned back. "I think I like you even more now."

Claire felt her pulse quicken.

"One large Supreme with banana peppers," Rosetta said, writing it down. "Good choice. I like a woman who knows what she wants."

As Rosetta walked away, Claire grinned. "I can't believe you actually like banana peppers on a pizza."

"This might be the start of a very exclusive club."

"A club of two?"

"The best kind," Gabe said, and something in his tone made her forget why she'd been nervous about this evening.

"So what about you?" Claire asked. "What made you give up the corporate life for Christmas trees?"

Gabe's expression grew thoughtful. "Have you ever felt like you're living someone else's idea of your life?"

"Story of my Atlanta years."

"That was me in Nashville. Good job, great money, nice apartment—everything I was supposed to want. But I'd sit in those conference rooms talking about quarterly projections, and I was dying inside." He shrugged. "Coming home was the best decision I ever made."

"Any regrets? Girlfriends you left behind?"

Gabe was quiet for a moment. "No regrets. And yes, there was someone. Amanda. She wanted the version of me that was climbing the corporate ladder, making six figures, and had the five-year plan mapped out. When I told her I was moving back here to run my family Christmas tree farm…" He met Claire's eyes. "Let's just say she made her priorities in life and in relationships very clear."

"I'm sorry."

"Don't be. She showed her true self and what really mattered to her, and it wasn't me." He paused. "What about you? Anyone in Atlanta?"

"A few casual relationships, but nothing serious. It was difficult to build a relationship when you're working seventy hours a week."

"Sounds lonely."

"It was. I convinced myself I was too busy for relationships, but the truth is I was too unhappy with my life to share it with anyone else."

"And now?"

Before Claire could answer, Rosetta appeared with their pizza.

"One large Supreme with extra banana peppers, made with love and forty years of experience," she announced, setting the steaming pie between them.

The pizza was perfect—golden crust, cheese bubbling, the banana peppers scattered like little yellow gems across the surface. Claire took her first bite and closed her eyes.

"This is going to sound ridiculous," she said, "but this is only the second time I've eaten dinner... or lunch for that matter, that I didn't cook myself since I moved here."

Gabe paused mid-bite.

"Between running the bakery and learning the business side of things, I barely have time for grocery shopping, let alone going out to eat."

"That's actually kind of sad. You should make time for things you enjoy that aren't work-related."

"My staff keeps telling me the same thing. Joyce actually took my apron yesterday and hid it and told me I wasn't allowed to work past three."

"Smart woman. We'll have to work on getting you out of that bakery and having some fun," he said with a grin. "What did you do in Atlanta for entertainment?"

Claire paused, slice of pizza forgotten, as she tried to remember. "I went to restaurants. Farmer's markets for ingredient inspiration. Museums occasionally."

"All food-related or work-adjacent," Gabe observed.

"I suppose they were. But I enjoyed them."

"I'm not criticizing. I just think it's important to have parts of life that exist purely for joy." He gestured around them. "Like sitting in a pizza place on a Saturday night with someone you'd like to get to know better and discovering you both have excellent taste in pizza toppings."

Claire smiled. "All right, Gabe Mills. Let's get to know one another a little better. What kind of terrible teenage trouble did you get into back in the day?"

Gabe grinned. "Junior year of high school, I decided I was going to be a rock star."

"A rock star?"

"Yep. I bought a guitar and started a band with three friends who couldn't play instruments either. We called ourselves 'Mistletoe Ma yhem.'"

Claire laughed. "Please tell me there are photos."

"Oh, there are photos for sure. My sister threatens to show them whenever she wants me to do her a favor."

"What happened to the band?"

"We played exactly one gig—the senior center talent show—and discovered that enthusiasm doesn't make up for a complete lack of musical ability."

"The senior center?" Claire was laughing so hard she had to wipe her eyes. "Oh, I bet they loved dramatic teenage rock music."

"The director of the senior center told my mom afterward that we showed 'real spirit' but should consider other hobbies."

"What about you?" Gabe asked. "Any embarrassing teenage phases?"

Claire felt heat rise in her cheeks. "The Great Hair Incident of sophomore year."

"Now I'm intrigued."

"I decided I was tired of being the responsible, predictable daughter who always followed the rules. So I convinced Hannah to help me dye my hair black with purple streaks using drugstore box dye."

"How did that work out?"

"Have you ever seen what happens when brown hair meets black box dye without bleaching first?"

"I'm guessing, not well."

"My hair turned into this horrible muddy jet black-greenish color. The purple came out looking like a bruised eggplant. I looked like I'd been in a fight with a paint store and lost."

Gabe was trying not to laugh, his shoulders shaking with the effort. "What did your parents say?"

"Dad took one look at me and asked if I was feeling okay. Mom just sighed and made an emergency salon appointment."

"Emergency appointment?"

"Yep. It took three hours and two hundred dollars to fix what Hannah and I had accomplished with twelve dollars of drugstore dye. The stylist said it was one of the most challenging color corrections she'd ever attempted."

"I bet you looked beautiful anyway," Gabe said quietly, and something in his tone made Claire look up to find him watching her with an expression that made her pulse skip.

"That's very kind, but photographic evidence suggests otherwise."

Their conversation flowed naturally through shared stories and gentle teasing, the kind of easy back-and-forth that felt both new and familiar. Claire found herself genuinely curious about his thoughts on everything from seasonal tourism to family traditions, while he asked thoughtful questions about baking and business that showed genuine interest beyond their professional partnership.

"Can I ask you something?" Gabe said as they finished their pizza.

"Sure."

"Do you miss it? The city energy, the opportunities?"

Claire considered this. "Sometimes I miss the variety of options. But I don't miss feeling lost in my own life. Here, everything I do matters to the people I care about. When Mrs. Phelps comes in for her weekly oatmeal cookie; that matters to me, and it's important to her. Or like you...when a family finds their perfect Christmas tree at your farm... that matters. We're both creating moments that become part of people's stories."

"We're both in the memory-making business," Gabe said.

"Exactly." Claire felt a flutter of excitement at how easily he understood. "Your trees and my baked goods might seem small in the grand scheme of things, but they become part of family traditions and a part of their memories."

"You're right." Gabe leaned forward slightly. "You know what's becoming one of my favorite memories?"

"What?"

"This. Right here. Talking with you, discovering we both have a questionable taste in pizza toppings, and learning that you once looked like you fought a paint store."

"Mine too."

"How's everything over here?" Rosetta's voice interrupted the moment as she approached their table.

"Wonderful," Claire replied, straightening in her seat. "The pizza was perfection."

"I'm so glad. Can I tempt you with dessert? The tiramisu's fresh."

"Actually, we should probably head out," Claire said, glancing at her phone to discover they'd been there nearly two hours. "But thank you for everything."

As they gathered their coats and Gabe insisted on paying despite Claire's protests, she found herself reluctant for the evening to end.

"Walk you to your car?" Gabe asked as they stepped into the crisp evening air.

"I'd like that."

They walked across the parking lot together, their breath creating small clouds in the chilly air while streetlights cast pools of warm illumination on the snow-dusted sidewalks. When they reached Claire's car, Gabe moved automatically to open her door.

"Thank you," Claire said before getting in.

"Claire... I was wondering... would you come with me Monday afternoon to check on the decorations at the community center? We should probably go through everything and see what we're working with."

"I will. What time?"

"Around one? I could pick you up."

"I'd love that."

They stood beside her car for another moment, neither quite ready to end an evening that had transformed from nervous first-date energy into something more.

"I had a really wonderful time this evening," Claire said finally.

"So did I," Gabe replied, meeting her eyes. "Better than wonderful, actually."

"Better than wonderful?"

"Perfect," he said simply. "Absolutely perfect."

As Claire drove home through the quiet streets of Mistletoe Falls, she caught herself replaying moments from the evening. She felt... lighter. Like she'd been holding her breath for months and could finally exhale. For two full hours, she hadn't thought about tomorrow's baking schedule or whether she was measuring up to Mae's standards or if the oven would cooperate for another day. She'd just been Claire—laughing, talking, and feeling butterflies like some teenager with her first crush. It was terrifying and wonderful and completely unfamiliar, and she had absolutely no idea what to do with any of it.

Chapter 13

The chainsaw's roar shattered the stillness of the crisp November morning as Gabe eased the blade through the base of the towering Fraser fir. Each steady, deliberate cut brought them closer to felling the tree destined to stand at the heart of Mistletoe Falls' holiday celebrations. Sawdust spiraled onto the snow-dusted ground while the fourteen-foot giant began to sway.

"Easy does it," Derrick yelled, while Jim Parker and two seasonal workers, Mike and Tony, stood ready with ropes and the specialized cart that would transport the tree safely to the waiting flatbed truck.

"There she goes," Gabe announced, stepping back as the Fraser fir began its stately descent exactly where they'd planned, landing with a soft whoosh across the canvas tarp they'd positioned to protect the branches during transport.

"Perfect cut," Derrick yelled with obvious satisfaction, immediately moving to examine the trunk while the other men began working to prepare the tree. "Clean, straight, exactly the right angle for the stand.

This beauty's going to look like it was born to stand in the town square."

Gabe switched off the chainsaw. The sudden quiet was filled by the sound of boots crunching through snow and the gentle conversation of men who'd worked together long enough to anticipate each other's movements.

"Gabe, you've been grinning like a fool all morning," Jim said as he secured ropes around the tree's base. "Either you're excited about this year's community tree, or something else has put you in a good mood."

"Maybe both," Gabe replied.

"Our boss here had himself a date Saturday night," Derrick said casually.

"A date?" Mike asked with obvious interest, pausing in his branch arrangement to study Gabe with renewed attention.

"It wasn't—" Gabe began, then caught himself. Why was he about to downplay something that had been the highlight of his weekend? "Claire Whitfield from Sugarplum Bakery."

"Claire Whitfield," Tony repeated with obvious approval, straightening from his work. "Now there's a fine woman who's pretty as a picture. Best baker in Tennessee, if you ask me."

"How'd it go?" Jim asked.

"Really well. Better than I expected."

"Better than expected," Derrick repeated with obvious amusement, hefting one end of the tree toward the cart. "That's quite a romantic assessment."

"What I mean is—" Gabe stopped, realizing that anything he said would probably provide additional ammunition for his friend's gentle teasing. "It was a good evening."

"Good evening," Jim said with satisfaction, moving to help guide the tree onto the specialized cart. "I remember when my wife and I had our first 'good evening' together. Thirty-three years later, she still makes my heart skip when she walks into a room."

The men worked together to secure the massive tree on the transport cart, their movements efficient from years of experience handling large trees destined for special occasions. The Fraser fir looked even more impressive horizontally than it had standing.

"So when are you seeing her again?" Derrick asked as they began wheeling the cart toward the truck, their boots crunching through snow while Baxter trotted alongside, obviously interested.

"Not sure," Gabe replied. "Lots of planning meetings coming up though."

"Planning meetings," Mike repeated with obvious skepticism. "Is that what we're calling dates nowadays?"

"They're legitimate planning meetings," Gabe protested, though he was smiling despite himself. "The ceremony's next Friday, and we've got volunteer coordination to figure out, refreshment logistics, decoration scheduling—"

"All excellent excuses to spend time with a woman you're sweet on," Tony observed. "My wife and I planned our entire wedding around opportunities to see each other more often."

"So when's your next planning meeting with Claire?" Derrick said with obvious intention as they reached the truck and began positioning the lifting equipment.

Gabe found himself checking his phone automatically, though they hadn't scheduled anything specific. "We should probably get together soon."

"Probably should," Jim agreed with a knowing smile. "Lots of details to coordinate."

They spent the next thirty minutes carefully loading the tree onto the truck, securing it with professional-grade straps and protective padding that would ensure it arrived at the town square in perfect condition. The process required careful attention and coordination, but Gabe's mind kept drifting to possibilities for seeing Claire again.

"There," Derrick said with satisfaction as they completed the tie-down process. "One magnificent community Christmas tree, ready for delivery and installation. Should make for quite the ceremony."

As the other men headed back to their various tasks around the farm, Derrick lingered beside the loaded truck, studying Gabe with the kind of attention that suggested he had more to say about the Claire situation.

"You know," Derrick said conversationally, "I haven't seen you this relaxed and happy since you moved back from Nashville. It's a good look on you."

Gabe considered this while watching Baxter investigate interesting scents around the truck's tires. "I feel... good, I guess. Like maybe things are falling into place in my life."

"Could that have anything to do with a certain beautiful baker who makes you smile every time her name comes up?"

"Maybe," Gabe admitted, "probably definitely."

"So ask her out again."

"We had dinner on Saturday. It's only Wednesday."

"So?" Derrick looked genuinely baffled by Gabe's logic. "If you enjoyed her company and want to spend more time with her, ask her out again. There's no rule about waiting a specific number of days between dates."

"I don't want to seem too eager."

"Gabe," Derrick said with the patience of someone explaining basic concepts to a confused child, "I don't think eagerness is going to scare her away."

"Besides," Derrick continued with obvious satisfaction at having made his point, "you've got legitimate reasons to get together if you feel you need an excuse. Final ceremony planning, coordination details, and making sure you're both prepared for next Friday's event. Perfectly reasonable."

"Perfectly reasonable," Gabe repeated, pulling out his phone.

"What are you doing?"

"Texting Claire."

Derrick grinned. "Now you're thinking like a man with functioning brain cells."

Gabe stared at his phone screen, the cursor blinking in the empty text message field. What had seemed straightforward in theory suddenly felt complicated in practice. How casual should he sound? How much should he emphasize the planning aspect versus simply wanting to see her?

Hey Claire, he typed, then deleted it. Too casual.

Claire, I was wondering if you'd like to get dinner tomorrow to go over ceremony details; he tried next, then deleted that too. Too formal.

"Having trouble with your text message?" Derrick asked with obvious amusement, noting Gabe's furrowed concentration.

"I can manage a two-hundred-acre farm, but composing a simple dinner invitation is apparently beyond my capabilities," Gabe muttered.

"Here's a radical concept: just say what you're thinking."

Gabe looked up from his phone. "What I'm thinking is that I want to see her again. I'd like to cook dinner for her at my place, and I'm nervous about whether that's too forward after one official date."

"Then say that. Well, maybe leave out the nervous part."

Taking a deep breath, Gabe typed, *Claire, would you like to have dinner tomorrow night at my place to go over final ceremony details? Or we could go out to eat—whatever you'd prefer. Let me know what works for you.*

He hit send before he could second-guess himself further.

"Done," he announced.

"See? Not so complicated." Derrick clapped him on the shoulder.

They began walking back toward the main barn area, Baxter falling into step beside them while the late morning sun created diamonds out of frost crystals clinging to nearby evergreen branches. The farm hummed with productive activity.

Gabe's phone buzzed.

"That was fast," Derrick observed with obvious amusement as Gabe immediately reached for his device.

I'd love dinner tomorrow! Actually, if you don't mind, I'd prefer your place. I could bring Chinese takeout from Dragon Palace if that sounds good? 6 PM?

Gabe read the message twice, a smile spreading across his face that felt completely beyond his control.

"Good news?" Derrick asked, noting his friend's expression.

"She wants to come over. She offered to bring Chinese takeout at six tomorrow."

"She chose your place over a restaurant," Derrick said with obvious satisfaction. "That's a woman who wants to spend real time with you."

Perfect, he texted back. *Looking forward to it.*

Me too, came her immediate reply, followed by a smiley face emoji that made him grin like a teenager.

"You know what this means, right?" Derrick said as they reached the barn area where other crew members were organizing equipment for afternoon tasks.

"What?"

"You've got approximately twenty-four hours to make sure your cabin is presentable for female company. When's the last time you had anyone over who wasn't family or farm-related?"

Gabe paused, considering this question with growing concern. "I honestly can't remember."

"Then you've got some housekeeping in your immediate future," Derrick said with a hint of amusement.

Gabe found his mind shifting between present responsibilities and tomorrow evening's possibilities. Claire would be in his home. In his personal space, seeing his books and furniture and the personal touches that revealed who he was.

The prospect felt simultaneously thrilling and terrifying.

"You're doing that grinning thing again," Jim observed as he walked past.

"Leave him alone," Derrick said. "Man's got a beautiful woman coming to dinner tomorrow night. Of course he's grinning."

"That's serious progress." Mike said with obvious approval.

"It's just dinner. Knock it off, you guys," Gabe protested as he grinned.

"Right," Derrick said with obvious skepticism. "Just like last Saturday night was just pizza. Can I give you a piece of advice?"

"What?"

"Be yourself tomorrow. Not the version of yourself that you think she wants, not the version that you think is impressive—just you. The down-to-earth, funny, and good person you are. That's the man she's interested in getting to know better. Quit overthinking this."

Chapter 14

The log cabin nestled among towering pines looked like something from a Christmas card, the windows glowing with light against the darkening winter sky while smoke drifted lazily from the fieldstone chimney. Claire sat in her car for a moment after putting it in park, taking in the scene that seemed almost too perfect to be real—the wraparound porch with its comfortable rocking chairs, the careful landscaping that showcased native mountain plants under a light dusting of snow, and the overall sense of permanence and peace that seemed to radiate from every carefully detail.

The front door opened, and Baxter bounded down the porch steps. His tail wagged with such vigor that his entire back end wiggled in harmony, and when she opened her car door, he immediately pressed his head into her outstretched hand with a contented sigh that suggested he'd been waiting specifically for her.

"Well, hello there, handsome," Claire laughed as she got out of the car, crouching to give him the attention he clearly felt was his due. "Did you miss me?"

"He's been watching for you out the front window ever since I told him you were coming," Gabe said from the doorway with a smile that made her pulse skip.

"Really? I hope I'm worth the wait."

"Definitely worth it," Gabe replied, moving down the steps to meet her halfway. "I should probably warn you that you might have a furry shadow all evening."

"I can handle it," Claire said, following him toward the porch while Baxter followed.

The interior of Gabe's cabin exceeded every expectation she'd formed during the drive up the mountain. The great room soared to exposed-beam ceilings that showcased traditional timber framing, while the massive fieldstone fireplace commanded attention all on its own. But it was the furniture that made her breath catch—every piece clearly handcrafted with the kind of attention to detail that spoke to genuine artistry rather than simple functionality.

"Gabe," she said, setting the takeout bags on the kitchen island, "did you make all of this furniture?"

Color rose in his cheeks as he followed her gaze to the oak dining table, the built-in shelving, and the coffee table in the living room crafted from reclaimed barn wood. "Most of it my dad and I built. Winter evenings get long up here, and I like working with my hands."

"You like working with your hands," Claire repeated, moving closer to examine the dining table. The craftsmanship was extraordinary—smooth surfaces that showed natural wood grain, joints so seamless they seemed to have grown that way, and proportions that made the substantial pieces feel graceful rather than overwhelming.

"This isn't hobby woodworking, Gabe. This is quality furniture." She ran her fingers along the table's edge, noting details that revealed hours of patient work. "How long have you been creating pieces like this?"

"Since I was a teenager, really. My dad and granddad had a workshop, and they both taught me." Gabe moved to the kitchen island and began unpacking their dinner while watching her explore his living space.

Claire continued her circuit of the living room, noting family photographs in frames that showed the same meticulous craftsmanship. The built-in storage maximized function while maintaining beauty, and everywhere she looked, evidence of someone who created lasting beauty through patient dedication.

"You were taught well," she said, pausing beside a shelf that held several hand-carved Christmas ornaments—stars, trees, angels—each one unique but clearly from the same artistic hand. "These are incredible."

"Those are just for fun," Gabe said. "I make new ones every year. Most of them end up as gifts for family or donations to community events."

"Just for fun," Claire repeated, picking up a delicate wooden angel with flowing robes and an expression of peaceful joy. The detail work was extraordinary—tiny feathers carved into the wings, fabric texture in the robes, and a face that somehow conveyed both strength and gentleness. "Gabe, you could sell these for serious money. They're works of art."

"I don't make them to sell," he said quietly, joining her beside the shelf. "I make them because it feels good to create something beautiful that might make someone else happy."

The simple honesty in his response made warmth bloom in her chest. Here was a man who spent his days growing Christmas trees to create family memories, his evenings crafting gifts for others, and his spare time coordinating community events—someone whose entire life seemed focused on bringing joy to people around him.

"Well," she said, carefully replacing the angel ornament, "your grandfather would be proud of what you've accomplished, and I'm sure your dad is too."

"Come on," Gabe said, gesturing toward the kitchen area where their takeout containers waited. "Let's eat before everything gets cold. I want to hear about your day."

The dining table, positioned to catch views of the surrounding forest through large windows, felt like the perfect setting for a casual dinner. Gabe had set out plates, added cloth napkins, and opened a bottle of wine, which suggested he'd put thought into making their evening feel special.

Baxter settled himself beside Claire's chair with obvious contentment, occasionally looking up while she and Gabe enjoyed their dinner.

"So tomorrow morning," Claire said, consulting the notes she'd brought along, "you're planning to deliver the tree around ten?"

"Yes," Gabe confirmed, serving himself more of the sesame chicken. "I'll bring the tree on a flatbed truck, and the guys will bring the lifting equipment, plus the specialized tree stand that can handle a fourteen-footer."

"I plan on watching the delivery and setup," Claire said.

"You're welcome to ride along with me, if you like. Then, it will probably take a few hours getting everything positioned and secured properly once we get to the town square."

The casual invitation to accompany him during tree transport felt significant in ways that had nothing to do with ceremony logistics.

"I'd love that," Claire replied. "I can have Joyce and the girls handle the bakery, and it'll give me a chance to see you in action."

"Fair warning—it might be a slow and bumpy drive in the delivery truck. Then, once we get to the town square, it involves a lot of technical discussion about positioning and balance. Probably not the most exciting way to spend a Friday morning."

"Are you kidding? I get to watch you and your crew transform the town square with what I'm pretty sure is the most beautiful Christmas tree Tennessee has ever seen. That sounds like witnessing magic to me."

"When you put it like that, it does sound pretty special."

They finished their dinner while working through the remaining ceremony details—volunteer schedules, equipment needs, weather contingency plans—but Claire found herself increasingly distracted by small details that revealed aspects of Gabe's character she hadn't anticipated.

"Should we move to the living room?" Gabe suggested as they finished clearing their plates. "I can add a few more logs to the fire."

"Sure."

Claire settled into one end of the leather sectional while Gabe added logs to the fire, Baxter immediately claiming the spot on the rug where he could maintain visual contact with both humans.

"This is perfect," Claire said, tucking her feet under her while the fire's warmth settled into her bones. "I can see why you love living up here. It's like being wrapped in peace and quiet."

"It took some adjustment after living in the city," Gabe admitted, settling beside her on the sofa. "But now I can't imagine living anywhere else."

"What's the biggest challenge you've faced since taking over the farm?" Claire asked.

Gabe was quiet for a moment, considering. "Honestly? Learning to trust my judgment. When you're the third generation, there's a lot of pressure to maintain traditions while also adapting to changing times. Every decision feels weighted with family history."

"Like what kind of decisions?"

"The decision to expand into offering more of a destination or total experience type farm atmosphere. Adding the petting zoo, the wagon, and sleigh rides, and that sort of thing. Adding the gift shop was terrifying," he admitted. "My grandpa and dad ran the farm as a traditional tree farm. I worried that expanding into retail might some-how dishonor their legacy or change what made this place special."

Claire nodded with understanding. "I felt the same way about updating Mae's menu. Every time I wanted to try something new, I worried I was being disrespectful to her memory."

"Yep. You get it. But then I realized that staying completely frozen in the past wasn't honoring them either—it was just being too scared to grow." Gabe looked at her with obvious interest. "What finally convinced you to trust your instincts?"

"Joyce, actually. She told me that Mae had spent decades developing her recipes and adding new items. She said Mae would be disappointed if I didn't continue the tradition and go with my gut instincts."

"Can I ask you something personal?" she continued.

"Sure."

"When did you first know you wanted to work with your hands? I'm looking at all this beautiful furniture you've created, and I'm curious when that passion started."

Gabe's expression grew thoughtful as he considered the question. "I was probably eight when my grandpa first let me into his workshop. It was this magical place—with tools hanging everywhere, the smell of sawdust and wood stain, and half-finished projects on every surface. He was working on a hope chest for my mom's birthday, and he let me sand one of the panels."

"That must have been special," Claire said softly, imagining a young Gabe carefully focused on his task.

"I was so proud of that sanded panel. I probably spent two hours making sure it was absolutely perfect." Gabe smiled at the memory. "Grandpa told me that wood had a memory—that every touch, every cut, every finish became part of its story. He said if you worked with respect and patience, the wood would show you what it wanted to become."

"That's beautiful philosophy."

"He was a wise man. I can remember as I got older, every spare moment I had, I'd ride my bike up to his place and spend hours in that workshop. Most kids my age were playing video games, but I was happiest with a piece of oak and a set of chisels."

Claire found herself completely charmed by the image of young Gabe pedaling eagerly to his grandfather's workshop. "What was the first piece you made completely by yourself?"

"A disaster," Gabe laughed. "I was twelve and decided I was going to surprise Mom with a jewelry box for Mother's Day. Grandpa let me work on it myself, only offering advice when I asked. The proportions were completely wrong, the lid didn't fit properly, and I used about three times more stain than necessary."

"But she loved it anyway?"

"She still keeps it on her dresser. Uses it for her everyday jewelry even though the lid sticks and it wobbles. She claims it's her most treasured possession because she can see my heart in every imperfect detail."

"That's what made you fall in love with woodworking—creating something that carried your heart... isn't it?"

He nodded. "What about you? When did you first know you belonged in a kitchen?"

Claire settled more comfortably into the sofa, surprised by how much she wanted to share this story with him. "I was probably six when Grandma Mae first let me help with real baking instead of just licking spoons. She was making teacakes for a church social, and she let me measure out the dry ingredients."

"Big responsibility for a six-year-old."

"Enormous responsibility. She had this ritual when she baked for church—she'd put on her favorite apron, tie her hair back just so, and arrange all her ingredients like a general preparing for battle. That day, she gave me one of her treasured aprons. She had to wrap it around my little body and secure it with safety pins so it stayed put, and she let me stand on a chair beside her."

"I bet you took it very seriously."

"Oh, I did. I measured the flour with the concentration of a scientist conducting crucial experiments. But the magical part was watching Mae taste the batter and somehow just know what it needed. A pinch more vanilla, an extra minute of mixing—she could sense what would make the difference between good and extraordinary."

"And you have the same instinct?"

"I do. I discovered it when I was about thirteen. Mae was sick with the flu, but she had promised a batch of snickerdoodles for her bridge club. I begged to try making them myself, using her recipe cards."

"Did it work?"

Claire laughed, remembering the mixture of terror and determination she'd felt. "I followed every instruction exactly, but when I tasted the dough, something felt wrong. Not bad, just... not quite right. So I added a tiny bit more cinnamon and a touch more vanilla, even though the recipe didn't call for it."

"And?"

"They were perfect. Better than perfect, actually. Grandma tasted one and asked what I'd done differently. When I told her, she got tears in her eyes and said I had 'the touch'—the ability to feel what food needed beyond what any recipe could teach."

"And that's when you knew?"

"That's when I knew. That was my magical moment when I knew what I wanted to do with my life. I also realized that baking wasn't just following directions—it was trusting my instincts. Pretty profound moment for a thirteen-year-old. I didn't even know I had instincts at that young of an age." Claire paused. "It sounds silly when I say it out loud, actually."

"It doesn't sound silly at all," Gabe said firmly. "It sounds exactly like what my grandpa taught me about wood. Some things can't be learned from books or instructions—they have to be felt."

Gabe shifted slightly on the sofa, and Claire became aware that they'd naturally moved closer together during their conversation. Near enough that she could see the green flecks in his eyes and catch the clean scent of his woodsy cologne.

"I love hearing about how you discovered your gift in life," he said. "It helps me understand what drives someone who puts so much heart into everything she creates."

"Same with you," Claire replied. "Learning about your grandpa's workshop and what woodworking means to you—it helps me see who you are in an entirely different way."

"Claire," Gabe said, his voice carrying a note of hesitation that made her look at him more closely. "I'm really glad you came tonight. Not just for the planning parts of the evening for the tree ceremony, but for... this. Getting to show you where I live, talking about things that matter. It's been a long time since I've felt comfortable sharing this much of myself with someone."

The honesty in his admission made her smile. "I'm glad I came too. Your home is beautiful, and seeing how you live, the things you've created with your own hands—it helps me understand who you are beyond the Christmas tree farmer and community coordinator."

"And what do you think about who I am?"

The question was asked quietly, with genuine curiosity rather than fishing for compliments, and Claire found herself wanting to give him the most honest answer possible.

"I think you're someone who creates beauty and joy for others through everything you touch. Your trees, your furniture, your approach to community events—everything shows the same care and attention to what makes other people happy. That's a rare quality."

"Thanks. That means more to me than you probably realize."

The firelight flickered across his face as he spoke, and Claire found herself studying the way the shadows highlighted the strong line of his jaw and the genuine warmth in his eyes. When had she started noticing details like the way he unconsciously ran his hand through his hair when he was thinking or how his whole expression changed when he smiled?

He slowly reached for her hand where it rested on the sofa beside her. His fingers brushed across her knuckles with gentle question, and when she didn't pull away, he carefully entwined their fingers together.

The simple contact sent warmth flooding through her entire body. His palm was slightly rough from farm work, his grip gentle but sure, and holding his hand felt both completely natural and thrillingly intimate.

They sat together in comfortable silence, fingers interlaced while the fire crackled and Baxter's gentle breathing provided a peaceful rhythm. The beautiful living room, the man beside her who'd revealed depths of himself with gentleness she hadn't anticipated, and the simple pleasure of holding hands made her heart sing in ways she'd never experienced.

Chapter 15

The massive delivery truck rumbled around the last curve onto Mistletoe Lane, its precious cargo secured beneath protective tarps while Police Chief Judd Anderson's patrol car led the slow procession with flashing lights. Gabe downshifted carefully as they approached the town square, Claire sitting beside him in the passenger seat, her notebook balanced on her knee as she coordinated final details over her phone.

Through the truck's windshield, Gabe could see the town square transformed into a staging area that looked like a cross between a construction site and a community celebration. Orange cones cordoned off the entire southern section, while Fire Chief Ray Martin's red truck blocked one of Mistletoe Lane's main intersections with the efficient precision of someone who'd orchestrated dozens of similar operations.

"This is so exciting," Claire said as Chief Anderson guided them toward the chosen spot to park the delivery truck.

Gabe began the careful process of backing the delivery truck into position while Chief Ray directed him with hand signals.

Claire watched out the window. City trucks, electrical cables, volunteers, and city officials were everywhere, and shop owners had emerged to witness the installation that would define their town's holiday season.

"There's Hannah," she said, waving at her friend, who stood outside Holly Belle Boutique with obvious excitement. "And my dad made it too."

Gabe followed her gaze to where Rob Whitfield stood beside a fire truck, gesturing toward the tree while deep in conversation with the city electrician, Todd Jones.

"Dad never misses a chance to help with projects that involve power tools or public safety," Claire said with fond amusement. "Mom's at school, but she made him promise to take pictures so she could share them with her students."

The truck settled into a satisfied rumble as Gabe set the parking brake and turned it off. Through the passenger mirror, he could see Derrick and Jim approaching with the specialized equipment trailer, followed by Tony and Mike in the smaller support truck.

"Here comes the cavalry," Gabe announced, opening his door to the crisp morning air.

Claire gathered her coordination materials and climbed down from the passenger seat, only to be intercepted by Joyce—armed with a hefty insulated coffee carafe and enough disposable cups to keep half the town running until lunchtime.

"Good timing," Joyce called out. "I made the dark roast. Carol's bringing some cookies in a few minutes. We figured everyone would need fuel for heavy lifting."

"Joyce, you're a saint," Gabe said gratefully, accepting a cup that warmed his hands. "This is going to be at least a three-hour operation."

"Three hours? Wow," Claire said.

"Getting a tree this size positioned exactly right requires measuring twice and moving once. No room for error," Gabe said with a grin.

Mayor Hayes appeared with his characteristic enthusiasm and a man Claire didn't recognize, who carried professional camera equipment.

"Morning, everyone!" the mayor called out with a booming cheerfulness that suggested he'd already consumed significant caffeine. "Beautiful day for making history. Gabe, Claire, I'd like you to meet Miles Livingston from the Tennessee Gazette. He's here to document our tree installation for the front page."

Miles, a thin man in his forties, immediately began photographing the truck and equipment and then scribbled notes in a pocket-sized notebook.

"Mayor Hayes tells me this is the largest community tree you've ever had in Mistletoe Falls," Miles said, clearly delighted by the story potential. "Mr. Mills, what made you decide to go with such an ambitious tree this year?"

Gabe glanced at Claire before responding. "Sometimes you find a tree that's so perfect, you just have to go with your gut instinct. This Fraser fir represents everything we want our community Christmas tree to embody—strength, beauty, and the kind of presence that creates lasting memories."

"And Ms. Whitfield, how has coordinating all this for the town been going?"

"It's been incredibly easy," Claire replied. "Gabe and I work together naturally, which makes managing all this feel more like a partnership. We've got an incredible team of volunteers helping with everything."

Miles scribbled furiously while Mayor Hayes beamed with the kind of civic pride.

"Alright, people," Fire Chief Martin interrupted with the practical authority of someone responsible for public safety. "We've got downtown traffic to think about. Let's get this tree positioned so we can reopen the intersections as soon as possible."

The next hour unfolded with the kind of choreographed precision that came from careful planning and experienced teamwork. Gabe coordinated the heavy lifting equipment, while Claire managed volunteer logistics and communication.

"Derrick, can you adjust the stabilizer angle about fifteen degrees?" Gabe called out while monitoring the tree's position through the lifting harness. "Jim, we need another six inches toward the gazebo for optimal sight lines."

"Claire, Todd needs you," Officer Anderson said, gesturing toward the town electrician, standing by with measuring equipment and safety gear.

"On it," Claire replied immediately, moving toward Todd while consulting her coordination notes. "Todd, we've got clearance for the electrical hookup, and I have all the town permits required for lighting installation and testing."

Todd Jones, a sturdy man in his fifties who'd handled the town's electrical needs for twenty years, nodded approvingly as he began measuring distances and calculating voltage requirements.

"This tree's going to require some serious power," he observed, stepping back to assess the Fraser fir's full dimensions. "But the electrical infrastructure can handle it. I'll need to run additional lines for safety redundancy."

"Whatever you need," Claire assured him. "We want everything perfect for the lighting ceremony."

The tree-raising itself required the kind of physical coordination that revealed character under pressure. Gabe's calm leadership kept everyone focused, while Claire's organizational skills ensured that each step proceeded smoothly without confusion or wasted motion.

"Easy, easy," Gabe directed as the massive tree began its vertical ascent, guided by ropes and steady experienced hands. "Let the equipment do the work. We're just providing direction and stability."

Claire watched the process with fascination.

"It's beautiful," she breathed as the tree reached its full height, branches spreading in perfect symmetry while early morning sunlight caught the rich green needles. "Even without decorations, it's already magnificent."

"Wait until next Friday," Rob Whitfield said, joining his daughter. "When those lights come on and the whole community gathers around, this tree's going to be spectacular."

"Dad, I'm so glad you came," Claire said with affection, leaning against her father's shoulder while they watched Gabe make final adjustments to the tree's positioning.

"Your grandma Mae would've loved watching you be involved in all this."

"I believe she would have, Dad. She's probably smiling down from heaven watching all this."

The final adjustments of the tree took another thirty minutes—securing the base, testing stability, ensuring safety clearances—but eventually Mayor Hayes declared the installation officially complete and ready for decoration.

"Ladies and gentlemen," he announced to the crowd, "I present Mistletoe Falls' 2025 community Christmas tree, courtesy of Mistletoe Christmas Tree Farm and coordinated by our fantastic ceremony team."

Spontaneous applause erupted, and Claire found herself grinning with pride at what they'd accomplished.

"We make a good team," Gabe said, approaching her as the crowd began to disperse and equipment was loaded back onto trucks.

"We really do," Claire agreed.

"What's next on our timeline?" Gabe asked.

"All that's on the agenda for this afternoon is loading the city vans with all the lights and decorations waiting at the community hall. Decorating begins tomorrow. Volunteers arrive at ten in the morning. Todd will be on hand to inspect the lights; the fire department is scheduled to arrive with a truck first thing, and we'll start with decorating from the top down using their ladder truck."

"Perfect, I'll take my truck back to the farm in a few minutes and then head over to the community center and help load the city vans."

As the town returned to normal activity and the equipment trucks departed, Claire and Gabe stood together in the town square, tired but satisfied. He reached for her hand as they stood looking up at the tree.

Chapter 16

Claire stood beside Gabe in the crisp morning air, both of them craning their necks to watch as firefighter Graham Smith maneuvered the massive gold star into position atop the community tree. The firetruck's extended ladder created a tower of gleaming metal against the blue sky.

"A little to the left, Graham," Chief Martin called through his radio, his voice crackling with static while early morning shoppers paused to watch the installation process. "Perfect—now secure it, and let's get the final ornaments on those top branches before we bring you down."

The past hour had transformed the town square into a winter wonderland construction site again, with the fire department systematically stringing lights from the tree's peak downward. Orange safety cones created a perimeter around the work area, while boxes of ornaments, strings of lights, garland, and other decorative materials waited in organized stations around the town square.

Graham's voice carried down from the platform as he secured the final oversized ornaments that required ladder truck access. "That's the last of the stuff for the top of the tree, Chief! It's ready for the ground crew!"

As Chief Martin began lowering the platform, Claire noticed more volunteers arriving. Arms full of decoration boxes, trailing extension cords, and assorted other items, they approached with the kind of enthusiasm that made major community projects successful.

"And here comes part of my family," Gabe observed with satisfaction, waving toward the approaching group heading directly toward them.

Claire's attention immediately focused on a tall, auburn-haired woman with infectious energy practically bouncing alongside a calmer man carrying supplies. Two children raced ahead with barely contained excitement that suggested Christmas decorating ranked among their favorite activities.

"Uncle Gabe!" called the little girl, launching herself toward him with a complete faith that he'd catch her midair leap.

Gabe swept the child into a bear hug that made her giggle with delight. "There's my favorite niece," he said, spinning her once before setting her feet back on the ground.

"I'm your only niece," nine-year-old Lily replied with a grin. She immediately turned her attention to Claire with curious brown eyes. "Are you Uncle Gabe's girlfriend?"

"Lily Davidson!" the auburn-haired woman scolded, though her tone held more amusement than genuine reproach.

"But I want to know," Lily protested.

"I'm Claire Whitfield. I own the Sugarplum Bakery right over there," she said, pointing.

"The bakery with the good cinnamon rolls?" seven-year-old Conner asked.

"Yep, that's my bakery," Claire said as she crouched to his eye level. "I'll have to make sure I put extra icing on yours the next time you come in."

"Really?" Conner's face lit up like she'd just promised him a personal visit from Santa.

"Really. But only if you promise to help us decorate this huge Christmas tree today, can you do that?"

"We're good tree decorators," Lily said with complete confidence.

"And I'm Brooke, the mother of these two walking tornadoes," the auburn-haired woman said, extending her hand.

"And I'm Shane," the man beside Brooke added, shifting decoration supplies to shake her hand. "Thanks for taking on the coordination nightmare of this community event. Brooke volunteered us to help before I could even ask what was involved."

"Community service builds character," Brooke replied cheerfully. "Besides, it's not every day we get to help create Christmas magic."

"Here come Mom and Dad," Gabe said with obvious affection.

The older man, clearly Gabe's father based on similar build and facial features, carried a toolbox as the woman beside him balanced a large basket in her arms.

"Rick and Sarah Mills," Gabe said as his parents reached their group. "Mom, Dad, this is Claire Whitfield."

Sarah set her basket down, and Claire found herself enveloped in a warm hug. "Claire! I remember you from when you were a wee little thing. You've grown into such a lovely young woman."

"Thank you, Mrs. Mills," Claire replied. "I remember coming to your farm with my family every Christmas. You always had the most beautiful trees."

"Still do," Rick said with pride, extending a work-weathered hand. "Gabe's taken the operation to levels I never imagined. What he's accomplished in the past four years makes this old farmer proud."

"I brought coffee and Danish for everyone," Sarah announced, beginning to unpack her basket onto a nearby table, ready for snacks and beverages.

"Danish?" Lily perked up immediately. "What kind of Danish?"

"Cherry, apple cinnamon, and cream cheese," Sarah replied, producing wrapped pastries that made several nearby volunteers begin gravitating toward their impromptu refreshment station.

"Snacks," Conner said. "Best Saturday ever."

"It's definitely in the top ten," Claire agreed, accepting a steaming cup of coffee from Sarah while watching the easy family dynamics unfold around her.

As Claire looked around, she became aware of more people arriving across the square—couples carrying ladders, families with children eager to help, and other residents who'd clearly decided that community Christmas decorating was worth braving November cold. The town square gradually filled with the kind of productive energy that made major community projects successful.

"Okay, everyone," Claire called out, raising her voice to address the growing crowd. "Thank you all for volunteering your Saturday morning to help make our tree lighting ceremony magical! There are clipboards on the table in the gazebo that list what decorating team you've been assigned. If you need anything, Gabe or myself can help you. Have fun, and again, thank you!"

Scattered applause and cheerful greetings rose from the assembled volunteers, along with several compliments about the tree's impressive size and beauty.

"Teams!" Lily declared with excitement. "I want to be on the ornament team!"

"The ornament team sounds perfect for you and Conner," Claire agreed, consulting her notes while the children practically vibrated with anticipation.

"What about the lights?" Conner asked.

"Light-stringing team," Gabe replied, pointing toward several volunteers who were already examining extension cords and testing connections.

"Uncle Gabe," Lily said, tugging on his jacket while cradling a beautiful ornament shaped like a snowflake, "will you help me hang this one really high? I want everyone to see it when they look at the tree."

"Of course," Gabe replied, hoisting her up so she could reach a branch about seven feet off the ground. "Where do you think it should go?"

"Right here," she declared, carefully positioning the ornament with serious concentration. "So when people stand in front of the tree, they'll see how pretty it is."

"That's absolutely perfect," Claire told Lily. "You've got great decorating instincts."

"Mommy and Grandma taught me," Lily replied with obvious pride.

The next several hours unfolded with the kind of chaotic fun that made community projects both challenging and deeply satisfying. Teams of volunteers worked together, transforming the town square into a Christmas wonderland, while laughter and conversation created a festive atmosphere.

Claire moved naturally between different volunteer groups—helping children select ornaments, coordinating with adults about light placement, troubleshooting decoration dilemmas, and serving as one half of the coordination team that kept everything running smoothly.

Joyce and Melanie appeared as the day was winding down, carrying supplies for a small army—trays of cookies, thermal containers of hot chocolate and coffee, and disposable cups.

"Cookies?" Lily asked immediately, abandoning her ornament hanging to investigate.

"Yes, sugar cookies," Melanie replied. "Plus some gingerbread and candy cane-shaped shortbread."

"They're gorgeous," Brooke said with genuine admiration, examining the detailed decoration work on the sugar cookies.

As volunteers gathered around the refreshment station, Claire found herself standing slightly apart from the group, watching the scene unfold with deep satisfaction. The magnificent Fraser fir now sparkled with hundreds of carefully placed ornaments and the light strings that would transform it into a beacon visible throughout downtown Mistletoe Falls.

Gabe approached Claire with a satisfied grin. "So," he said, glancing up at the decorated tree and then back at her, "how does it feel to be halfway through creating the most spectacular tree lighting ceremony Mistletoe Falls has ever seen?"

"Pretty incredible," Claire admitted, following his gaze to take in the full scope of what they'd accomplished. "And exhausting, and exhilarating, and slightly overwhelming all at the same time."

"Good overwhelming?"

"Definitely a good overwhelming." Claire paused. "Gabe, your family is wonderful. I enjoyed working with them today."

"They adore you," Gabe replied, stepping closer so their conversation became more private despite the activity continuing around them. "Watching you today with my family..." He paused, seeming to search for the right words. "I realized something important."

"What's that?"

Gabe's hand found hers, their fingers interlacing with the natural ease that had developed between them. When he smiled, it was with the kind of genuine happiness that transformed his entire expression.

"I realized that when someone fits so naturally into your life, when everything feels effortless and right... that's when you know you've found someone truly special."

Chapter 17

The day before Thanksgiving, Claire stepped out of the bakery and watched the scene in the town square unfolding. City trucks lined Mistletoe Lane while uniformed city workers unloaded equipment.

"My goodness," Joyce said as she exited the bakery with Carol, "they've got more equipment here than we used for my granddaughter's outdoor wedding."

Claire's gaze immediately found Gabe near the largest city truck, his flannel sleeves rolled up despite the cold as he helped two city workers wrestle a substantial tent frame toward the square's perimeter.

"There's your coordination partner," Joyce observed, following Claire's line of sight. "Looking very capable and... what's the word I'm looking for?"

"Professional," Claire said.

"I was going to say handsome," Joyce replied cheerfully.

Gabe straightened from his tent-wrestling duties, his face breaking into a smile when he noticed them. "Morning, ladies!" He called as he gestured toward the equipment scattered around the square. "Hope you're ready to transform this into something that looks intentional."

"We are," Claire said as she crossed Mistletoe Lane.

"We have coffee and muffins for the work crew," Joyce added, already moving toward the nearest empty table in the square.

As Joyce distributed refreshments efficiently, Claire naturally gravitated toward where Gabe was working. The area where the first refreshment booth's tent frame lay in pieces across the snow-covered grass like an elaborate puzzle waiting for assembly.

"How long does tent setup usually take?" She asked, studying the array of poles, stakes, and heavy canvas that would soon become shelter.

"Maybe thirty minutes per booth," Gabe replied, pulling work gloves from his back pocket.

Mayor Hayes approached with characteristic enthusiasm, Frank Whitman following behind. Both men surveyed the tent components with obvious eagerness to contribute.

"Morning, you two!" Mayor Hayes boomed, rubbing his hands together. "Ready to create some serious Christmas magic? Frank came to help us this morning. He's assembled every type of temporary structure known to mankind."

"That was forty years ago, Roger," Frank replied with good humor, examining the tent instructions with the careful attention of someone who'd learned that reading directions prevented embarrassing mistakes. "But I suppose it's like riding a bicycle—once you know how to put up a tent, you never forget."

The next hour unfolded with collaborative comedy that made community projects both challenging and entertaining. The first tent's assembly required input from six different people who each had opinions about pole placement, anchor point selection, and the proper technique for achieving weather-resistant tension.

"No, no, that corner needs to go toward the gazebo," Mayor Hayes directed while Frank held a substantial tent pole and Gabe worked to secure the opposite corner. "Wind patterns, you know—don't want the whole thing taking flight during the ceremony."

"Roger, the wind doesn't care which direction we point the tent," Frank replied patiently.

"Actually," Gabe said, "Mayor Hayes has a point about wind patterns. But I think we'll be fine as long as we get proper anchoring and stake the guy-lines correctly."

Claire watched how naturally Gabe managed the different volunteers' personalities, providing direction without diminishing anyone's contributions. When Frank's technique for tent pole insertion proved inefficient, Gabe quietly demonstrated a better method while praising Frank's attention to detail. When Mayor Hayes became overly enthusiastic about guy-line tension, Gabe channeled that energy toward productive tasks that utilized the mayor's genuine desire to help.

"You're really good at this," she said quietly during a brief lull while the mayor and Frank debated optimal table placement within the completed first tent.

"Good at what?" Gabe asked, pausing in his inspection of tent stakes to give her his full attention.

"Managing people. Making everyone feel valuable while keeping projects moving forward." Claire gestured toward where Mayor Hayes was now measuring table distances with obvious satisfaction. "It's like watching a master class in collaborative leadership."

Color rose slightly in Gabe's cheeks at her observation. "Years of managing seasonal employees during the Christmas tree season. You learn that people work better when they feel heard and appreciated, even if their suggestions need gentle... redirection."

"Is that what you call it?" Claire teased, remembering the mayor's earlier wind pattern theories. "Gentle redirection?"

"Diplomatic problem-solving," Gabe corrected with a grin that made her chest flutter. "Much more professional-sounding."

"Claire!" Joyce called from the second tent site, where she and Carol had begun organizing table arrangements with military precision. "We need your input on the hot beverage stations."

The refreshment booth planning absorbed the next hour as they worked through practical details. Each of the three booths required coffee and hot chocolate dispensers positioned for easy access, table space for cookie displays and serving supplies, electrical connections for equipment, and storage areas for backup supplies that would prevent mid-ceremony emergencies.

"This booth handles the gazebo-side crowd," Claire explained to Joyce while they arranged tables within the completed tent. "I imagine this area will be popular with families with small children and elderly folks who want easy access to seating. We'll need extra paper goods here, I imagine."

"And that booth naturally catches the overflow, and those happy with hanging around the outer perimeter of the ceremony," Carol added, pointing toward the second tent.

"What about the third booth?" Gabe asked, joining their logistics discussion while Todd Jones began running electrical lines between tent locations.

"Couples and serious tree-viewing," Claire replied. "I imagine that booth area will be hit with all the media that will be in attendance and well... probably a lot of families as well. Maybe we should--"

"Claire, it's hot chocolate, coffee, and cookies, not a wine tasting. Let's not get too bogged down with details and just overstock each booth anticipating a crowd," Joyce said with a grin.

Eventually, after a few more hours, the refreshment booths stood ready, the electrical systems functioned perfectly, and every detail reflected the kind of collaborative excellence that made community events memorable.

"So," Gabe said as they completed their final walk-through, "tomorrow's Thanksgiving."

"It is. Are you cooking for your family, or is your mom handling the turkey duties?"

"Mom's in charge of the main event, but I'm making my grandpas' famous cornbread stuffing," Gabe replied with a grin. "Famous because it's the only dish I make that my family actually requests."

"I'm sure it's delicious," Claire said, trying to imagine Gabe in his kitchen, carefully preparing stuffing while Baxter supervised hopefully from nearby.

"What about you? Traditional Whitfield family Thanksgiving?"

"Very traditional. Mom starts cooking at dawn, Dad spends the morning watching a parade on television and offering 'helpful' kitchen advice, and Rachel and I handle the desserts. We're making Grandma Mae's sweet potato pie recipe and a pumpkin pie, plus maple pecan tarts with caramel-flavored whipped cream."

"Sounds good."

They stood together in comfortable silence for a moment, watching the last volunteers finish cleanup.

"So," Gabe said, "Friday morning—your first official baked goods delivery to the farm."

"Yep. Are you nervous about opening day?"

"More excited than nervous," he said. "Then we've got the tree lighting ceremony that night."

"We do," Claire agreed. "I'm going to miss all this once it's all over... the planning and the extra time we've spent together."

Gabe stepped a little closer. "After Friday's ceremony is over and we've pulled off the best tree lighting Mistletoe Falls has ever seen... maybe we could find other reasons to spend time together."

"Other reasons?"

"Reasons that don't involve community service," he clarified. "Reasons that are just about us wanting to be together."

"I'd like that. A lot."

Chapter 18

Claire guided the bakery's delivery van around the last curve leading to Mistletoe Christmas Tree Farm, her pulse quickening as the property unfolded before her like a scene from the most elaborate Christmas movie ever filmed. Even though she'd visited multiple times during the past few weeks, nothing had prepared her for the transformation that opening day energy created across every visible inch of Gabe's operation.

The entrance pillars gleamed with fresh garland and oversized red velvet bows, while professionally painted signs announced "Grand Opening - North Pole Trading Post" in elegant script surrounded by holly and pine branches.

I feel like a kid again, Claire thought.

Staff members in matching red vests worked steadily with last-minute preparations, while the sound of cheerful holiday music drifted across the property from hidden speakers that created a festive atmosphere.

The North Pole Trading Post practically glowed with welcoming light, its windows showcasing artfully arranged displays that promised the kind of authentic Christmas shopping experience that couldn't be replicated in any mall or chain store.

She parked near the Trading Post's service entrance as planned, immediately spotting Gabe emerging from the main barn with Brianna close behind. But it was Baxter who reached her first.

"Did you miss me, sweet boy?" Claire said, climbing down from the driver's seat while Baxter practically vibrated with joy.

"I believe he did. You're his favorite person nowadays," Gabe said, approaching with a grin that made her chest flutter.

Claire opened the van's rear doors to reveal neat rows of white bakery boxes.

"My goodness," Brianna said. "This looks like enough to supply a small restaurant."

"Opening day seemed like the time to make a strong first impression," Claire said.

Working together, the three of them transferred Claire's baked goods from the van inside the Trading Post.

"Where do you want the sample cookies?" Claire asked, surveying the Trading Post's interior, which looked even more impressive filled with the energy of opening day preparation.

"Right here, center stage," Brianna replied, gesturing toward the beautiful display case positioned to catch customers' immediate attention.

The next twenty minutes transformed the Trading Post's food service area. Claire arranged cookies and then moved on to other baked good displays, while Gabe ensured the coffee and hot chocolate equipment functioned perfectly, and Brianna added final touches that made everything look even more festive.

"These sugar cookies are works of art," a voice said from behind them, and Claire turned to see Derrick as he examined the decorated Christmas trees, stars, and snowflakes through the display case glass. "Customers are going to lose their minds when they see these."

"Melanie spent extra time on the decoration details," Claire replied. "We wanted opening day for your customers to be extra special."

"Mission accomplished," Derrick said, accepting coffee from Gabe while the four of them stepped back to survey their completed setup. "This looks like something from a high-end resort gift shop, not a rural Christmas tree farm."

"We're not competing with high-end—we're creating our own category," Gabe said with a smile.

"The five-minute countdown begins now!" Brianna said. "Ready for the big moment, boss?"

"More than ready," Gabe replied, though Claire caught a hint of nervous excitement in his voice.

At ten o'clock, Gabe unlocked the Trading Post's main entrance and stepped aside as the first families began flowing through the doorway with the eager energy of people who'd been eagerly awaiting this experience. Claire positioned herself near the food service area where she could observe customer reactions.

The next hour unfolded like watching Christmas magic come to life through other people's eyes. Children pressed their faces against the cookie and baked goods display cases with obvious wonder, while parents asked thoughtful questions about ingredients and flavors. A mother with twin toddlers actually gasped when she tasted the sample snickerdoodle.

Claire enjoyed observing the customer interactions while watching families discover the Trading Post's carefully curated selection of gifts and decorations. Every few minutes, she caught glimpses of Gabe moving through the crowd with natural ease, greeting customers personally, and ensuring everyone felt welcomed.

"This partnership was definitely the right decision," Brianna said during a brief lull, approaching Claire with obvious satisfaction at how smoothly everything was functioning. "Your baked goods are a hit."

"Mission accomplished. It feels good to be part of this," Claire admitted.

"Claire!" a familiar voice called, and she turned to see Lily and Conner racing toward her with Brooke following at a more measured pace, all three of them clearly delighted to encounter her during their farm visit.

"Uncle Gabe said you made all the cookies!" Conner said. "Which one's the bestest one?"

"Now that's a tough question," Claire said with mock seriousness, crouching to meet his eyes. "But I'd say the decorated Christmas tree cookies are pretty high on my list. In fact, I think you both need to try one and tell me if I'm right."

"Really? We can have one right now?" Lily asked, practically bouncing on her toes.

"Of course you can," Claire said with a smile.

"Will you be at the tree lighting ceremony tonight?" Lily asked, inspecting her decorated cookie as if it were a rare treasure.

"I wouldn't miss it," Claire assured her.

"It's gonna be like a magic show!" Conner declared his grin widening at the thought.

As the morning wore on, the Trading Post buzzed with a steady stream of shoppers, each one drawn into the festive charm Gabe had so carefully crafted. Claire found herself lingering near the windows, taking it all in—the cheerful chaos, the scent of fresh pine drifting in every time the door opened, the sound of distant laughter carrying from the fields.

Outside, visitors climbed aboard wagon rides led by friendly staff, bundled against the cold as they toured the snow-dusted farm. Beyond that, families strolled through the nearest tree grove, pausing to run gloved hands over fragrant branches before choosing their perfect Christmas tree.

"Pretty amazing, isn't it?" Derrick said, appearing at her side.

"Incredible," Claire agreed, her gaze still sweeping the scene. "I knew Gabe had built something special here, but seeing it alive with families enjoying every detail—it's something else entirely."

"He's got a gift for knowing what makes experiences memorable," Derrick replied, pride threading through his voice.

Around eleven-thirty, the opening day rush eased into a steady flow, and Claire realized it was time to head back to the bakery. The thought of leaving the farm's magical hum was almost disappointing, but practical responsibilities called.

"I should head back to town," she told Gabe as she made her way toward him.

"Already?"

"Duty calls," she said with a regretful smile, stacking her empty delivery containers. "I need to swing by the community center to check on ceremony prep, then get back to the bakery. It's an all-hands-on-deck kind of day."

"Tonight," Gabe repeated, his gaze locking with hers, a spark of anticipation in his voice. "Hard to believe we're finally going to see everything come together."

"Yep—tonight's the night," Claire agreed, feeling a flutter of excitement threaded with nervous energy.

"Thanks for staying a little while this morning," Gabe said, stepping closer until the surrounding bustle faded to background noise.

"I wouldn't have missed this for anything."

"I'll see you tonight?"

"You'll see me tonight," she promised, letting their fingers twine briefly before she pulled away. Families continued wandering the farm, oblivious to the small, charged moment between them.

At the van, Baxter stationed himself by the door as if he might block her departure.

"I'll see you soon, buddy," she said, giving his head a fond pat. "Be a good boy and help your daddy today."

The drive back to town gave her time to savor the morning's success. She hummed along to a Christmas tune on the radio, replaying customer smiles, cheerful chatter, and the smooth teamwork that had made their first official partnership day even better than she'd imagined.

This time last year, I was miserable in Atlanta; she thought as Mistletoe Falls' familiar downtown came into view. *Now I'm humming Christmas carols after spending the morning watching families discover the magic of a Christmas tree farm gift shop that I helped stock.*

Tonight's going to be magical, she realized with growing excitement *—the icing on the cake.*

Chapter 19

Gabe approached the refreshment booth through a gentle snowfall that had turned Mistletoe Falls' town square into a living Christmas card. His breath formed small clouds in the crisp evening air, and the square hummed with the anticipatory excitement of families gathered for the tree lighting ceremony. The refreshment booth glowed with warm light against the deepening twilight, where Joyce handed out steaming cups of hot chocolate and coffee to a steady line of customers.

Beside one of the serving tables, Claire straightened already-perfect napkin dispensers, her gaze sweeping the crowd as if ticking items off an invisible checklist. Even surrounded by falling snow, twinkling lights, and the hum of happy conversation, her perfectionist instincts wouldn't let her stop fine-tuning every detail.

"Claire, honey, quit fussing with those napkins and go enjoy your evening," Joyce said with gentle firmness, shooing her away as she passed a cup of hot chocolate to a waiting customer. "I've got this booth running like clockwork, and the volunteers helping me are perfectly capable. You have more important things to do than rearrange supplies that don't need rearranging."

"But what if you run out of coffee? Or the cookies—shouldn't I check the cookie supply? And—" Claire reached for a stack of disposable cups that looked perfectly adequate to Gabe.

"Young lady," Joyce interrupted, her tone a blend of maternal patience and no-nonsense authority, "I've been serving refreshments at community events since before you were born. We have backup coffee, extra cookies, and enough caffeine on hand to keep half of Tennessee awake until New Year's. Now, march yourself over to that beautiful tree you helped create and enjoy the ceremony."

Gabe bit back a smile, watching Claire wage an internal battle between her need to control every detail and the dawning realization that Joyce was absolutely right. The booth ran like a well-oiled machine—customers received steaming cups with warm smiles, and everything unfolded exactly as they'd planned.

"She's right, you know," Gabe said, stepping beside her. Snow had dusted her dark hair with tiny crystals that caught the glow of the nearby streetlamps, making her look as though she belonged in the scene as much as the twinkling lights and falling snow. "Your staff and the volunteers have everything under control. You deserve to actually experience the ceremony instead of managing it."

"But what if—" Claire began, then stopped herself with a rueful laugh that sent a pleasant warmth through his chest. "I'm being ridiculous, aren't I?"

"You're being you," he replied gently, reaching for her hand in the casual way that had become second nature. "Which means caring so much about creating something perfect for everyone else that you forget to enjoy your own success."

Her fingers slid into his, their warmth settling over him like a familiar comfort.

"Joyce, you're absolutely right," Claire said. "But if you need anything—"

"I'll text you," Joyce replied. "Now go on, both of you."

They left the bustle of the refreshment booth behind, moving through the growing crowd toward the towering Christmas tree that anchored the town square like a living monument. Claire tucked naturally against his side, her hand warm in his. Snow drifted down in lazy flakes, while the sound of carolers near the gazebo blended with the cheerful conversations of people reveling in the night's festivities.

"Look at all these people," Claire said with wonder, her gaze sweeping the square, awe shining in her eyes. "I knew we were expecting a big turnout, but this is incredible."

Gabe followed her gaze. Couples strolled hand in hand beneath the falling snow while children darted between legs, their laughter rippling through the crisp air. Elderly residents sat on benches along the perimeter, bundled against the cold as they chatted and watched the activities going on around them. Visitors from neighboring towns snapped photos of the gazebo draped in garland and the towering Christmas tree, their faces lit with delight.

Near one of the refreshment booths, he spotted Melanie passing out cookies to a line of customers that included several familiar faces. "There's the Abbotts," Gabe said, nodding toward a family of five. "They've bought trees from us for five years, but Mrs. Abbott told me this is the first time they've made it to the lighting ceremony."

"And look—" Claire pointed toward the third refreshment booth, where Carol manned the counter with calm efficiency while a local news reporter leaned in for an interview. "Looks like we're getting media coverage for our little ceremony."

"Little ceremony," Gabe echoed with a grin, sweeping his arm toward the packed square. "Claire, we've got well over a thousand families here, three television crews from what I've heard, and at least two newspapers. This isn't little—this is the kind of event that puts towns on the tourism map."

"Gabe! Claire!" Brooke's voice carried above the cheerful din as she approached with Shane and the kids in tow, all of them bundled in winter coats and glowing with the kind of family excitement that made nights like this unforgettable.

Lily darted ahead of her parents, launching herself toward Gabe and Claire with the fearless enthusiasm of a nine-year-old who had decided they were firmly in her circle of favorite grown-ups.

"Uncle Gabe, everyone's talking about how beautiful the tree is!" she announced, bouncing on her toes as snowflakes caught in her auburn hair. "Tommy Dunmore says it's the most beautifulist Christmas tree he's ever seen, and his family goes to New York City every year to see their big tree!"

"Tommy Dunmore clearly has excellent taste," Claire said with mock seriousness, crouching to meet Lily's eyes. "But I think our tree has something those big-city trees don't."

"What's that?" Conner asked, appearing at his sister's side, curiosity written all over his face.

"It was grown right here in Mistletoe Falls, with love and patience, and decorated by friends and neighbors working together," Claire explained.

"Plus," Lily added, "you and Uncle Gabe picked it together. That makes it extra special—like, practically old married couple special."

"Lily Davidson," Brooke chided gently, though her amused smile undercut any real reproach. "We don't go around making announcements about other people's personal business."

"They hold hands and smile at each other," Conner said with the absolute certainty of a seven-year-old. "Dad says that means—"

"That means they like each other, and that's all that matters right now," Shane cut in smoothly.

Claire's cheeks warmed to what felt like four different shades of red under the children's scrutiny.

"We should probably find good spots for the ceremony... you know, like old married folks," Gabe murmured with a chuckle, leaning closer so only she could hear.

As they moved through the crowd together, Gabe caught the approving nods and warm smiles sent their way. Word had clearly spread about their partnership on the ceremony—and, judging by the looks, the community was rooting for them in more ways than one.

"Gabe, Claire—wonderful job tonight," called Tom Morrison, pausing his conversation with a group of longtime residents to offer his congratulations. "This tree is the finest we've ever had, and the whole setup is just spectacular. You two have outdone yourselves."

"I've never seen such a beautiful celebration. It's wonderful seeing this many folks turn out," added Mrs. Phillips, with a look of deep satisfaction.

As they moved through the crowd, the same theme repeated—warm compliments, heartfelt thanks, and sincere congratulations from customers, neighbors, and visitors alike. Every word confirmed what Gabe and Claire were already feeling: their efforts had given the town something truly special.

"Attention, everyone!" Mayor Hayes' amplified voice rang out from the gazebo platform. "Could I have your attention for just a few moments?"

The buzz of conversation gradually faded into an expectant hush. Parents drew children close, couples leaned toward each other, and a ripple of anticipation passed through the square. Gabe slipped his arm around Claire's shoulders. She leaned in without hesitation, and together they faced the gazebo—surrounded by the glow of twinkling lights, the soft swirl of falling snow, and the shared pride of knowing they had helped create the night's magic.

"Welcome, friends, neighbors, and visitors," Mayor Hayes began, his voice carrying easily through the crisp evening air. "Tonight we gather for more than just the lighting of our community Christmas tree. We celebrate the spirit of collaboration, dedication, and love that makes Mistletoe Falls truly special."

Scattered applause rippled through the crowd, underscored by the warm hum of genuine pride rather than polite formality.

"This year's ceremony represents something extraordinary," the mayor continued, gesturing toward the magnificent Fraser fir that towered above them like a regal sentinel. "Through the partnership between Sugarplum Bakery and Mistletoe Christmas Tree Farm—coordinated by Claire Whitfield and Gabe Mills—and with the help of many dedicated volunteers, we've seen the kind of teamwork that creates lasting holiday memories."

He paused, letting the words settle over the crowd like a blessing. "So before we light our tree and officially welcome the Christmas season to Mistletoe Falls," he concluded, his expression one of obvious satisfaction, "let's recognize the dedication that made this magical evening possible. Claire and Gabe, would you step forward?"

"He wants us to—" Claire began, glancing up at Gabe, her surprise threaded with a flicker of nervous excitement.

"Come on," Gabe said softly, his hand finding hers with quiet assurance. Together they started toward the gazebo as the applause swelled around them, the sound as warm and bright as the lights strung through the square.

The brief walk to the platform felt both longer and shorter than it should have—every step punctuated by familiar faces offering congratulations, warm smiles, and words of appreciation, while the flash of cameras lit their path like tiny bursts of starlight. Beside him, Claire moved with natural grace despite the hint of a flutter in her expression, and when they reached the steps, Mayor Hayes extended a hand to help her up.

"Ladies and gentlemen," he announced as they joined him, "Claire Whitfield of Sugarplum Bakery and Gabe Mills of Mistletoe Christmas Tree Farm—the two folks who coordinated this event and led teams of volunteers that made tonight's magic possible!"

Applause, cheers, and appreciative calls rose in a wave that wrapped around them like the embrace of the whole town. Gabe spotted his parents, sister, and the kids clapping enthusiastically near the tree, while Joyce, Melanie, and Carol had stepped out from behind the refreshment booth to beam their support at Claire.

"Thank you," Claire began, accepting the microphone from Mayor Hayes. Her voice carried a note of nervousness, but as she spoke, confidence warmed each word. "This ceremony represents so much more than lighting a Christmas tree. It celebrates the community spirit that makes Mistletoe Falls special—neighbors helping neighbors, businesses working together, and everyone contributing their unique gifts to create something beautiful that belongs to all of us."

Her words rang clearly through the crisp evening air, and pride swelled in Gabe's chest at how effortlessly she had distilled the heart of their weeks of collaboration.

"Gabe and I discovered that the best partnerships happen when people share the same values and vision," she continued, glancing at him with a look that held both professional respect and something warmer, something personal. "Thank you for trusting us with this responsibility and for making tonight so special."

She passed the microphone back to Mayor Hayes as applause once again filled the square.

"And now," Mayor Hayes announced with a theatrical flourish, "the moment we've all been waiting for. In ten seconds, our magnificent community Christmas tree will officially welcome the holiday season to Mistletoe Falls!"

The crowd erupted into a unified countdown, children's voices tumbling over one another with giddy excitement while the deeper tones of the adults kept the rhythm steady. Anticipation shimmered in the snowy air like static before a storm.

"Ten! Nine! Eight!"

Beside him, Gabe felt Claire's fingers tighten around his, the simple pressure holding a world of shared accomplishment and something warmer that had nothing to do with the temperature.

"Seven! Six! Five!"

"Four! Three! Two!"

Just before "one," he glanced at her—and for a moment, the bustle and noise blurred into the background. The glow from the surrounding lights caught in her eyes, her expression alive with joy, and he thought she had never looked more beautiful.

"One!"

The square erupted in cheers as the tree blazed to life, thousands of lights sweeping outward in cascading waves of gold and white until the Fraser fir stood like a luminous sentinel at the heart of town. Gasps of delight rose from the crowd, the golden star at its peak flaring brilliantly as though it had captured every light below and sent it back out into the night.

But Gabe barely noticed the tree's dazzling transformation. His attention was fixed entirely on Claire, who stood transfixed by the moment, wonder and quiet satisfaction etched across her features. Drawing her closer, he settled his arm more securely around her shoulders and pressed a gentle kiss to the top of her head.

For Claire, the world seemed to fall utterly still.

The cheers and applause faded to nothing, the snowflakes hung suspended in midair, and even the brilliant glow of the Christmas tree softened into the background—secondary to the warmth of Gabe's lips against her hair and the solid, reassuring weight of his arm holding her close.

When she looked up, her eyes shone, and the gentle curve of his smile told her everything she needed to know. All the hopes she'd been quietly carrying, too fragile to name, had just crystallized into something beautiful and unmistakably real.

Around them, Mistletoe Falls celebrated the official start of the Christmas season. But for Claire and Gabe, the magic wasn't in the lights or the music—it was in the quiet certainty that they'd found something rare and worth keeping in each other.

Chapter 20

"Mark, can you double-check the wagon harnesses before we open?" Gabe called to his seasonal worker, who was stacking gear near the barn. "Yesterday's opening day put everything through its paces, and I want us ready for a busy Saturday."

"On it, boss," Mark replied.

The farm was already alive with motion and purpose. The success of opening day, paired with the glow of last night's spectacular tree lighting, had left the crew buzzing with energy instead of worn out.

Gabe glanced up from his equipment checklist as the Sugarplum Bakery delivery van rolled into view.

Baxter immediately abandoned his side, tearing across the yard with the boundless enthusiasm he reserved for one particular visitor.

"Well, hello there, my favorite farm ambassador," Claire called, climbing down from the driver's seat. She crouched to give Baxter the attention he demanded, rubbing behind his ears as his tail wagged like a metronome. "Did you miss me? It's been a whole twenty-four hours since I saw you last."

Baxter pressed his entire head into her hands, making soft, almost conversational sounds—like he was recounting every important thing that had happened since yesterday.

"Good morning," Gabe said as he approached, genuine pleasure threading through his voice.

"Morning yourself," Claire replied, straightening from her Baxter appreciation session. Her cheeks were pink from the cold, her eyes bright with the alert energy of someone who'd been up for hours. She rounded the van to the passenger side, opening the door and retrieving a white bakery box, a thermal coffee cup, and an individually wrapped cinnamon roll.

"I figured you wouldn't have time for your usual Saturday morning trip to town, not with opening weekend keeping you busy here at the farm," she said.

Gabe stopped mid-step. "You brought me my Saturday morning order."

"Yep. Black coffee, a cinnamon roll, and a mixed half-dozen muffins Melanie picked out special," Claire confirmed, holding the items out with a smile that sent a slow, warm stretch through his chest. "All on the house... just because."

Gabe accepted the box and coffee, struck by the simple thoughtfulness of it. "You didn't have to do this."

"I wanted to," she said.

"Well," Gabe said, taking a sip of the perfectly hot coffee, "this officially makes you the most thoughtful business partner in Tennessee."

"Just business partners?" Claire's teasing tone held a glimmer of something more.

He met her gaze, matching her playful challenge. "Among other things."

Claire smiled. "I should probably get the delivery inside before Brianna starts wondering where her inventory is," she said, moving toward the van's rear doors with Baxter trotting beside her in his role as loyal escort. "I brought extra sample cookies today, too. Figured with it being Saturday, you're going to be swamped."

"Let me help with that," Gabe said immediately, setting his coffee and the packaged baked goods on a table near the gift shop.

Working with a peaceful rhythm, they began unloading the van.

"Morning, Claire," Brianna called as they stepped into the Trading Post. "Yesterday's baked goods sold out by two in the afternoon—completely exceeded my predictions."

"Wow, that's great! Melanie sent extra sample cookies today," Claire said, heading straight for the display cases. "Plus some new gingerbread stars she finished late last night. Wait until you taste them."

She began arranging the cookies with practiced precision while Brianna kept up a cheerful stream of updates about yesterday's customer reactions and the expected rush ahead.

"The families were raving about the quality," Brianna said, accepting a stack of boxes from Gabe as he came back through the door. "I had at least a dozen people ask for business cards and information on special orders."

"That's awesome," Claire said with clear satisfaction, stepping back to admire her finished cookie display.

"Claire," Gabe began, "what would you think about coming to the farm tomorrow... as a customer?"

She paused mid-adjustment, turning toward him with a curious tilt of her head. "As a customer?"

"You know... a full tree farm experience," Gabe explained, feeling a little like a teenager asking someone to a school dance. "An afternoon of fun, picking out a Christmas tree for your apartment and a tour of the property."

"A real Christmas tree and a tour," Claire repeated, her eyes lighting with genuine excitement.

"The most authentic Christmas tree experience possible. I could show you parts of the farm you haven't seen yet—the pond, the walking trails, some of the scenic overlooks that make this place special."

"That sounds absolutely wonderful," she said without a second's hesitation, her whole face brightening.

"Around one?"

"One o'clock tomorrow sounds perfect," Claire agreed, then paused, a hint of embarrassment tugging at her smile. "But I should warn you, I have no clue how to care for a live tree. When I was growing up, my parents always took care of that. So you'll have to give me a lesson in tree care."

"I can do that."

Through the Trading Post windows, Gabe noticed the first families of the day beginning to arrive.

"I should probably let you get back to work," Claire said as she gathered her empty delivery containers. "Looks like you're in for a busy Saturday."

"Probably. But I'm already looking forward to tomorrow."

"Just us exploring the farm and picking out a tree," Claire said, her smile warming something deep in his chest. "No committees, no schedules, no responsibilities except enjoying ourselves."

"Exactly," Gabe replied, walking with her toward the exit while Baxter fell in step beside them. "Though I should warn you—Baxter will probably insist on supervising the entire tree selection process."

"I'm counting on it," Claire laughed, pausing to give the dog one last fond rub before climbing into the driver's seat.

She started the van, the gentle hum of the engine breaking the quiet bubble that had formed between them. Gabe lingered by the open window.

"Thanks for thinking of me this morning," he said. "I appreciate you bringing my breakfast."

"That's what people do when someone matters to them," Claire replied warmly. "I wanted to make sure your Saturday started right."

"Mission accomplished," Gabe assured her, stepping back from the van—fighting the sudden urge to lean in and close the distance with a kiss.

"See you tomorrow," Claire said, shifting into gear.

"Have a good day, Claire."

"You too."

He watched as the van pulled away.

"You've got it bad," Brianna said with obvious amusement as she joined him outside the Trading Post.

"That obvious?" Gabe asked.

"Completely obvious," Brianna confirmed cheerfully, nodding toward the stream of vehicles pulling in. "But right now, we've got trees to sell and Christmas magic to make. You can moon over Claire later."

Chapter 21

Claire stepped out of her SUV, and into the crisp enchantment of fresh snow crunching beneath her boots. The blanket of white that had fallen earlier in the day had transformed Mistletoe Christmas Tree Farm into something straight from the cover of a Christmas card. Pine-scented air filled her lungs, cool and invigorating, while the distant laughter of families exploring the fields provided the perfect soundtrack to what felt like stepping into a winter wonderland.

"Perfect timing," Gabe called, emerging from the main barn with Baxter bounding ahead like a furry missile of pure joy. "I was starting to worry you'd changed your mind about spending the afternoon with a tree farmer and his overly enthusiastic dog."

"Never," Claire replied, crouching to give Baxter the welcome he clearly expected. Over the dog's head, she couldn't help noticing how Gabe looked entirely in his element—work boots, warm flannel, and that confident, calm smile that sent an unexpected skip through her pulse. "Though I have to admit, I'm a little nervous about picking out my first real Christmas tree as an adult."

"Christmas trees aren't a test you can fail," Gabe said with an easy smile. "It's all about finding the one that feels right to you."

When he reached for her hand with the natural ease that had become second nature between them, the familiar flutter of awareness stirred in her chest. "That's very philosophical for a Sunday afternoon."

"I'm a deep thinker," Gabe replied with mock seriousness, then gestured toward the barn, a spark of excitement breaking through his casual demeanor. "Come on, I have a surprise."

Baxter trotted beside them as they crossed the yard toward the barn's wide entrance, his tail wagging like he knew exactly what was coming. The distant sounds of the farm wrapped around them—families calling to one another among the trees, the low rumble of wagon tours, and employees' cheerful voices guiding customers toward their perfect Christmas memories.

"So, what's the plan?" Claire asked as they reached the barn doors. "Do we just wander until something speaks to me, or is there an actual science to picking a Christmas tree?"

"A little of both," Gabe said, pulling open the heavy wooden door, his eyes crinkling with barely suppressed amusement.

Claire stepped through the doorway and stopped so abruptly that Baxter nearly bumped into the back of her legs. Her breath caught, eyes going wide with unguarded wonder.

Beneath a canopy of twinkling lights that bathed the space in warm, golden radiance stood a holiday-red sleigh that looked as if it had been lifted straight from the pages of a Christmas storybook. Hitched in place were two magnificent dapple-gray Percherons, their steady breaths forming white clouds in the cool air while the soft jingle of brass bells marked each shift of their weight. Pine garlands curved gracefully along the sleigh's frame, plaid wool blankets lay neatly folded across the seats, and behind it, a small flatbed trailer waited for the Christmas tree they would choose together.

"Gabe..." Claire's voice was breathless, her awe impossible to hide as she slowly approached the sleigh. "This is... absolutely magical. I wasn't expecting..." She trailed off, at a rare loss for words, then laughed softly in wonder. "How did you even know I'd love something like this?"

"Call it a lucky guess," Gabe replied, though the pleased curve of his mouth said otherwise. "I figured today should be memorable. Besides," he added, his grin sending a flutter through her chest, "this is what I call the couples' experience—private tours for people who want something special instead of the regular wagon rides."

"Wow. And you can actually drive this?"

"Handle a team, you mean? Absolutely." Gabe moved to the horses with an easy confidence, running his hand along the nearest Percheron's neck. The massive animal leaned into the touch like it had been waiting for him all day. "Jim Parker manages most of their care and training, but he taught me enough to take special guests out on private tours. Duchess and Duke here are gentle as lambs—and they know these trails as well as I do."

"Duchess and Duke. They're beautiful. And enormous."

"Percherons are gentle giants. Perfect for sleigh rides—steady, patient, and incredibly reliable. Want to say hello before we head out?"

Claire approached Duchess with tentative reverence, extending her hand the way she'd seen done in movies. The mare lowered her head with dignified grace, warm breath puffing against Claire's fingers before she allowed a slow, velvety stroke along her nose. A soft nicker vibrated through the air, the sound oddly soothing.

"She likes you," Gabe said, the corners of his mouth lifting.

"Just like Baxter," Claire replied, glancing down at the Border Collie mix now stationed beside the sleigh like a furry bodyguard. "Speaking of which, can he come with us?"

"Try keeping him away. He'd be personally offended if we left him behind."

He offered his hands, steady and warm, to help her into the sleigh. Claire felt the brief, grounding pressure of his grip at her waist before settling into the plush seat cushions. The plaid blankets promised cozy warmth against the crisp afternoon air, and with a quick bound, Baxter joined her, claiming his place at her side like he'd been part of the plan all along.

"This is incredible," Claire said, running her hand over the sleigh's polished wood and gleaming brass fittings as Gabe climbed onto the driver's seat at the front. "I feel like I'm starring in my own Christmas movie."

"That's the idea," Gabe replied, gathering the reins. "Ready for the Christmas tree adventure of a lifetime?"

"More than ready," Claire said, leaning back into the cushioned seat as anticipation bubbled in her chest like champagne.

With a soft click of his tongue, the horses surged forward in smooth, powerful strides, carrying them out of the barn and into the snowy afternoon. The sleigh glided over the fresh powder with surprising grace, brass bells chiming in a cheerful rhythm that seemed to announce their passage to every corner of the farm.

"So," Gabe called over his shoulder as they followed a well-groomed path winding between rows of evergreens, "tell me about your perfect tree. Size, shape—what would make Claire Whitfield's ideal Christmas centerpiece?"

Claire considered her gaze sweeping over the postcard-perfect scenery. In the distance, families moved among the trees, their laughter floating on the crisp air. Employees in red vests lifted children toward higher branches while parents debated the merits of one tree over another.

"Well," she began thoughtfully, "I live in an apartment, so nothing too enormous. Something I can actually get up the stairs and through my doorway without too many problems."

"Size restrictions noted," Gabe said with a grin. "What else?"

"Full branches for hanging tons of ornaments and..." Claire stopped mid-thought, a sudden spark of inspiration straightening her posture. "Actually, I just had an entirely different idea."

"Different how?"

"What if we skip the tree for my apartment and find one for the bakery instead?" The words spilled out in a rush, her excitement building as she pictured it. "The bakery has those gorgeous high ceilings and big windows, and I've got boxes of Grandma Mae's Christmas decorations in the basement. Imagine a huge, beautiful tree right in the customer area—it would be perfect."

Gabe turned in his seat to look at her, his expression lighting with the same delight she felt. "Claire, that's a brilliant idea. Are you sure?"

"More than sure," she said, bouncing slightly against the cushioned seat. Her enthusiasm was apparently contagious—Baxter's tail had started wagging as if he approved. "Let's find something really special, something that'll make the whole bakery feel like Christmas morning."

"Absolutely," Gabe said, guiding the horses onto a winding path toward a hillside where older, more mature trees rose against the snow. Around them, the sounds of the farm continued like a festive symphony—distant laughter, the occasional buzz of a chainsaw, and the cheerful chatter of families building their own holiday memories. Claire couldn't help being impressed by the seamless way Gabe's operation handled so many moving parts without losing a bit of charm.

"There," Gabe said, drawing the horses to a stop beside a grove of magnificent Fraser firs that stood like proud sentinels. "These beauties have been growing for about twelve years. Perfect for commercial spaces—great needle retention, gorgeous shape, and enough presence to command a room."

Claire stepped down from the sleigh with Gabe's steadying hand, her boots crunching into the pristine snow. She moved toward the grove, immediately enchanted by the trees' rich green needles and elegant symmetry. Each one soared eight to ten feet high, its branches full and evenly spaced—ready to hold strings of lights, heirloom ornaments, and the magic of Christmas itself.

"They're all beautiful," she murmured, drifting among them with Baxter trotting faithfully at her side. "How am I supposed to choose between perfection... and more perfection?"

"Take your time," Gabe said, retrieving a chainsaw from the sleigh's storage compartment and giving her space to wander. "Walk around, see which one feels right. Sometimes the perfect tree chooses you."

Claire moved slowly through the grove, the crisp air nipping at her cheeks as she imagined each tree standing proudly in Sugarplum's dining area, sunlight spilling through the windows while customers sipped coffee and enjoyed fresh pastries beneath its branches.

Then she stopped.

The tree ahead stood like a masterpiece in nature's gallery—nine feet of perfect symmetry, every branch full and evenly spaced, the proportions so flawless they seemed almost dreamlike.

"This one," she called, her voice bright with certainty and joy. "Gabe, this is it. Can you picture it in the bakery's front windows, with families sitting at the tables, soaking in the magic while they enjoy their morning treats?"

Gabe joined her, his expression one of clear satisfaction as he brushed a hand along the needles. "Your customers are going to love it."

"I can already see it. Mae had this collection of vintage glass ornaments, every color you can imagine, plus handmade angels her mother created. Oh, Gabe, I'm so excited!"

"Then let's make this happen," Gabe said, pulling the starter cord with practiced ease until the chainsaw roared to life. "Want to help me cut down your perfect bakery tree?"

"Really? I can help?"

"Absolutely. It's your tree—you should be part of bringing it home."

The next twenty minutes unfolded in a blur of crisp air, fresh pine scent, and Gabe's patient, steady instruction. He showed her where to position the blade for the right trunk angle, explaining how a clean cut would help the tree sit perfectly in its stand.

"Here—put your hands right here," Gabe said, stepping in behind her and placing his hands over hers on the handles. The solid warmth of his chest at her back was enough to make her breath catch. "Feel the way the saw moves? We're guiding it, not forcing it. Let the saw do the work."

Claire leaned into the rhythm, her concentration narrowing until the world felt like just the two of them, the tree, and the hum of the chainsaw. When the Fraser fir gave a slow, regal sway and fell exactly where they'd planned, she let out a joyful cheer.

"We did it!" she laughed, stepping back to admire the fallen tree while Baxter trotted over to sniff it with the curiosity of someone who'd just discovered a brand-new jungle gym. "I can't believe I actually helped cut down a Christmas tree!"

"Natural talent," Gabe said with clear pride, setting the chainsaw aside before grabbing the trunk to drag it toward the waiting trailer.

"This is even more fun than I imagined," Claire admitted, helping him maneuver the tree into place, her cheeks pink from the cold and her pulse still quick with excitement. "I feel like a kid again."

She glanced at the magnificent tree after it was secured for transport, and a sudden practical thought slipped in. "Gabe, this tree is going to completely transform the bakery atmosphere. But..." She gave him a mock-serious look. "How in the world am I going to get this massive thing from here to downtown—and actually inside the building?"

"That's what delivery trucks are for," Gabe said with gentle amusement, securing the final tie-down strap before giving her his full attention. "Claire, you don't think I'd let you wrestle a nine-foot tree into the bakery by yourself, do you?"

"You'd do that?" she asked softly, searching his face.

"Claire, of course, I'd do anything to make you happy."

The way he was looking at her, like her happiness was the most important thing in his world, sent a rush of emotion straight through her. Before she could think better of it, she launched herself forward, wrapping him in an impulsive bear hug.

The force of her enthusiasm, combined with the slippery snow beneath their feet, sent them both tumbling onto the snow-covered ground, arms and legs tangling as startled laughter spilled between them.

Baxter, clearly convinced this was the best game ever invented, bounded into the pile with gleeful barking, attempting face-licks and full-body wiggles that turned the moment into joyful chaos.

"Oh my goodness," Claire gasped between laughs, trying to push herself up while Baxter climbed determinedly over both of them. "I'm so sorry, I didn't mean to—"

"If this is what happens when I cut down your perfect tree," Gabe interrupted, grinning as he helped wrangle the overexcited dog, "I'm going to have to make tree cutting a regular tradition."

Claire laughed so hard she could barely breathe, snow clinging to her hair and coat. She was sitting in an undignified heap beside the most wonderful man she'd ever met, while his dog beamed as though he'd orchestrated the entire scene.

"Baxter, you ridiculous fur ball," she managed between giggles, finally coaxing him to settle between them instead of on top of them. "We're trying to have a moment here."

"I think we're having exactly the right kind of moment," Gabe said warmly, helping her to her feet before brushing snow from her coat in gentle, lingering sweeps. "The kind you tell stories about for years."

As they walked back toward the sleigh, snow still clinging in stubborn patches and Baxter trotting proudly at their side, Claire felt something stir deep in her chest. The afternoon had awakened a feeling she hadn't experienced in years—pure, uncomplicated joy in simple pleasures and the magic of sharing them with someone who made her feel truly seen.

"This day has been perfect," she said as Gabe helped her back into the sleigh, his hands warm and steady at her waist. "Thank you for doing this for me."

"My pleasure," Gabe replied, climbing onto the driver's seat while Duchess and Duke shifted eagerly in their traces, as if they too were ready for the return trip. "So, what's next on your tour? We could visit the pond, take the trail to the scenic overlook, or I could show you the fire pit where we serve hot chocolate and roasted marshmallows during evening rides."

Claire glanced toward the horizon, imagining each option—hot chocolate by the fire, sweeping views from the overlook—but her gaze inevitably drifted back to the magnificent Fraser fir riding proudly on the trailer behind them. The thought of it standing in the bakery's front windows, dressed in Grandma Mae's ornaments, sent a little thrill through her chest.

"You know what I really want to do? I want to get this gorgeous tree back to the bakery and start decorating it. I'm so excited I can barely sit still."

"Are you sure?" Gabe teased, though his eyes said he understood completely. "No fire pit with hot chocolate? No scenic overlook later at sunset? You've got to promise me you'll come back for the full farm experience."

"Oh, I absolutely promise," Claire said, her grin so bright it made his chest tighten. "But right now, all I can think about is seeing this tree in Sugarplum's front corner—covered in Mae's beautiful ornaments—filling the bakery with the kind of Christmas magic that makes people want to linger over their coffee and remember what the holidays are really about."

"Then let's get your tree home," Gabe said with obvious satisfaction, clicking his tongue to signal the horses forward.

Chapter 22

"Easy, easy," Gabe called, backing through the Sugarplum Bakery's front door with his hands wrapped around the trunk end of Claire's nine-foot Fraser fir. "Turn it just a little—no, the other way—there we go."

Claire wrestled with the top end, her cheeks flushed with a mix of effort and laughter as they maneuvered the massive tree through a doorway clearly designed for customers, not Christmas forests. "I think this thing has grown since we cut it down."

"Trees don't grow after you cut them," Gabe replied, his voice full of amusement—though the weight in his arms suggested she might be onto something. Out in the open grove, the nine-footer had seemed perfectly manageable. In here, it felt like they were trying to thread a needle with a telephone pole.

"Tell that to this tree," Claire muttered, stumbling a little when the top end suddenly cleared the frame.

Without the usual bustle of customers and clink of coffee cups, the bakery felt different—quieter, almost intimate.

"Where do you want it?" he asked, scanning the dining area.

Claire stood in the center of the room, slowly turning as if picturing the possibilities. "That corner, by the front windows," she decided at last, pointing to where two walls of floor-to-ceiling glass met. "Good natural light during the day, visible from the street, and it won't block the flow to the counter."

"Perfect. I hope you have a sturdy tree stand. We'll need something substantial to keep this beauty upright."

"Tree stand," Claire said with sudden recollection, snapping her fingers. "Mae kept all the Christmas decorations in the basement—there's definitely a stand down there. I'll be right back."

She disappeared through the basement door, her footsteps echoing down what sounded like wooden stairs, leaving Gabe alone with the tree and the comforting quiet of the empty bakery. He took in the space, imagining how this towering Fraser fir would change the room—how every customer who came in for coffee or a pastry would be greeted by the warm glow of Christmas magic.

"Found it!" Claire's voice floated up from the basement. "I think it weighs more than the tree."

"Need help?" Gabe called toward the open door.

"I've got it," came her determined reply.

Several moments later, she emerged carrying a cast-iron tree stand that looked like it could have anchored a California redwood. A few strands of hair had escaped her ponytail, and a faint smudge of dust streaked her cheek, but her expression was pure triumph.

"This thing is older than I am," she declared. "Mae always said it was the best tree stand money could buy—holds anything up to twelve feet, never tips over, and lasts forever."

"Built back when they made things to last," Gabe said, crouching to examine the hefty construction with genuine appreciation.

"Mae's father gave it to her for her first Christmas after she got married. She used it every year after that."

"Well then," Gabe said with a grin, "let's get this beauty standing proud."

The next twenty minutes unfolded in the kind of easy, wordless teamwork Gabe was coming to recognize as uniquely theirs. Claire steadied the tree while he adjusted the stand, both of them moving around each other with an unspoken rhythm—anticipating, shifting, and compensating without having to speak. It wasn't just getting the job done; it was a small, quiet dance that felt as natural as breathing.

"A little more to the right," Claire directed, standing back to assess the tree's positioning while Gabe tightened the final adjustments on the stand. "Perfect. Now rotate it just slightly... stop! That's it exactly."

Gabe stepped back, brushing his hands together as he admired their handiwork. "This tree is going to make every customer feel like they're having coffee in a Christmas wonderland."

"I can already picture it covered with ornaments," Claire said, circling the tree with a sparkle in her eyes, viewing it from every possible angle as if committing the sight to memory.

"Speaking of ornaments," Gabe said, glancing at his watch and realizing how quickly the afternoon had slipped away, "we should probably fuel up before we tackle decoration duty. Pizza delivery?"

Her face lit up. "Yes, please. I've been dying to try this place called Antonio's that just opened up. I've heard their Margherita pizza with fresh basil and mozzarella tastes like something straight out of an Italian cookbook."

"Sold. What's their number?" Gabe pulled out his phone and then chuckled. "We have a thing for pizza, don't we?"

"I guess we do," Claire said with a laugh, disappearing behind the counter to rummage for the menu.

While she searched, Gabe found himself watching her—really watching her. Even after wrestling a nine-foot tree through a narrow doorway and hauling a cast-iron stand up from the basement, with her ponytail slightly mussed and a faint dust smudge on her cheek, she was beautiful. More than that, she was happy—radiantly, genuinely happy—and something warm and lasting settled in his chest at the sight.

"Large Margherita, extra basil," Claire said, returning with the menu card. "Oh... and let's try some garlic knots."

"Done," Gabe said, placing the order. The promise of delivery in forty-five minutes gave them the perfect window to tackle their next task.

They headed for the basement to retrieve Mae's ornament collection—a treasure trove of carefully preserved Christmas decorations, each box labeled in Mae's neat handwriting. It was all organized with the kind of meticulous care Gabe was beginning to recognize as a hallmark of Whitfield women, past and present.

"Mae labeled everything," Claire said, running her fingers along neat rows of boxes stacked with almost military precision. "Lights, garland, ornaments by color, ornaments by type. Look at this. She even has a box marked Emergency Backup Decorations."

"Emergency backup decorations," Gabe repeated with a grin. "I like a woman who plans for every contingency."

"She always thought three steps ahead of everyone else and somehow made it look effortless."

They carried the ornament boxes upstairs and set them in a careful semicircle around the tree. Claire headed for the coffee station behind the counter, glancing over her shoulder. "Coffee? I was thinking hazelnut blend, Christmas music, and enough ornaments to make this tree absolutely magical."

"Sounds like a plan," Gabe replied, lifting the lid on the first box—and instantly understanding why Claire had been so excited.

Inside were ornaments unlike anything in a department store—delicate glass spheres in jewel tones that caught the afternoon light, hand-painted figurines with old-world charm, and carved wooden pieces polished smooth from decades of careful handling. It was a collection that spoke of history, travel, and the kind of tradition that made Christmas feel timeless.

"These are incredible," he said, lifting a fragile glass angel whose flowing robes and golden wings seemed lit from within. "This looks like something from a European Christmas market."

"That one's from Prague," Claire called from the coffee station, where the scent of hazelnut was beginning to mingle with the fresh pine of the tree. "Mae and my grandfather took a trip to Europe for their twenty-fifth anniversary. She came back with ornaments from every country they visited."

With two steaming mugs in hand, she reached for the discreet sound system hidden behind the display cases and pressed a button. Gentle instrumental Christmas melodies—guitar, piano, and soft strings—spilled into the bakery.

Crossing the room, Claire joined Gabe by the tree and passed him one of the mugs. He accepted it with a quiet word of thanks, savoring a sip before glancing at the unopened ornament boxes. "Where should we start?"

"Christmas lights first," Claire announced, lifting the lid on a box to reveal perfectly organized strands of warm white lights. "Mae always said lights were the foundation—everything else was just decoration, but lights created the magic."

"Smart woman," Gabe agreed, taking his end of the first light strand as Claire crouched near the base of the tree. "How many strands are we talking about here?"

"Mae's rule was one hundred lights for every foot of tree height," Claire said, her smile tinged with fondness at the memory. "So this nine-footer gets nine hundred lights—minimum."

They set to work, weaving the warm white strands through the branches with practiced teamwork—Gabe circling one way, Claire the other—ensuring every angle caught the glow without a single tangle.

"So, what are Christmas celebrations like for your family?" Claire asked as they worked their way up the tree's lower section. "With your parents retired and Brooke's family in the mix, where does everyone gather? Do you host at your house, or is there a set tradition?"

Gabe considered the question while threading lights between branches. "Christmas Eve is always at Mom and Dad's cottage. Christmas morning has usually been at Brooke and Shane's since the kids were born." He paused, a small smile tugging at his mouth. "But this year, I volunteered to host Christmas at my cabin for the first time. We'll gather in the afternoon so Brooke's kids can have their Christmas morning at home."

"That's exciting," Claire said, pausing in her light-stringing to glance at him with genuine interest. "Are you nervous about hosting?"

"Terrified," Gabe admitted with a laugh. "Mom keeps offering to 'help with the planning,' which really means she doesn't trust me not to serve frozen dinners for Christmas. So far, she's in charge of all the side dishes, Brooke's bringing dessert, and I'm responsible for baking the ham."

"I'm sure you'll do wonderfully. Though if you need an extra set of hands, I'd be happy to help."

"I may just take you up on that," he replied with a grin.

They fell into a comfortable rhythm, the combination of soft Christmas music, the aroma of fresh coffee, and the shared task creating an atmosphere of easy contentment.

"So, what will Christmas be like for you this year?" Gabe asked as they finished the middle section of lights and began working toward the tree's peak. "I mean, being back in Mistletoe Falls after all those years away—your first Christmas home again."

Claire paused mid-strand, considering the question with obvious thoughtfulness. "Honestly? I'm still figuring that out," she admitted. "Christmas Eve morning, the bakery will be open until noon. After we close, it'll just be me upstairs in my apartment, enjoying peace and quiet... maybe some hot chocolate and a good book. I'm looking forward to actually having time to enjoy myself instead of working in a restaurant all day like I did in Atlanta."

"That actually sounds perfect," Gabe said, picturing her curled up in her cozy apartment while the bakery's Christmas tree glowed downstairs. "What about Christmas Day?"

"Mom's planning a big family lunch at their house," Claire replied, her voice warming with anticipation. "Dad, Mom, Rachel, and me—just like it used to be when I was growing up, except now I get to bring dessert instead of just helping in the kitchen. Mom's already warned me she's making enough food to feed half the county."

"Will you miss the excitement of a city Christmas?"

"Not even a little bit," Claire said without hesitation. She smiled as she secured another strand of lights. "Christmas in Atlanta was all about work. The restaurant I was in stayed open Christmas Eve and Christmas Day, so I rarely got to come home to celebrate. This year, I can actually enjoy the season instead of just surviving it. Plus,"—she gestured around the bakery— "I get to create Christmas magic for other families instead of missing out on my own."

"Sounds like coming home was the right decision."

"Best decision I ever made," Claire said, plugging in the lights they'd just finished stringing.

The tree burst into warm golden radiance, transforming the corner of the bakery. Hundreds of tiny bulbs created depth and sparkle among the Fraser fir's perfect branches, while their reflection in the front windows doubled the luminous effect.

"Oh," Claire breathed, stepping back to admire it. "It's absolutely beautiful. Even without ornaments, it's already perfect."

"This is probably the most romantic pizza dinner I've ever had," Claire said, gesturing toward their softly lit surroundings as she reached for another garlic knot. "Christmas tree, gentle music, coffee brewing—it's like something straight out of a Christmas fairy tale."

"A romantic pizza dinner... I have to agree," Gabe said, his eyes lingering on her.

After dinner, they returned to ornament hanging with renewed energy and the kind of easy conversation that happens when two people realize they share far more than just mutual attraction. Claire told stories of family Christmas mornings as she hung delicate glass balls, while Gabe recounted childhood decorating mishaps that had her laughing until her sides ached.

"My sister decided she was old enough to be in charge of decorating when she was seven," Gabe was saying as he carefully positioned a wooden snowflake ornament. "She had very specific ideas about color coordination and wouldn't let anyone else touch the tree."

"How did that work out?" Claire asked, standing on tiptoe to reach a high branch. Gabe instinctively moved closer, ready to steady her if she wobbled.

"Complete disaster," he said with a grin. "She got so focused on making every ornament perfectly positioned that she over-decorated one side and left the other side bare. It looked like the tree was wearing a fancy dress on one side and pajamas on the other."

"Poor Brooke. What did your parents do?"

"Dad told her it was the most unique tree he'd ever seen, and Mom suggested maybe next year she could be the 'decoration coordinator' instead of doing it all herself. Diplomatic victory for everyone."

As they worked through Mae's carefully organized ornament collection, Gabe grew increasingly impressed by the variety and craftsmanship. Hand-blown glass ornaments from Germany nestled beside delicate beaded snowflakes, while carved wooden figurines shared space with simple paper angels that had clearly been made by loving hands long ago.

"These are amazing," he said, studying an intricate glass ornament shaped like a miniature Christmas tree. "Every single piece tells a story."

"That's what Mae loved about Christmas decorating," Claire replied, accepting the ornament and finding the perfect spot among the tree's middle branches. "She said every ornament should have meaning—either because of who gave it to you, where you found it, or what it represented about that particular Christmas."

"What's the story behind this one?" Gabe asked, holding up a simple wooden star painted in soft gold.

Claire's expression softened with obvious affection as she took the ornament. "Dad made that in his high school wood shop class. It was supposed to be a Christmas gift for Mae, but he was so nervous about whether she'd like something handmade that he almost didn't give it to her."

"But he did."

"He sure did. He told me she cried when she opened it," Claire said with a fond smile. "Told him it was the most beautiful ornament she'd ever received because he'd put his heart into making it just for her. Grandma Mae hung it on the tree every single year in the most prominent spot. I can still hear her saying, The best gifts come from the heart, not the wallet."

They continued decorating, moving easily around each other as they worked through box after box of family treasures while Christmas music played softly in the background. Gabe found himself watching her almost as much as the ornaments—her face lighting up when she uncovered a decoration she hadn't seen in years, the quiet hum of her voice joining familiar carols, the effortless way she placed each piece like it had been waiting for that exact spot all along.

And somewhere between the laughter, the coffee, and the sparkle of the tree lights, he realized this night was becoming one of his favorite memories. Not because of the perfectly decorated Fraser fir in front of them—but because of the woman beside him and the sense that they weren't just hanging ornaments. They were building something that might last far beyond this Christmas.

"Last ornament," Claire announced, lifting a delicate glass angel with flowing robes and golden wings. "This one always goes at the very top, just below the tree topper."

"Family tradition?" Gabe asked, accepting the angel and turning it gently in his hands, studying the intricate detail.

"Mae's tradition," Claire corrected with a fond smile. "She always said angels belonged close to heaven, watching over everyone gathered around the tree. This one has been the last ornament hung for as long as I can remember."

Gabe reached up and positioned the angel with deliberate care, securing it so the soft lights shimmered across its golden wings. From its place near the tree's peak, it seemed to hover protectively over the cascade of ornaments below.

"It's perfect," Claire whispered, her voice hushed as though they'd just completed something sacred. "Absolutely, completely perfect."

"Want to see how it looks with the overhead lights off?"

Claire nodded, and with a soft click, the bakery's overhead lights dimmed away. The Fraser fir became the room's sole source of light, its hundreds of tiny bulbs casting a shimmer of color that danced across the ornaments. Glass, wood, and metal caught the glow and sent it back in a thousand glints, like a galaxy of stars suspended among the branches. At the very top, the angel seemed almost alive, its golden wings bathed in warm light, radiating a quiet, watchful grace over the entire room.

"It's beautiful," Claire said, stepping to Gabe's side.

In the darkened bakery, the world seemed to shrink to the warm golden glow of the Christmas tree and the soft strains of music weaving through the air. Gabe felt something shift deep in his chest—quiet but undeniable. This wasn't just attraction anymore. It wasn't simply enjoying her company or admiring her dedication. This was falling in love—completely, irrevocably—with a woman who made everything better simply by being herself.

"Claire," he said, turning toward her in the tree's light.

"Mmm?" she replied, looking up at him with eyes that caught and held the glow like tiny stars.

Gabe extended his hand in silent question. She placed hers in it without hesitation, and he drew her gently closer until they stood face to face, surrounded by the tree's golden halo.

"Dance with me," he said quietly—less a request, more a hope.

Claire's smile was answer enough, but she nodded too, letting her free hand rest on his shoulder as his settled at her waist. They began to sway in time with the music, wrapped in the kind of Christmas magic that made the rest of the world fall away.

"You know," Claire said after a moment, her voice touched with soft laughter, "we probably look completely ridiculous to anyone walking by—dancing in a bakery by the light of a Christmas tree."

"Completely ridiculous," Gabe agreed, smiling as he said it. "And I don't care even a little bit."

"Good, because I don't care either."

The music flowed around them, tree lights painting the room in soft light. Gabe memorized everything—the way her hair shimmered under the lights, the ease with which she fit against him, and the contentment in her eyes that told him she was exactly where she wanted to be.

After several songs, during a pause between carols, Gabe felt his heartbeat kick up, his mind circling something he'd been wanting to ask since yesterday's sleigh ride. The glow of the Christmas tree, the warmth of Claire in his arms, the quiet certainty that his feelings were returned—if there was ever a perfect moment, it was now.

"Claire," he said softly, his voice carrying just enough nervousness to make her glance up at him in curiosity.

"Yeah?"

"Would you..." He hesitated, feeling absurdly like a teenager working up the nerve to ask someone to prom. Then, with a quiet breath, he pushed through. "Would you go to the Mistletoe Ball with me?"

Her face lit with immediate, unmistakable delight, and relief washed through him before she even spoke.

"I would love to. I was hoping you'd ask."

"You were hoping?" Gabe asked, grinning at the admission.

"I've been thinking about it ever since Hannah mentioned she already bought her dress," Claire confessed, a faint blush coloring her cheeks even as her eyes sparkled with amusement. "But I didn't want to assume you'd want to take me."

"Claire," Gabe said, his tone turning earnest as his hands tightened gently at her waist, "there's no one else I'd rather take to the Mistletoe Ball. Honestly, there's no one else I'd rather spend an evening with."

Her breath caught, and she studied his face with a mix of wonder and growing joy that made his chest feel too full.

"The Mistletoe Ball," she repeated softly, almost as if tasting the words. "Our first official formal date."

"Our first formal date," he agreed with a smile, then added with quiet humor, "Though I have to admit, I'm a pretty big fan of our informal ones too. Pizza in bakeries, tree decorating, sleigh rides—you're setting a high bar for romance."

"Well," Claire said, her eyes dancing with playful mischief, "I guess that means I'll just have to find the most magical dress I can for our first ball together."

"I can't wait to see it," Gabe said truthfully—already imagining her in the glow of the ballroom, already knowing that no matter what she wore, she'd be the most beautiful woman there.

Chapter 23

"I need a good cup of coffee and some serious girl time," Hannah declared as she breezed through Sugarplum Bakery's door with her usual flair, trailing a swirl of crisp December air in her wake.

Claire looked up from the register, where she'd been reviewing the day's receipts, and her face immediately brightened. Hannah's auburn hair was perfectly styled despite the wind outside, and her green eyes carried that familiar sparkle of mischief—a sure sign she had more on her mind than a quiet coffee break.

"Well, hello to you too," Claire laughed, moving toward the coffee station. "Let me guess—you've had one of those Mondays where nothing goes right, and you need caffeine intervention before tackling whatever crisis is brewing next?"

"Actually, the boutique's been surprisingly calm," Hannah replied, unwinding a cream-colored scarf and draping it over the back of a stool. "But I had this sudden urge to catch up with my best friend—especially since she's been glowing like a Christmas ornament lately—and coffee felt like the perfect excuse."

"Glowing like a Christmas ornament?" Claire repeated with a teasing smile. "That's quite the description."

"It's quite a transformation. Ever since you started spending time with a certain handsome tree farmer, you've had this... happiness that lights up your whole face."

Claire tried to keep her expression casual, but her smile only grew. "Speaking of Gabe..."

"What?" Hannah's head snapped up. "Did something happen? Please tell me something happened."

"He asked me to the Mistletoe Ball," Claire admitted, her voice unable to hide the excitement bubbling beneath her words.

Hannah's mouth fell open. "He finally asked?"

"He did."

"And you said yes—obviously—because you're not completely insane," Hannah said, her voice rising with delight.

"I said yes," Claire confirmed, though her fingers fidgeted with a dish towel as anticipation tangled with nerves. "But Hannah, I have no idea what I'm doing. The last formal dance I went to was senior prom—and that was almost ten years ago. I don't even own anything remotely appropriate for a ball."

Hannah's eyes lit with the kind of dangerous enthusiasm Claire had learned to recognize—and, occasionally, fear—over years of friendship.

"That is exactly why best friends exist. We are going shopping. Right now. This minute."

"Right now?" Claire glanced around the bakery, noting the handful of customers lingering over afternoon coffee while Joyce wiped down tables in the dining area. "Hannah, I can't just abandon my responsibilities to go dress shopping on a Monday afternoon."

"Joyce!" Hannah called toward the dining area with shameless determination. "Tell Claire she needs to go shopping for a ball gown immediately—and that you've got everything under control here."

Joyce looked up, amusement dancing in her eyes at Hannah's theatrical urgency. "Claire, honey, if you don't go with this girl right now and find a dress that'll make Gabe Mills forget his own name, I'm going to be personally disappointed in your priorities."

"But the afternoon rush—" Claire began.

"Will be handled perfectly fine by me, Melanie, and Carol," Joyce interrupted with maternal firmness. "We can survive without your fussing over details that don't need fussing. Go shopping. Have fun. Buy something beautiful."

"See?" Hannah said triumphantly, looping her scarf back around her shoulders. "Best friend and surrogate mother approval. We're going to The Velvet Boutique; we're going to find you the most gorgeous dress in Mistletoe Falls, and you, Claire Whitfield, are going to feel like a princess at this ball."

Claire found herself swept along by Hannah's infectious enthusiasm, barely having time to grab her coat and purse before being shepherded toward the door. She called a quick goodbye to Joyce, who waved them off with an expression that suggested she was thoroughly enjoying every second of the unfolding drama.

The late-afternoon air was crisp and invigorating, nipping at Claire's cheeks as they walked the few blocks toward The Velvet Boutique. Christmas decorations twinkled from every storefront and lamppost, their reflections shimmering across frosted shop windows while their breath rose in small white clouds.

"I'm nervous," Claire admitted as they turned onto Jingle Bell Lane, her hands buried deep in her coat pockets. "What if I look ridiculous? What if I can't remember how to walk in heels? What if the whole thing is too formal and I feel completely out of place?"

"Claire," Hannah said with gentle firmness, linking her arm through her friend's, "you're going to look absolutely beautiful because you are beautiful. And if you're worried about feeling out of place, remember you'll be with Gabe, who clearly thinks you're amazing exactly as you are."

"But what if—"

"No what-ifs," Hannah interrupted, stopping in front of The Velvet Boutique's elegantly dressed windows. Inside, mannequins modeled gowns in jewel tones and soft pastels, each one looking like it belonged on the cover of a winter gala invitation. "We're going to find you a dress that makes you feel confident and gorgeous, and then you're going to dance with the most wonderful man in Mistletoe Falls and have the magical evening you deserve."

The moment they stepped inside, The Velvet Boutique wrapped Claire in an atmosphere of pure elegance. Soft lighting cast a golden glow over everything; mirrors reflected sparkling glimpses of fabric and light, and evening gowns hung along the walls like works of art. Silks, satins, and velvets shimmered in colors that captured every shade of winter beauty—from icy silver to deep cranberry—promising possibilities she hadn't dared to imagine.

"Welcome to The Velvet Boutique," called a voice from behind an elegant display of accessories. A woman emerged with the graceful poise of someone who knew exactly how to make each customer feel as though they were the most important person in the room. "I'm Victoria. Are you shopping for a special occasion today?"

"The Mistletoe Ball," Hannah announced before Claire could speak. "We need something that's going to make this young lady feel like the belle of the ball."

"The Mistletoe Ball," Victoria repeated with genuine delight, her experienced gaze sweeping over Claire in a quick but thorough assessment. "How wonderful! It's such an elegant event. Are you leaning toward something classic and timeless, or would you prefer a bit more contemporary flair?"

"I honestly have no idea," Claire admitted, feeling suddenly out of her depth amid the shimmering gowns and sophisticated atmosphere. "I spend most of my time in jeans and t-shirts. This is... very new to me."

"Well," Victoria said warmly, her eyes twinkling, "then we'll explore a few possibilities and see what speaks to you. Sometimes the right dress chooses you instead of the other way around."

The next hour played out like the perfect scene from a romantic comedy's makeover montage. Victoria and Hannah whisked Claire from one shimmering display to the next, plucking gowns that ranged from sleek, sophisticated black numbers with clean, timeless lines to rich jewel-toned creations that glowed under the boutique's golden lighting. Each trip into the fitting room felt like a performance, with Hannah stationed just outside like an eager personal stylist—ready to gasp dramatically, burst into applause, or offer a well-placed, good-natured critique.

"You look beautiful," Hannah declared as Claire stepped out in a fitted black dress with cap sleeves, "but this says business dinner, not magical Christmas ball."

"Too serious," Victoria agreed, already gliding toward another rack. "Let's find something with more personality."

They moved through a rainbow of deep, wintry hues—emerald green that made Claire's skin glow, sapphire blue that brought out the richness of her dark hair, deep burgundy that added warmth and sophistication. Each gown revealed a different side of her, but none created that unmistakable, heart-stopping moment they were chasing.

"Okay," Hannah said, taking advantage of a quiet pause while Claire lingered in the fitting room catching her breath. "I need to ask you something, and I want you to be completely honest."

"Shoot," Claire called through the curtain.

"How do you really feel about Gabe?" Hannah's voice was soft but intent, tinged with that uncanny best friend instinct. "I mean beyond liking him or thinking he's nice. What's really going on in your heart?"

Claire froze halfway through unzipping the dress.

"I'm serious, Claire," Hannah pressed gently. "Because watching you light up when you talk about him, seeing how happy you've been lately—this isn't just a little crush, is it?"

"No," she said softly, her voice almost reverent. "It's not casual at all. Hannah, I think... I think I'm falling in love with him. I've never felt like this about anyone before. Not even close. When I'm with Gabe, it feels... right. Effortless. Like I'm exactly where I'm meant to be. And that terrifies me, because it's so much deeper than I ever imagined it could be."

"Oh, Claire." Hannah's voice brimmed with joy as she swept aside the fitting room curtain without hesitation. "Come here."

The boutique's elegance faded into the background as Hannah pulled her into a fierce, protective hug that spoke of years of unwavering friendship.

"I am so happy for you. So incredibly happy. You deserve this kind of love, Claire. You deserve someone who makes you shine. And now, we're going to find a dress worthy of a woman who's falling head over heels for the most wonderful man in Mistletoe Falls."

Victoria, who had tactfully kept her distance during the tender exchange, approached with a gown draped carefully over her arm. "I think," she said, a knowing smile playing at her lips, "this might be exactly what we've been searching for."

The dress was nothing short of breathtaking—a deep forest green that immediately brought to mind the fragrant evergreens of Christmas and the rich color of Gabe's eyes. The luxurious crepe fabric promised to drape like a dream, while the off-the-shoulder sleeves and gently flowing skirt spoke of elegance and movement, made for gliding across a dance floor.

"Oh," Claire breathed, her fingertips brushing over the soft material as if it were something rare and precious. "It's beautiful."

"Try it on," Hannah urged, stepping back with a spark of anticipation in her eyes.

The moment Claire slipped the gown over her head, she felt it—an almost magical sense of belonging. The forest green caught warm gold flecks in her brown eyes she'd never noticed before, and the flattering cut skimmed her figure in a way that felt both graceful and comfortable.

Stepping out into the soft light of the boutique, she turned toward the three-way mirror—and gasped.

"Is that... really me?" she whispered, slowly turning to see the gown from every angle.

"That's you," Hannah said, her voice brimming with delight, "looking absolutely stunning—and exactly like someone who's about to dance with Prince Charming."

In the mirror, the woman staring back wasn't just the practical bakery owner who spent her days in flour-dusted clothes and sensible shoes. She was sophisticated. Elegant. Radiantly feminine.

"The color is perfect with your complexion," Victoria said with professional satisfaction, her keen eye clearly pleased. "And the cut?

Absolutely ideal for your figure. When you walk into that ballroom, every head will turn."

"Gabe's going to forget how to speak," Hannah added, grinning as she circled Claire to admire the gown from every possible angle. "One look at you in this dress, and he's going to know—beyond a shadow of a doubt—that he's the luckiest man in Tennessee."

Claire's gaze stayed fixed on her reflection, hardly recognizing the woman in the mirror. Warmth bloomed in her chest, genuine, unguarded excitement at the thought of dressing up... and doing it for someone who mattered.

"I love it," she said at last, her voice carrying a mix of wonder and confidence. "I actually love how I look in this dress."

"Then it's perfect," Victoria declared, already gliding toward the accessories display with renewed purpose. "Now, let's complete your fairy tale—shoes, jewelry, the works."

The next thirty minutes blurred into a whirl of shimmering options and shared laughter. They settled on delicate silver heels—graceful without being precarious—and pearl drop earrings that echoed the gown's understated elegance, and a slender silver bracelet that caught the light with every movement, adding the final note of quiet magic to Claire's transformation.

As Victoria placed her dress in an elegant garment bag along with her other items, a light, effervescent feeling rose in Claire's chest, like champagne bubbles threatening to spill over.

"I can't believe I'm actually going to the Mistletoe Ball," she murmured as they completed the purchase, the evening suddenly becoming real now that she had the perfect dress in hand.

"Believe it," Hannah said, looping her arm through Claire's as they stepped out into the December evening. "And believe you're going to have the most magical night of your life."

They walked back through the twinkling lights of downtown Mistletoe Falls, Claire's fingers curled protectively around the dress bag. Excitement and nerves tangled inside her, the night ahead shifting from a source of anxiety to something she could hardly wait to experience.

"Thank you," she said as they paused outside Sugarplum Bakery. "For everything—pushing me to go shopping and helping me find the perfect dress."

"That's what best friends are for."

"Hannah," Claire said with a sudden burst of apprehension, "I only have eleven days to figure out hair, makeup, walking in these shoes, and how to act like someone who belongs at an elegant social event."

Hannah laughed, brushing away her concern. "Eleven days is plenty. And you won't need to 'act' like anyone but yourself. Gabe asked you to this ball because he likes exactly who you are."

After their goodbyes, Claire stood for a moment outside the bakery and drew in a deep, steadying breath.

The Mistletoe Ball.

Dancing with Gabe in the most beautiful dress she'd ever owned.

It felt like she was living a dream.

Chapter 24

"Well, hello there, handsome," Claire called as she stepped down from the bakery van, immediately crouching to greet Baxter, who bounded toward her with his usual enthusiasm. "Did you miss me? I know, I know—it's been a whole twenty-four hours since you last saw me."

Gabe approached, watching the familiar ritual of Baxter claiming Claire's full attention while she scratched behind his ears.

"You're going to spoil him completely."

"Too late for that," Claire replied cheerfully.

She circled to the van's passenger side and pulled out a white bakery box, a thermal coffee cup, and a carefully wrapped cinnamon roll. "Your Saturday-morning cinnamon roll, coffee, and muffins."

"I'm definitely getting used to this personal delivery service," Gabe said, accepting the offerings with obvious pleasure. "Black coffee, cinnamon roll... and let me guess—Melanie's selection of six mixed muffins?"

"Carol's selection this time," Claire corrected with a grin that sent a warm ripple through his chest. "She insisted on including a new caramel crunch muffin she's been working on. Said you're the official taste tester since you have such dependable opinions about baked goods."

Claire hefted the first stack of bakery boxes from the van while Baxter supervised, tail swishing in approval. Working easily in tandem, she and Gabe transferred the goods to the Trading Post. Inside, the gift shop was already humming with life as Brianna adjusted displays, tested the register, and set the stage for another festive, bustling day.

"I brought extra decorated sugar cookies, a double batch of snickerdoodles, and a variety of muffins today, Brianna."

"Perfect—I anticipate we'll be busy," she said, testing the temperature on the hot chocolate dispenser.

Gabe leaned against the counter for a moment, watching Claire work. She moved through the Trading Post with easy familiarity, as if it were simply an extension of her own bakery. Her dark hair was pulled back in a practical ponytail, and her cream-colored sweater set off the warmth in her complexion. She looked absolutely beautiful to him.

"What's the weather forecast looking like?" Brianna asked without looking up from her task.

"Clear skies, cold temperatures, and a chance of snow this afternoon," Gabe replied, an idea beginning to take shape in the back of his mind. "Perfect conditions for anyone wanting to try something adventurous on a Saturday."

Through the front windows, he could see his staff moving about preparing for the day.

"Claire," Gabe continued, setting down his coffee cup and crossing to where she was arranging the cookie display. "What would you say about playing hooky from work today?"

She straightened, eyes widening. "Playing hooky?"

"Let's go ice skating out at Frost Hollow Lake. Both of us take the afternoon off from being responsible business owners and just... have fun together."

"You want to play hooky. You, Gabe Mills—the man who works seven days a week during the Christmas season—want to abandon your responsibilities on the busiest day of the week to go ice skating."

"I want to spend the afternoon with you," he replied simply. "Just us—ice skating, probably falling down a lot, and drinking hot chocolate when we get too cold. Something purely fun."

"But what about the bakery? What if there's a rush, or—"

"Go," Brianna urged, making shooing motions with her hands, her eyes bright with matchmaking satisfaction. "Both of you—go have fun. The gift shop and the bakery will still be here when you get back."

"What do you say?" Gabe asked, extending his hand toward her. "Ready for an adventure?"

Claire glanced from his outstretched hand to Brianna's encouraging smile, then back to Gabe.

"I've never been ice skating," she admitted, placing her palm against his with the easy trust that had grown between them.

"Neither have I... but it sounds fun," Gabe said with a grin.

* * *

The drive to Frost Hollow Lake wound along mountain roads that looked as though they'd been lifted from a Christmas card. Snow-laden pines lined the route like silent sentinels, and the distant peaks of the Great Smoky Mountains rose against the winter sky in breathtaking contrast. The beauty made conversation unnecessary, turning the quiet between them into something warm and natural.

Claire sat in the passenger seat, her hand resting on the console between them so Gabe could easily reach for it during the straight stretches. She'd called Joyce from the Trading Post parking lot, enduring good-natured teasing about taking the rest of the day off, while Gabe had checked in with Derrick—who'd responded to his announcement with good-natured approval and assurances that everything at the farm would be handled flawlessly.

"I can't believe I'm actually doing this," Claire said as they turned onto the final road to Frost Hollow Lake, her tone a mix of wonder and nervous excitement. "Playing hooky on a Saturday afternoon to try something I've never done before... with someone who's never done it either."

"Worried?" Gabe asked.

"Terrified," Claire admitted with a laugh. "But the good kind of terrified—like when you're about to try something that might be amazing, but you have no idea if you'll be completely awful at it."

"Well," Gabe said as Frost Hollow Lake came into view through the trees, "if we're completely awful at it, at least we'll be awful together."

The lake spread before them like a natural mirror, reflecting the blue December sky, its surface transformed by cold mountain temperatures into a pristine skating rink that gleamed in the afternoon sunlight. Couples and families dotted the frozen expanse, gliding across the ice with varying degrees of skill, their voices carrying through the crisp air in calls of encouragement and bursts of laughter.

Around the lake's perimeter, benches offered resting spots for skaters and onlookers, while park-maintained walking paths provided easy access to different areas. The entire scene radiated winter magic and community joy, and Gabe found himself understanding exactly why Frost Hollow Lake had become one of Mistletoe Falls' most beloved seasonal traditions.

"It's so pretty here," Claire breathed, her gaze sweeping the panoramic view as her expression shifted from nervous anticipation to genuine wonder. "Look at all those people having fun. They make it look so easy."

"Famous last words," Gabe replied with gentle humor, pulling into a parking spot near the log cabin that housed the Peppermint Patty Snack Shack.

The snack shack embodied everything Gabe loved about Mistletoe Falls' way of creating magic—rustic charm blended with practical function, a community gathering place that felt welcoming rather than commercial. The cabin's exterior boasted hand-carved wooden signs advertising skate rentals, hot drinks, and "Warmth for Frozen Fingers and Toes," while cheerful red-and-white striped awnings added a festive splash of color against the weathered wood.

Through the wide front windows, Gabe spotted families and couples warming up between skating sessions, their cheeks flushed from cold air and exercise as they sipped hot chocolate and chatted around rustic wooden tables positioned for perfect lake views.

"Ready to embarrass ourselves publicly?" Claire asked as they approached the entrance.

"As ready as I'll ever be," Gabe replied, holding the door for her.

Inside, warmth wrapped around them. A cheerful woman behind the rental counter glanced up from organizing skates, her face lighting up at the sight of new customers.

"Welcome to Peppermint Patty's!" she called with genuine enthusiasm. "First time visiting us?"

"First time skating ever," Claire admitted.

"Oh, how wonderful!" the woman replied. "I'm Patty, and I love helping first-timers discover the joy of ice skating. Let's get you fitted with skates that'll make learning as comfortable as possible."

The next twenty minutes unfolded under Patty's patient guidance. She fitted them with rental skates, explained basic safety tips, and offered warm encouragement. Other customers chimed in with advice and lighthearted stories of their own skating mishaps that made stepping onto the ice feel far less intimidating.

"The key is balance and patience," Patty explained. "Don't worry about speed or looking graceful—just focus on staying upright and enjoying the experience. The lake ice is perfect today, smooth as glass."

"Any advice for first-time teachers?" Gabe asked.

"Stay close to one another, but don't be overprotective," Patty advised. "Let her find her own balance while being ready to catch her if needed. Most people learn faster when they feel supported but not smothered."

After a few more safety tips and Patty's encouraging words, they made their way to the lake's edge. A designated beginners' area offered a gentle entry onto the ice. Claire gripped Gabe's arm with visible apprehension as they stepped from solid ground to frozen surface, her first tentative slide sending her off in unpredictable directions.

"Okay," she said with a shaky laugh, both hands now clutching Gabe's forearms while her skates wobbled beneath her. "This is much harder than it looks."

"Take your time," Gabe said gently, focusing on keeping his own balance while offering steady support. "We're not trying to win any speed skating competitions."

Their first few minutes barely qualified as skating—more a careful shuffle across the ice—but the halting progress was punctuated with shared laughter and murmured encouragement. Claire leaned on Gabe for stability, but his own unsteady footing meant they often ended up holding each other upright.

"I think I'm getting it," Claire announced after managing three consecutive glides without grabbing for his arms. "Watch this—"

Her confident declaration was immediately followed by a spectacular loss of balance. She windmilled backward toward what would have been a solid fall—if Gabe hadn't caught her around the waist, pulling her against his chest as they both fought to stay upright.

"Nice save," Claire said breathlessly, her face inches from his as they stood pressed together on the ice, her hands braced on his shoulders, his arms secure around her waist.

For a moment, they stayed motionless in their impromptu embrace, the sounds of other skaters mingling with the crisp beauty of the mountain afternoon.

"Should we try again?" Claire asked softly, though she made no immediate move to step away from his steady warmth.

"In a minute," Gabe replied, allowing himself to enjoy holding her while they both caught their breath.

The next hour passed in a blur—gradual improvement, the occasional spectacular fall they learned to laugh at rather than fear, and a growing confidence that allowed more real skating than cautious stumbling. Claire proved to be a quick study once she stopped overthinking the mechanics, and Gabe discovered that years of farm work had given him a balance that translated surprisingly well to the ice.

By the time they took their first warming break at Peppermint Patty's, both were flushed from the cold air and exercise, their hands slightly numb despite warm gloves, yet glowing with the satisfaction of mastering something new together.

"Hot chocolate for the brave beginners," Patty announced, setting steaming mugs before them at a window table with a perfect view of the lake. "How did it go? You looked like you were having a good time."

"Better than expected," Claire said, curling her hands around the warm ceramic as her cheeks slowly returned to their usual color. "I only fell four times, and Gabe caught me three of those."

"Natural protective instincts," Patty said with a smile. "You two make a lovely couple on the ice."

"We make a lovely couple everywhere," Gabe said.

"Yes," Claire replied softly, "we do."

The rest of the afternoon passed in a comfortable rhythm—skating sessions followed by breaks to warm up or sitting watching other couples gliding across the lake and enjoying the easy laughter that came with shared discovery. Each time they stepped back onto the ice, their coordination improved, their movements smoothing into real skating rather than cautious shuffling.

During their final session, as shadows stretched across the lake and the winter light took on the golden glow of an approaching mountain sunset, Gabe found himself skating slowly beside Claire. She moved with a new natural grace, her earlier uncertainty replaced by obvious pleasure.

"I can't believe how much fun this has been," she said, gliding in time with him. "I kind of like playing hooky from work."

"Think you'll want to come back?" Gabe asked, reaching for her hand as they made an easy circuit around the lake's perimeter, the snowy mountains framing a picture-perfect scene.

"Definitely," Claire said, her fingers lacing through his. "Though I have to admit, I think a lot of my enjoyment has to do with the company."

Chapter 25

Claire pushed through Sugarplum Bakery's door with both arms full of shopping bags, the little brass bell announcing her return from what had started as a routine morning delivery to Gabe's farm but had turned into an impromptu candy-buying expedition for tomorrow's Sleigh Parade. The bags rustled with candy canes, chocolate coins, and wrapped caramels—enough sweet ammunition to delight every child lining Mistletoe Lane when she and Gabe rode through town in his horse-drawn sleigh alongside the other participating merchants.

The past six days had fallen into the most wonderful rhythm Claire could have imagined—morning deliveries to the farm that always included a few stolen moments with Gabe while Baxter supervised, and evening phone calls that stretched later each night as they discovered new reasons to enjoy each other's company.

Tomorrow night's Mistletoe Ball felt like the natural culmination of everything that had been building between them—their first formal event together, a chance to dance somewhere more elegant than her bakery floor, an evening that promised to be magical in every way.

But as Claire glanced around the familiar warmth of her dining area, something felt... different. Off.

Four people in expensive business attire occupied the corner table usually claimed by her morning regulars. Laptops sat open beside neatly stacked file folders, the group's quiet conversation accompanied by the faint click of keyboards. One woman wore a tailored navy suit that probably cost more than Claire's monthly clothing budget, while the three men had the polished, big-city look of people accustomed to boardrooms rather than small-town bakeries.

"Joyce," she said, approaching the register. "Sorry it took me longer this morning—I grabbed candy for tomorrow's parade."

Joyce accepted the bags with a knowing smile. "You're practically glowing talking about that parade. I swear, every time you mention doing something with that man, you light up like our Christmas tree."

"I'm excited," Claire admitted, then lowered her voice. "Who are those people? They look like they're planning a corporate takeover."

Joyce's expression shifted to something more serious. "They've been here for over an hour, honey. Asked for you specifically, so be prepared—I'm not sure what they want. Very polite, bought coffee and pastries, but they've got that look."

"What look?"

"The look of people who want something important... like they're hunting for it."

Before Claire could ask more, Joyce disappeared through the swinging doors into the kitchen with the candy bags, leaving her alone at the register just as one of the businesspeople—the woman in the navy suit—approached with a confident stride.

"Excuse me," the woman said with a warm smile. "Are you Claire Whitfield?"

"I am," Claire replied, straightening her shoulders. "How can I help you?"

"My name is Katherine McPherson, and I'm a representative from the Heartland Cooking Network. Would you have a few minutes to speak with me and my associates? I promise it will be worth your time."

Claire's eyebrows lifted before she could stop them. The Heartland Cooking Network was one of the fastest-growing food channels on television, known for showcasing authentic American cooking and celebrating small-town food traditions. She'd watched their programs during slow afternoons at the bakery, always impressed by the production quality and their genuine appreciation for family recipes.

"Of course," Claire managed, still trying to process why a television network would want to talk to her. "Would you like to speak here in the dining area, or would you prefer my office for privacy?"

"Your office would be perfect if you don't mind. This is a conversation that might require some confidentiality."

Claire led the group through the kitchen to her small but neatly organized office, gesturing toward the chairs she kept for supplier meetings while willing the nervous flutter in her chest to settle. Katherine McPherson took the seat across from her desk with practiced poise, while the three men arranged themselves with the efficient ease of people accustomed to important meetings.

"Ms. Whitfield," Katherine began, opening a leather portfolio, "let me start by saying that the Heartland Cooking Network has been following your work here at Sugarplum Bakery with considerable interest."

"Following my work?" Claire echoed, genuinely puzzled. "I'm sorry, but I have no idea what you mean. I run a bakery in a small tourist town. We're hardly television material."

"Actually, that's undoubtedly what makes you television material," Katherine replied, her enthusiasm carrying the smooth confidence of a seasoned television executive. "My team was in Mistletoe Falls a few weeks ago to film a segment on your annual Christmas tree lighting ceremony for our holiday special programming."

The tree-lighting ceremony. Pieces of a puzzle Claire hadn't even realized existed began clicking into place.

"We were impressed by the community involvement, the authentic small-town atmosphere, and—most of all—the exceptional quality of the refreshments provided," Katherine continued. "Naturally, we investigated the source of those incredible baked goods, which led us straight to Sugarplum Bakery."

"We've done our research, Ms. Whitfield," one of the men added, glancing at notes on his tablet. "Your family's bakery has been part of this community for several years. Your grandmother Mae Whitfield was something of a local legend, we've learned, and you've carried on that tradition while adding your own innovations, we've been told. The combination of family heritage and culinary creativity is precisely what our viewers are looking for."

Claire's mind raced; the words were both flattering and completely surreal. "I'm honored that you enjoyed our baked goods, but I'm still not sure why you're here."

Katherine's smile widened, as though she'd been waiting for this exact moment. "Ms. Whitfield, the Heartland Cooking Network would like to offer you your own cooking show."

The words seemed to hang in the air, solid and shimmering, something Claire could almost reach out and touch—but couldn't quite believe. Her own cooking show. On national television. The concept was so far beyond anything she'd ever imagined that her thoughts stalled entirely.

"I'm sorry," she said slowly, "could you repeat that?"

"Your own cooking show," Katherine confirmed, clearly enjoying Claire's stunned reaction. "We're thinking of calling it Claire's Country Kitchen, and we believe it has the potential to become one of our flagship programs."

She opened her portfolio and began arranging glossy presentation materials across Claire's desk—mock-up logos, sample promotional images, and detailed production schedules that made the whole idea feel suddenly, startlingly real.

"The concept focuses on family recipes, small-town traditions, and the kind of authentic home cooking that our viewers enjoy," Katherine explained as the materials seemed to multiply across the desk. "You'd demonstrate techniques and recipes passed down through generations while sharing the stories behind them. Think of it as preserving American culinary history while teaching viewers how to create that same magic in their own kitchens."

Claire's gaze moved over the presentation materials, noting how polished everything looked—how completely they'd thought through each detail. The mock-up logo featured her name in elegant script, framed by illustrations of rolling pins, mixing bowls, and a cozy kitchen scene that evoked the warmth of families gathered together to make memories.

"Production would be based primarily in our Nashville studios," one of the men added, "with monthly visits to Mistletoe Falls for location segments that highlight your bakery and the community traditions that inspire your cooking. We're envisioning a comprehensive media package—cooking show, cookbook deals, potential product lines, and national recognition for both you and Sugarplum Bakery."

"Nashville," Claire repeated, the word tasting strange. Nashville was three hours away. Nashville meant leaving Mistletoe Falls regularly. Nashville meant... an entirely different life than the one she'd been building here.

"The financial package is quite substantial," Katherine said, sliding a sealed envelope across the desk with the kind of casual confidence that implied the numbers inside were impressive.

Claire's fingers hovered above the envelope, her mind already racing through possibilities—new ovens, upgraded equipment, finally having the kind of professional kitchen that could match her ambitions.

But another part of her mind, the part that had been humming with contentment since returning from her morning delivery to Gabe's farm, wondered what accepting this opportunity would mean for the life she'd been building in Mistletoe Falls.

"Why me?" she asked, lifting her gaze from the presentation materials to meet Katherine's eyes directly. "You could choose established chefs, people with television experience, or celebrities who already have national recognition. Why a small-town bakery owner who's never been on camera in her life?"

"Authenticity," Katherine replied without hesitation. "Ms. Whitfield, viewers are tired of celebrity chefs and manufactured personalities. They want real people sharing real family traditions in real kitchens. You represent something that can't be created or purchased—genuine connection to heritage, community, and the kind of home cooking that actually brings families together."

"Plus," another team member added, his tone bright with enthusiasm, "your story has all the elements our viewers love. A young woman returns home to honor her grandmother's legacy, continues running a family business successfully, and becomes a pillar of her small-town community. It's exactly the kind of inspiring narrative that builds loyal audiences."

Claire felt the weight of it all pressing in—the magnitude of what they were offering, the way her quiet Thursday morning had turned on its head. Just moments ago, her biggest worry had been whether she'd bought enough candy for tomorrow's parade. Now she was staring at an offer that promised national exposure and financial security beyond anything she'd ever imagined.

"This is..." she began, then stopped, realizing she had no words for what this was. "This is completely unexpected. I need time to think about it."

"Of course," Katherine said smoothly, as though she'd anticipated the response. "This is a life-changing opportunity, and we want you to feel completely comfortable with your decision. However, our production schedule for next year is tight, so we'll need your answer within one week—by December twenty-third."

One week. Seven days to decide whether to accept an offer that could transform her career while potentially unraveling the life and relationships she'd been building in Mistletoe Falls. Seven days to weigh financial security against personal happiness, professional success against the quiet contentment she'd found in her small-town community.

Katherine gathered the presentation materials into a neat folder, then handed Claire a stack of business cards and a comprehensive information packet—thick enough to demand serious study time.

"Everything you need to make an informed decision is in that packet," Katherine said. "Production schedules, financial details, creative concepts, and answers to questions you haven't even thought to ask yet. Please take the time you need, but remember—opportunities like this don't come along often."

After the Heartland Cooking Network team departed with promises to check in next week, Claire sat alone in her office, staring at the folder and business cards. The familiar sounds of the bakery carried on around her—Joyce managing the front counter, customers chatting over coffee, the steady hum of kitchen equipment that had been the soundtrack to her life for the past ten months.

Everything was exactly the same as it had been an hour ago, yet something fundamental had shifted. Now she faced a choice that could alter the entire course of her future.

Claire picked up Katherine McPherson's business card, running her thumb over the embossed Heartland Cooking Network logo as her mind tried to process the magnitude of what had just happened. Her own cooking show. National recognition. Financial security that could solve every practical problem she'd faced since inheriting the bakery.

But as she pictured herself in a Nashville television studio, demonstrating recipes for the cameras, her thoughts kept circling back to Gabe. To the morning deliveries that had become the highlight of her day. To ice skating adventures, sleigh rides, and the way he made her feel like the most interesting person in the world simply by listening to her talk.

To tomorrow night's Mistletoe Ball and the dress hanging in her apartment closet upstairs. To dancing with the man who made her heart skip just by taking her hand. To the quiet, wonderful life they'd been building together—one shared conversation and stolen moment at a time.

Claire opened the information packet, telling herself she owed it to her future to understand exactly what she was considering. But with each page detailing production schedules and travel requirements, with each paragraph describing the demands of television work, the weight of the decision pressed more heavily on her chest.

The financial offer was indeed substantial—enough to make her breath catch. Enough to replace every piece of equipment in the bakery, to renovate the entire kitchen, and to secure its future in ways she'd only dared imagine during her most ambitious moments.

But it was also enough to change everything about the life she'd been creating in Mistletoe Falls.

As the afternoon wore on and customers came and went, Claire found herself watching the familiar rhythms of her bakery with new eyes—Mrs. Harvey stopping by for her apple muffin, the Wilson twins arguing good-naturedly over cookie choices, her employees moving with practiced ease to keep everything running smoothly.

By closing time, she'd made one decision: she would keep this opportunity to herself while she processed what accepting it might mean. Not out of deception, but from a need to think clearly—without outside pressure or well-meaning advice that could cloud her judgment.

The thought of telling Gabe made her chest tighten. Would he be excited for her? Try to talk her out of it? See, as she was beginning to, that accepting might mean choosing a life with little room for the quiet happiness they'd been building together?

Tomorrow night, they would dance at the Mistletoe Ball—celebrating their first formal date and the relationship that had grown from a business partnership into something precious and irreplaceable. How could she fully enjoy that magical evening while carrying the secret of a decision that might change everything?

At day's end, Claire locked the bakery's front door and climbed the stairs to her apartment, the information packet clutched like a document that could hold either her dreams or her undoing. Settling into her favorite chair by the front windows, she could see the town square's Christmas tree twinkling through the glass.

It stood as a symbol of everything she loved about her life in Mistletoe Falls... and everything that might change.

Opening the packet again, she felt the full weight of her options pressing in from all sides.

Chapter 26

Gabe spotted Claire weaving through the organized chaos of parade preparations, her arms wrapped around a wicker basket filled with what appeared to be enough candy to satisfy half the children in Mistletoe Falls. Even from twenty yards away, her smile lit up when she saw him beside the sleigh, but something in her posture—the way her shoulders stayed just a touch too straight—pricked at his attention.

"Morning, beautiful," he called.

"Morning yourself, handsome," she replied, a little breathless from hauling what was clearly a substantial load. "I may have gone overboard with the parade candy. Melanie said we needed enough for the whole route, but I think I bought enough to supply a small army."

Gabe stepped forward to take the basket, their fingers brushing briefly as he took hold of the handles. The basket proved heavier than expected, packed with wrapped caramels, candy canes, chocolate coins, and an impressive variety of colorful hard candies.

"Better too much than running out halfway through," he said, settling it on the sleigh's floor. "Did you raid every candy store between here and Knoxville?"

"Just the ones in Mistletoe Falls," Claire laughed, taking his hand as she climbed into the sleigh, careful on the narrow step. "Joyce made me promise not to let any child go home empty-handed, so I figured generous is better than sorry."

Once they were both seated, Gabe reached behind them for the plaid wool blanket and spread it across their laps. She tucked the edges around her legs and instinctively shifted closer to share the heat.

"Ready for your first Mistletoe Falls Sleigh Parade?" he asked.

"Ready as I'll ever be for candy distribution duty," Claire replied, her eyes sparkling with excitement. "Fair warning though—my aim is terrible."

"The kids won't care," he assured her with a grin, clicking his tongue just as the parade marshal's whistle cut through the morning air. "More candy on the ground just means more scrambling fun."

The sleigh eased forward; the Percherons settling into their steady parade pace while brass bells chimed in time with their steps. The sound blended with the merry jingle from other sleighs along the route, creating a soundtrack of pure Christmas spirit. Ahead, Mayor Hayes waved from an elegant Victorian-style sleigh draped in evergreen garland and red velvet ribbons. Behind them, Hannah and several other boutique owners rode in a rustic farm wagon piled high with wrapped gifts and seasonal treats, their laughter carrying on the crisp winter air.

"This is incredible," Claire said, her voice brimming with wonder as they rounded the first corner and Mistletoe Lane came into view, lined with families, visitors, and neighbors gathered for the morning's festivities. "Look at all these people! And everyone looks so happy."

The sight never failed to hit Gabe square in the chest—hundreds of folks bundled in winter coats and bright scarves, kids bouncing on their toes while parents balanced coffee cups and cameras, elderly residents holding the best bench spots like prized parade real estate. It was small-town life at its best, the kind of celebration that felt magical instead of limiting.

"This is what I love about Mistletoe Falls," he said. "People don't just show up for each other—they throw themselves into it and enjoy every second."

Claire reached forward, scooping a handful of candy from the basket. "Okay, so what's the technique here? Gentle underhand toss, or full-scale candy bombardment?"

"Depends on the target," Gabe replied with mock gravity, pausing in his waving to demonstrate the proper form. "Little kids get gentle tosses that land within grabbing distance. Teenagers? You've got to make the throw challenging—it's a sign of respect for their coordination. Adults mostly just want to see their kids happy, so focus on maximum squeals and smiles."

"Got it," she said, lobbing her first candy cane toward a cluster of elementary-age kids. They dove for it with delighted shrieks. Claire's eyes widened in delight. "Oh, my goodness—they actually fought over it! That's adorable."

The next twenty minutes unfolded with Claire embracing her role as candy distributor with the same precision she brought to bakery displays.

As the sleigh wound from the town square into the quieter residential streets, Gabe found himself more entertained by her laughter than the parade itself. She tossed candy with the enthusiasm of someone who'd just discovered a new favorite pastime, grinning at every delighted squeal that followed.

Here, among porches strung with lights and families gathered on front lawns, the atmosphere turned more intimate. Between candy tosses, Claire's curiosity shifted toward the community itself—asking about the houses they passed, the families who'd lived here for generations, and the traditions that stitched the town together.

"That blue house with the white trim," she said, pointing toward a well-kept Victorian framed by old oak trees, "Joyce told me the Hendricks family has lived there for four generations. Can you imagine? Four generations in the same place, watching the town grow and change around them."

"That's what I love about this place," Gabe said, guiding the Percherons around an eager knot of children spilling into the street. "People put down roots and stay. They invest in each other instead of constantly looking for something better somewhere else."

Something in Claire's expression shifted—just a flicker, gone almost before he could name it. Most people wouldn't have noticed, but Gabe had learned her subtle tells. Whatever his words had stirred, she smoothed over with a quick return to her bright parade smile, leaving him with the faint sense he'd brushed against something she wasn't ready to share.

"Are you nervous about tonight?" Claire asked, her voice carrying a hint of forced lightness as she steered the conversation elsewhere.

"Tonight?" Gabe repeated, though he knew exactly what she meant.

"The Mistletoe Ball, you goof."

"Not nervous," Gabe said honestly, giving her gloved hand a quick squeeze while keeping one hand steady on the reins. "Excited. Very excited. Though I have to admit, I'm wondering if I'll remember how to dance like a civilized human being instead of someone who spends most of his time with horses and Christmas trees."

"I'm sure you'll do fine," Claire said, her smile softening into something more genuine. "Though I should probably warn you, I may step on your feet at least once. It's been a while since I've danced in heels."

"We'll figure it out together," Gabe assured her, noticing how the mention of the evening seemed to ease the tension he'd sensed in her posture earlier. "Besides, if we're both terrible dancers, at least we'll be terrible together."

Claire laughed then—this time with her usual warmth.

They finished the parade route with the candy basket empty and both of them flushed from the cold, their cheeks aching from too much smiling. And as their sleigh rolled into the designated end area behind the community center, Gabe found himself wishing it didn't have to end just yet.

"I can't believe how much fun that was. The children's faces, the families waving, the whole community coming together—I just love this town," Claire said as he brought Duchess and Duke to a gentle stop. Her cheeks were flushed from the cold, her eyes sparkling with genuine joy.

"Me too," Gabe replied, climbing down from the driver's seat before helping her from the sleigh. His hands settled at her waist as she stepped down, and even after her boots touched solid ground, he found himself reluctant to let go.

"I should probably get back to the bakery," Claire said, though she didn't immediately step away from his steadying hold. "Friday afternoons are always busy, and Joyce will need help with the weekend prep."

Gabe hesitated, not wanting to see her walk away when the morning had felt so right—so natural, as if they both belonged exactly here.

"Pick you up at seven tonight?"

"Seven is perfect," Claire confirmed, finally stepping back, though her smile stayed warm. "I'll be ready."

He watched her walk toward downtown, the empty candy basket swinging at her side, her dark hair catching the winter sunlight. The morning replayed in his mind—the way she'd deflected his comment, the faint tension beneath her laughter, the brightness in her voice that had felt just a little too deliberate.

Maybe he was imagining it. Maybe the anticipation of their first formal date was making him oversensitive. Maybe she was simply tired from a long week.

But as he began unhitching Duchess and Duke from their parade harness, the feeling lingered—that quiet, persistent sense that something was off with Claire.

Chapter 27

Claire stood before her bedroom mirror, smoothing the fabric of her dress while her heart pounded with anticipation. The woman staring back looked as though she'd stepped out of a fairy tale—elegant, confident, and radiantly feminine in a way her usual jeans and flour-dusted aprons never revealed.

"You, Claire Whitfield, are going to enjoy this evening," she told her reflection firmly. "The Heartland Cooking Network can wait. Tonight is yours."

The dress transformed her completely. The deep green made her eyes seem brighter, while the off-the-shoulder design gave her a grace and sophistication she rarely felt. Hannah had been right about everything—the color, the cut, even the silver heels that added just enough height without making her feel unsteady.

A soft knock at her apartment door sent butterflies fluttering wildly in her stomach. Gabe.

She grabbed her small silver purse and cream-colored wrap, then hurried through the living room to answer. The greeting she'd prepared vanished the moment she opened the door.

Gabe stood there in a charcoal black suit that fit his broad shoulders perfectly, a crisp white shirt, and a burgundy tie that brought out the warmth in his complexion. The look in his eyes made her breath catch—wonder, admiration, and something deeper that sent her pulse racing.

"Claire." Gabe's voice was soft, filled with amazement that sent warmth blooming in her chest. "You look... gorgeous."

"Thank you," she managed, her gaze sweeping over him in return. The suit only emphasized his natural confidence, making him look as though he belonged in elegant ballrooms every bit as much as in Christmas tree fields. "You clean up pretty well yourself, Mr. Mills."

"May I?" He extended his arm with old-fashioned courtesy, the gesture making her feel cherished rather than helpless.

"You may." She slipped her hand into the crook of his arm, letting him guide her down the stairs. His steady attention to her balance in the heels made her feel both cared for and treasured.

The December evening was crisp and clear, and stars twinkled above the glow of downtown lights. Gabe's freshly washed truck gleamed beneath the streetlamps, and he opened the passenger door for her.

"I have to admit," Claire said as Gabe climbed into the driver's seat, "I'm a little nervous about tonight."

"Good nervous or bad nervous?" he asked, starting the engine and glancing at her in the soft glow of the dashboard lights.

"Good nervous. Like Christmas morning nervous. Excited, but not quite sure what to expect."

"Well, set your nervousness aside. I have a feeling we're going to have a great evening." His smile made her chest flutter.

The drive to Mistletoe Lodge took them through downtown Mistletoe Falls, where Christmas lights twinkled from every building and the magnificent community tree they'd chosen together dominated the town square like a beacon of holiday magic.

"Look at that," Claire said, gesturing toward the tree as they passed. "I still can't believe we actually did that—chose it, planned the ceremony, and pulled off the whole thing without any major disasters."

"We make a pretty good team," Gabe replied, giving her hand a gentle squeeze as he turned onto Lodge Road.

Mistletoe Lodge emerged through the trees like something out of a winter wonderland, its rustic stone and timber construction outlined by thousands of twinkling lights. The circular drive was filled with cars, and couples in elegant attire moved toward the main entrance, where warm light spilled from the massive windows and the sound of live music floated into the crisp evening air.

"Goodness, my sister has really outdone herself. She really takes her job here seriously," Claire said, taking in the lodge's transformation. Every window box overflowed with evergreen arrangements and red ribbon, while the wide front porch was draped in garland and lit with lanterns that cast pools of golden light.

Gabe helped her from the truck, offering his arm as they joined the stream of guests heading toward the welcoming entrance. The massive front doors stood open, revealing a foyer adorned with towering Christmas trees, elegant floral arrangements, and enough twinkling lights to make everything look dusted with stardust.

"Claire! Gabe!" Rachel's voice carried across the foyer as she approached, her elegant navy dress and poised demeanor marking her as the evening's hostess. "You both look absolutely stunning. Claire, that dress is perfect on you."

"Thanks, sis," Claire replied, accepting her sister's quick hug. "Rachel, this is Gabe—Gabe, my sister Rachel. She's the manager here at Mistletoe Lodge."

"Nice to finally meet the man my sister speaks so highly of," Rachel said, extending her hand.

"It's nice to meet you too," Gabe replied.

"Rachel, this is incredible. The lodge looks wonderful," Claire said.

"That was the goal," Rachel answered with a pleased smile. "Now, both of you go on and enjoy the ball. The ballroom is straight through those doors."

The ballroom took Claire's breath away. The soaring timber-beamed ceiling was draped in evergreen garland and a canopy of twinkling lights above the polished dance floor. Round tables surrounded the dancing area, each with a winter floral centerpiece that glowed with candlelight, which added to the romantic feel of the room.

A live band played on a small stage at the far end. Couples glided across the dance floor with varying degrees of skill and obvious enjoyment, while others mingled around the perimeter or gathered at tables to watch the festivities.

"Would you like something to drink?" Gabe asked, guiding her toward the refreshment area where servers offered everything from hot cider to champagne.

"Maybe in a little bit." She glanced around, her eyes shining. "Gabe, this is absolutely beautiful. I feel like I'm in a Christmas dream."

"Would you like to dance?"

Her pulse quickened at the invitation, but she nodded without hesitation. "I'd love to."

Gabe led her onto the dance floor with confident steps, one hand settling at her waist while the other held hers. The band was playing a slow waltz—nothing too complicated, perfect for couples more interested in closeness than precision.

"Claire, you're the most beautiful woman here tonight," Gabe murmured, guiding her through a turn that sent her skirt sweeping gracefully around her legs.

"You're not looking around very carefully," she teased, though his words warmed her like hot chocolate on a snowy day.

"I don't need to look around," Gabe said with a simple honesty that made her breath catch.

As the waltz eased into a gentle swing number, they laughed their way through figuring out the steps, tripping once or twice before finding an easy, shared rhythm. Claire felt herself sinking into a joy so complete it left no room for anything else. The ballroom, the music, the elegant clothes—everything wrapped around them in a haze of magic and celebration, making ordinary concerns feel distant and unimportant.

"How was work today?" Gabe asked during a slower song that allowed for easier conversation. "You seem a little tired. I hope you're not pushing yourself too hard with all the Christmas rush."

Claire's smile faltered for just a fraction of a second, but she recovered quickly with the kind of lighthearted deflection that had become second nature over the past day.

"No work talk tonight," she said with mock firmness, reaching up to straighten his tie while they swayed together. "Tonight is about dancing and enjoying each other's company. Work can wait until tomorrow."

"Deal," Gabe agreed readily, though the flicker of concern in his eyes told her he'd noticed more than she wished. "But you know you can talk to me about anything that's bothering you, right?"

"I know," Claire said, meaning it completely. "But right now, all I want to think about is how wonderful this evening is... and how lucky I am to be here with you."

Gabe's arm tightened slightly around her waist, their joined hands settling against his chest. Claire was close enough to catch the clean scent of his soap mingled with the musky cologne that always seemed to cling to him.

"Claire," he said softly, his voice carrying something that made her look up and meet his gaze.

"Yeah?"

"I know we've been taking things slowly, getting to know each other," he said. "But I need you to know that this—tonight, being here with you, the way you make me feel—it's not casual for me. Not even close."

Her heart stumbled and then steadied again as his words landed deep and true. "It's not casual for me either," she whispered.

The admission lingered between them, wrapped in the music and light, while other couples danced around them and the rest of the world faded to a soft, blurred background.

Gabe cupped her cheek, his thumb brushing lightly across her skin as his eyes searched hers for permission. He leaned in slowly, giving her every chance to pull away—but instead, Claire rose onto her toes to meet him halfway.

When their lips touched, the rest of the world—the music, the other dancers, the glittering ballroom—faded into nothing. The kiss was everything a first kiss should be: gentle, sweet, and perfect in its tenderness. Gabe's lips were warm and sure against hers, carrying all the unspoken promises they'd been building toward through weeks of quiet connection and trust. Claire melted into the moment, her free hand coming to rest against his chest while his arm drew her closer.

When they finally parted, Gabe rested his forehead against hers, and they continued to sway to music that felt as if it had been written for them alone.

"That was worth waiting for," he murmured.

"Definitely worth waiting for," Claire agreed—though even as she spoke, a small voice deep inside reminded her of the choice still looming, the opportunity that could pull her away from this perfect moment... and from everything that had made it possible.

Around them, the Mistletoe Ball carried on in a swirl of music, laughter, and Christmas elegance, but Claire felt as though she were suspended in a quiet bubble of happiness—one created entirely by Gabe's arms around her and the realization that she'd stumbled upon something precious and rare. Something that made every other consideration fade to the edges.

Something that made the choice looming ahead feel impossibly harder.

As the band eased into another slow song and Gabe smiled down at her like there was nowhere else he'd rather be, Claire willed away thoughts of television studios, national recognition, and looming contract deadlines. Tonight was about this man, this moment, and the undeniable sense of belonging she felt in his embrace.

Everything else could wait until tomorrow.

Chapter 28

C laire fumbled with the bakery box of decorated Christmas cookies, nearly losing her grip.

"Get it together," she muttered to herself, steadying the box against her hip just as Baxter bounded toward her with his usual uncontainable enthusiasm.

"Morning, beautiful," Gabe called, his voice carrying easily through the crisp December air. The warmth in his tone made her pulse skip. "Sleep well?"

"Like a baby," she said—then instantly felt heat rise in her cheeks at how breathless she sounded. The truth was, she'd barely slept at all. Partly because she kept replaying every moment of their evening together and partly because the Heartland Cooking Network packet had sat on her nightstand all night like a ticking time bomb.

Gabe came forward to take the delivery boxes from her, and when their fingers brushed in the handoff, the same electric awareness from last night hummed between them. From the way his gaze lingered on hers, she knew he felt it too.

"Have I told you how absolutely stunning you were last night?"

"Only about a dozen times," Claire replied with a smile that felt more natural than the nervous one she'd worn moments ago. "Though I don't mind hearing it again."

"Good," Gabe said, his answering smile sending another flutter through her chest, "because I plan to mention it several more times."

They carried the delivery into the Trading Post together, the morning sunlight streaming through wide windows to spill golden pools across the polished wooden floor. Brianna was adjusting displays with the kind of smooth efficiency that made opening preparations look effortless.

"Well, well," Brianna said with barely concealed delight as she took in their obvious happiness. "Don't you two look like the picture of contentment this morning? I take it the Mistletoe Ball was everything you hoped it would be?"

Claire felt her cheeks warm as Gabe's hand settled gently at her lower back.

"It was perfect," Claire said. "The decorations were beautiful."

"Mm-hmm. I'm sure the decorations were lovely."

Claire turned to the display case, arranging fresh cookies, only to realize her usual systematic approach had deserted her. Christmas tree cookies ended up mixed in with snowflakes, and candy canes wandered into the wrong sections entirely. Romantic awareness tangled with the heavy decision she'd been avoiding, leaving her hands clumsy in a task she could normally do without thinking.

"Everything okay?" Gabe asked. "You seem a little... distracted this morning."

"Just tired," she answered quickly. "Good tired, though. Last night was wonderful, Gabe. Really wonderful."

"It was," he agreed, reaching over to straighten a cookie she'd set askew.

"Good morning, you two!" Derrick's cheerful voice cut in as he entered the Trading Post with an armload of fresh evergreen arrangements. "Hope I'm not interrupting anything important."

"Not at all. Just helping with the delivery," Gabe said.

"Claire, these cookies look incredible," Derrick said, leaning toward the display with genuine admiration. "More of Melanie's work?"

"Yes," Claire replied, relieved to be on a safer topic. "She spent extra time on the details."

The next thirty minutes passed with the easy rhythm they'd developed over weeks of morning deliveries, but beneath the familiar motions, Claire felt a constant hum of awareness. Every casual touch, every shared glance carried a charge that hadn't been there before last night. When Gabe handed her the empty boxes to carry back to the van, their fingers lingered just a breath longer than necessary. When she laughed at one of Derrick's stories about yesterday's customers, she caught Gabe watching her with a quiet intensity that made her feel both beautiful and cherished.

Yet beneath the happiness, anxiety gnawed at her chest like a steady ache. The Heartland Cooking Network packet haunted her thoughts, demanding an answer she didn't know how to give. How could she choose between the career opportunity of a lifetime and the quiet, irreplaceable happiness she'd found here? And how could she explain it to Gabe when she hadn't made sense of it herself?

"Gabe," she said suddenly, the words escaping before she could second-guess them. "Could we take a walk? I need to talk to you about something."

Something in her tone made him look up from the inventory clipboard, his expression shifting instantly to concern. "Of course. Everything alright?"

"I hope so," Claire said, meaning it more than he could know.

Gabe passed the clipboard to Derrick with a brief note about checking the far tree fields, then held the Trading Post door for her. Baxter immediately fell into step ahead of them.

The December morning was crisp and clear, the kind of brilliant blue sky that made the snow-covered landscape gleam. Their breath formed pale clouds in the cold air as they followed the path toward the scenic overlook, but Claire barely registered the surrounding beauty. Every step seemed to tighten the knot in her stomach. She was too busy searching for the right words to explain something she barely understood herself.

After several minutes of quiet, Gabe's voice broke the stillness. "So," he said gently, "what's on your mind?"

Claire's pulse kicked into overdrive. She stopped beside the split-rail fence overlooking the rolling tree fields, the sharp winter air biting at her cheeks. "I had visitors at the bakery the other day," she began carefully. "Business visitors. From the Heartland Cooking Network."

She watched his expression shift—curiosity giving way to surprise and then to something that might have been concern.

"The television network?" he asked. "What did they want?"

"They offered me my own cooking show," Claire said, the words spilling out faster than she'd intended.

"Claire, that's... incredible." His voice carried genuine admiration, but also something quieter beneath it. "National television, professional recognition—that's the kind of opportunity that could change everything for you. For the bakery."

"That's what they said," Claire replied, watching him closely, trying to read the mix of emotions in his eyes. "The financial package is... substantial. Enough to replace all my equipment, renovate the kitchen, and secure the bakery's future in ways I've only dreamed about."

"Wow." He let the word out on a slow breath. "What about the details? How would it actually work?"

Claire hesitated, bracing herself. "Production would be based in Nashville, with monthly visits back here for location filming. They want to feature the bakery and community traditions, but most of the shooting would happen in their studios."

The light in Gabe's expression dimmed, just slightly, like clouds passing over the sun. "Nashville," he repeated, his voice lower now. "That's a three-hour drive. How often would you have to be there?"

"They weren't completely specific," Claire admitted, "but from what I gathered, it would be regular enough to count as a serious time commitment. And there's more—cookbook deals, potential product lines... all the things that come with national recognition."

Gabe nodded slowly. "And the monthly filming here in Mistletoe Falls?" he asked. "What would that look like?"

"Television crews, equipment, constant cameras. Disruption of the normal flow of the bakery. They'd want to film everything—baking, customer interactions, and community events. The whole place would become a stage instead of just a business."

"I see." His tone was even, but the faint tightening in his shoulders didn't escape her notice. "Claire, it's an incredible opportunity—national recognition for your skills, financial stability, and a chance to share Mae's legacy with people all over the country."

"But?" she prompted, hearing the unspoken weight in his carefully even tone.

"But nothing," Gabe replied, though the subtle shift in his voice told her otherwise. "This is your decision—your career, your future. What matters is what you think."

Frustration prickled at her chest, sharp against the worry that had been building the past few days. In the space of a few sentences, he'd shifted from engaged partner to polite bystander, and the distance felt like a sudden drop in temperature.

"Gabe, I'm asking for your opinion because it matters to me."

He leaned against the fence, gaze fixed on the snow-dusted tree fields instead of her face.

"My opinion? I think you'd be crazy not to give it serious thought. Offers like this don't come along every day."

"That's not what I mean, and you know it," Claire said, stepping closer until the frosty air between them felt charged. Baxter lay down at their feet with the patient air of a dog who knew this conversation wouldn't end quickly. "I'm asking what you think it would mean for... us."

Gabe was quiet for a long moment, his hands gripping the fence rail until his knuckles whitened. When he finally spoke, his words came slow deliberate.

"Claire, what we have is... wonderful. But it's still new. I don't think it's fair for me to influence a decision that could define your career."

The words landed like a splash of cold water—true enough to sting, but lacking the personal anchor she'd hoped for.

"So you think I should take it?" she asked quietly.

"I think," Gabe said at last, turning to meet her eyes with warmth edged in something that felt like resignation, "you should choose whatever will make you happiest in the long run. Not just what feels right today, but what you'll be proud of five years from now."

Claire searched his face, noting the careful distance behind his sincerity. "And if what makes me happiest is turning down this offer and staying here—building the life I've started in Mistletoe Falls?"

"Then that's what you should do," Gabe said, and for just an instant—before he masked it—she saw a flicker of hope light his features. The sincerity in his voice wrapped around her like warmth against the winter air, but beneath it she heard something else—an edge of caution, a subtle pulling back.

"You're pulling away and protecting yourself," she said, the truth settling between them even as she spoke it aloud.

"What?"

"You're being supportive and saying all the right things, but you're bracing yourself for what happens if I take the offer. You and I both know that if I sign that contract, I'll be in Nashville for a significant amount of time, and that would change everything between us."

Gabe's jaw tightened slightly, but he didn't deny it. "Maybe I am. Maybe I've learned that it's better to be realistic about what people choose for their lives."

"Gabe," she said softly, reaching for his hand where it gripped the fence, "I'm not Amanda."

"I know." His voice was low and steady. He let her take his hand but didn't quite relax into the contact. "You're nothing like Amanda. But Claire, this opportunity is real, and it's significant. You'd be foolish not to consider it seriously."

He gave her fingers a gentle squeeze before releasing them. "Come on. We both need to get back to work, and you have big things to consider without me swaying your decision. I want you to know—I appreciate you trusting me with this. Whatever you decide, I believe it'll be the right choice for you. And I'll support you every step of the way."

They started back toward the Trading Post in a silence. Her hand was still in his, but the connection felt more tentative, as though some invisible thread had loosened.

With each step, the weight of her decision pressed harder against her chest. It wasn't just about her career anymore. Whatever choice she made would shape the precious thing that had been growing between them.

At her van, Gabe's voice broke the quiet. "When do you need to decide?"

"December twenty-third," Claire said.

"That's next Thursday," he said after a moment. "Five days."

"Five days," she echoed, the words tasting both impossibly close and endlessly far away.

He opened the driver's door for her, his hand lingering briefly at her elbow as she climbed in. The goodbye kiss he pressed to her lips was warm, still tender—but just a shade more careful than last night's.

As she pulled away, the road ahead blurred slightly, her thoughts circling the same realization: something between them had shifted. Not broken, but strained.

Five days to make a choice that could determine not just her career, but whether the man she was falling in love with would trust her enough to let their relationship grow.

Five days to decide what would truly make her happy—not just in this moment, but for all the moments that would follow.

Chapter 29

The firewood split with a sharp crack, each swing harder than the last. But no matter how many logs he cleaved in two, Gabe couldn't silence the voice in his head—Amanda's voice—calling this farm life he loved "limiting." The word clung to him like burrs, digging deeper each time he thought about Claire and the offer that might pull her toward Nashville. Would she someday look at his world the same way?

Thwack.

Another log burst apart, the pieces skittering over the frozen ground. Gabe wiped the sweat from his forehead despite the December chill, his breath curling in pale clouds while his shoulders burned from two hours of steady work.

Baxter sat a few yards away, his eyes tracking his every move. The Border Collie mix had tried all his usual tricks to pull Gabe out of his thoughts—dropping a slobbery tennis ball at his feet, showing off his best spins and paw shakes, and even attempting to herd him away from the woodpile. Each attempt had been met with the same quiet dismissal.

Now the dog simply watched with the patient resignation of someone who knew his human couldn't actually chop a problem into smaller, more manageable pieces.

"I know what you're thinking," Gabe said, settling another log onto the splitting block. Baxter's ears perked at the sound of his voice. "But this is perfectly normal firewood prep. Nothing unusual about being ready for winter weather."

Baxter tilted his head, unconvinced, as if to say that normal people didn't attack firewood like it had personally wronged them.

Gabe brought the ax down hard, the blade biting through the oak with such force that both halves flew in opposite directions. One chunk skidded to a stop near Baxter, who flinched back and fixed him with a look that was equal parts glare and wounded pride.

"Sorry, buddy," Gabe muttered, collecting the stray pieces. But his mind was already miles away, circling the same conversation on repeat.

Production would be based in Nashville... regular time commitment... national recognition...

Each phrase had landed like a warning bell, a quiet reminder of how bigger, shinier opportunities had a way of pulling people away. Not because Claire didn't deserve every single bit of success—she did—but because he'd already lived through the moment when someone decided his life and his dreams weren't enough to hang around for.

He swung again, but the ax glanced off the edge of the log and buried itself in the splitting block with a dull thunk. Baxter startled to his feet at the sound, as if ready to step in and save his human from himself.

"Great," Gabe muttered, working the ax free from the splitting block. His hands trembled—whether from exertion or something deeper, he wasn't sure.

Footsteps crunched over the snow-packed gravel. Derrick appeared with the unhurried stride of someone who'd witnessed more than one of Gabe's "woodpile therapy" sessions. A thermos of coffee dangled from his hand, and without waiting for an invitation, he settled on a nearby stump. Baxter trotted over immediately, grateful for the attention his human wasn't offering.

"Morning," Derrick said, glancing at the growing mountain of firewood. "Beautiful day for... whatever it is you're doing to that poor oak."

"Just catching up on splitting," Gabe replied, aiming for casual but landing closer to unconvincing.

"Uh-huh." Derrick poured coffee into two steaming cups. "And I'm sure the fact you've split enough wood to heat half of Mistletoe Falls has nothing to do with whatever's got you wound tighter than a watch spring."

Gabe accepted a cup, wrapping his chilled hands around the heat. "Sometimes, a man just needs to keep busy."

"Sometimes," Derrick agreed. "And sometimes a man needs to talk about what's eating him before he either pulls something or traumatizes his dog."

Baxter looked between them, ears perked, clearly voting in favor of this intervention.

"Claire got an interesting business proposition," Gabe said at last.

"What kind?"

"Heartland Cooking Network offered her a TV show," Gabe said, picking up the ax again more for something to do than out of necessity.

"National exposure. Filming in Nashville. Life-changing for someone with her talents."

"And you're happy for her?"

"Of course I'm happy for her," Gabe replied, bringing the ax down with deliberate precision, splitting the log in one clean stroke. "She deserves the recognition. The financial security. Everything she's worked for."

"Right," Derrick drawled. "So you're celebrating by chopping firewood."

Gabe paused, recognizing the sarcasm for what it was—a refusal to let him dodge. He set the ax down.

"Nashville's three hours away," Gabe said. "Production schedules aren't exactly flexible. Building a national brand doesn't leave much room for... other priorities."

"Like?" Derrick prompted.

"Like me. Like last-minute drives or spontaneous hikes. Like dating without having to reserve a time slot. Like spending Saturday mornings talking about everything and nothing."

"Like falling in love with someone who might choose bigger opportunities over small-town life," Derrick said, cutting to the heart of it with the plainspoken honesty that made him such a valuable friend. "Amanda made her choice. But Claire isn't Amanda."

They sat in silence for several minutes while coffee steamed in the cold air. Baxter moved between them, leaning against one man and then the other, offering wordless comfort with the steady weight of his presence.

"You know," Derrick said at last, "I think you're forgetting a few key differences between Claire and Amanda."

The mention of Amanda's name made Gabe's jaw tighten involuntarily. "Such as?"

"Such as Amanda never gave this place a chance. She was embarrassed by your connection to it—wouldn't even come here with you, remember? Treated Mistletoe Falls like some backwoods sideshow that might tarnish her precious corporate image. Claire's not like that. She chose this life, Gabe. Walked away from the city because she wanted something real. Something she could root herself in."

"Amanda said she wanted someone with 'real ambition'—right up until I showed some by choosing what mattered to me over a corporate paycheck," Gabe said, the old bitterness threading through his voice no matter how hard he tried to keep it neutral.

"Amanda wanted a trophy boyfriend," Derrick countered, his tone firm. "Someone who looked good on her arm at corporate events and could help her climb the social ladder. She never cared about you—just the image you fit into." He leaned forward slightly, holding Gabe's gaze. "Claire's different. She actually lives the values she talks about. She's up before dawn to bake and run her business. She organizes community events because she wants people to feel connected. She spent hours decorating a Christmas tree in her bakery just to make her customers smile. That's not ambition for show—that's heart."

Gabe's grip tightened around the coffee cup, but he found himself nodding despite the unease still gnawing at him. Derrick was right. Claire's place in Mistletoe Falls had never felt like a temporary arrangement. She'd woven herself back into the community with the quiet assurance of someone who wasn't just passing through. And yet, the shadow of Nashville lingered in his thoughts like a storm on the horizon.

"But this opportunity is huge," Gabe said quietly. "How do I compete with that?"

"Maybe you don't," Derrick replied. "Maybe you trust that what you're building with her means something, too."

"And if it doesn't?"

"Then you'll survive it," Derrick said with calm certainty. "Same way you survived Amanda. Same way you came back here when everyone in Nashville thought you'd thrown your life away."

Baxter dropped his tennis ball at Gabe's feet, hopeful for play. Gabe scratched behind his ears. "I'm going to support her decision... whatever it is."

He tossed the ball; Baxter bounded after it, snow scattering in his wake.

"I'll be honest with you—and maybe it's selfish—but I hope she tears the contract up," Gabe admitted. "I don't want things to change between us. And the time we'd be apart if she took this opportunity... it's not just hours... it would be days, even weeks at a time. It would change everything."

"Wanting things to stay the same isn't selfish—it's human," Derrick said. "The real question is what you do with that wanting."

"What would you do if you were me?" Gabe asked.

"I'd be honest," Derrick said without hesitation. "Tell her you love her, that you want her happy, and that you're scared. Give her your real opinion if she asks for it. Let her see the truth in your eyes, then trust her to decide, knowing exactly where you stand."

The simplicity of it hit Gabe harder than he expected. Claire would choose what was right for her—he couldn't control that. His only job was to be honest... and to trust her with the truth.

"When did you get so smart about relationships?" Gabe asked.

"Watching other people make mistakes," Derrick replied with a grin. "And my mom gives excellent advice—when I actually ask for it."

Baxter trotted back, this time dropping the tennis ball precisely halfway between them, his gaze flicking from one man to the other as if he were officiating. The diplomatic gesture made them both laugh, easing some of the heaviness.

"I've got a lot to think about," Gabe said at last.

Derrick gave a satisfied nod and walked toward the main farm buildings.

Gabe stayed by the woodpile, the ax fitting back into his grip as naturally as his own thoughts. Each strike sent a log splitting cleanly apart, but the questions in his head refused to break so easily. Would telling Claire exactly how he felt give her the clarity she needed—or would it push her away?

Chapter 30

"Claire! Honey!" Joyce's voice carried gentle urgency as she reached over to switch off the industrial mixer that had been churning far too long. "I've been calling your name for the past minute. This cinnamon roll dough has been mixing for nearly ten minutes."

Claire blinked, the kitchen's familiar soundtrack rushing back all at once—the hum of the ovens, the clatter of prep work, the quiet murmur of her staff. She'd been standing beside the massive mixer, staring blankly at the dough hook while her mind replayed yesterday's conversation with Gabe for what felt like the hundredth time.

"Oh, no." Her gaze dropped to the overworked dough, now far too stiff for anything resembling a tender breakfast pastry. "Joyce, I'm so sorry. I completely zoned out. I don't know what's wrong with me today."

"I do," Joyce replied, her tone a mix of compassion and the quiet authority of someone who'd raised three children and navigated countless workplace crises. "Something's weighing heavy on your heart, and pretending otherwise is only making it worse. Carol, sweet-heart, can you start a fresh batch of cinnamon roll dough? Claire needs a few minutes to gather herself."

Across the kitchen, Carol looked up from the muffin batter she was stirring, dark curls slipping from beneath her baker's cap. "On it," she said, already moving toward the flour bins with calm efficiency. "And Claire, don't worry. We've all had days when our hearts just don't want to cooperate with our hands."

"Speak for yourself," Melanie called from the decorating station, piping delicate garlands onto a batch of Christmas tree cookies. "Remember last month when you tried to make chocolate chip muffins but used salt instead of sugar because you were wrapped up in that mystery novel during breaks?"

"That was one time," Carol replied with good humor, "and those muffins were only slightly inedible."

"Slightly inedible is generous," Sadie chimed in from the front counter, where she was arranging fresh pastries in the display case. "Even the raccoons in the dumpster out back wouldn't touch them."

Despite the tangle of emotions twisting inside her, Claire smiled at the familiar banter. It was the kind of easy, good-natured teasing that made Sugarplum Bakery feel more like a family kitchen than a business. These women had become her anchor, offering stability and laughter in ways that reached far beyond their job descriptions.

"Why don't you and I take a coffee break in your office?" Joyce suggested, already heading toward the coffee station. "You look like you need to talk through whatever's got you so scattered."

Claire followed her into the small office, gratefully accepting the steaming mug of hazelnut coffee before settling into the chair. Usually, the room—with its neat files, cozy décor, and framed family photographs—brought comfort and clarity. Today, it felt more like a refuge from choices far bigger than she was ready to face.

"Now then," Joyce said, settling into the chair across from Claire's desk. "What's going on? And don't tell me it's just holiday stress."

Claire hesitated, fingers curling around her coffee mug. "If someone offered you everything you thought you wanted professionally—but saying yes meant big changes to the parts of your life that make you happiest—what would you do?"

"That depends," Joyce replied thoughtfully, "on whether what I thought I wanted was the same as what I actually needed."

Claire's brow furrowed. "What do you mean?"

"Well," Joyce leaned back, folding her hands in her lap, "when I was a little younger than you, I had the chance to manage a fancy restaurant in South Carolina. Good money, prestige, everything I thought would prove I'd 'made it.' But taking it meant leaving Mistletoe Falls, leaving Lester, leaving the community I love."

Claire leaned forward with growing interest.

"I spent three sleepless weeks making pros and cons lists, asking everyone's opinion, driving myself—and poor Lester—half crazy," Joyce said with a rueful smile. "Finally, my mama sat me down and asked one simple question: 'Joyce, honey, when you picture your life a few years from now, which choice makes you happier and feels more like it fits who you are?'"

"And?"

"And I realized that the fancy restaurant was what I thought I should want, not what actually made my heart sing. Managing someone else's kitchen, following corporate policies, living in a city where I didn't know my neighbors—none of that sounded like the life I'd dreamed of building."

"So you stayed."

"I stayed," Joyce confirmed, warmth in her eyes. "And I've never regretted it for a single day. But Claire—my answer fit my life. The question you need to ask is... what makes your heart sing?"

Taking a deep breath, Claire laid it all out—the Heartland Cooking Network offer, the generous financial package, the Nashville production schedule, and the confusion that had been knotting her thoughts ever since.

"The money is incredible, Joyce. More than enough to completely renovate the bakery kitchen, replace every piece of equipment, and give me true financial security. But the more I picture the reality..." She trailed off, trying to sort the tangle in her mind. "I'd be traveling to Nashville for long stretches, disrupting the bakery's rhythm, and having camera crews here every month."

Joyce nodded, her expression thoughtful. "Sounds like you're weighing what you'd gain against what you might lose."

"I am. And then there's Gabe," Claire admitted, her voice softer, threaded with the uncertainty she'd been trying to keep hidden. "When I told him about the offer, he was careful with his reaction—supportive, but... distant. Like he was putting up a wall."

"Honey," Joyce said after a moment of quiet, "that man's been hurt before. His ex walked away because he chose a life here over a big-city career. You've got an opportunity that could pull you toward the city for long stretches. I imagine he's worried he'd be competing with that life all over again. Maybe he's thinking the television offer wouldn't just change your schedule—it could change what you two have together. Can you really blame him for protecting himself?"

"No," Claire said softly. "When I think about my life here—the customers who know my name, my work family, Gabe, the way this community has embraced me—I want all of that." She paused, the weight of the decision pressing in again. "But then I think about what this opportunity could mean financially. Joyce, the money would solve every single equipment problem I have."

"Money's important, but it's not everything," Joyce said gently. "It comes and goes. What else is on your mind?"

"That's just it—I don't know," Claire admitted, her voice laced with genuine uncertainty. "Part of me is excited about the idea of a television show. Who wouldn't be? It's recognition for everything Grandma Mae built, and it could share her recipes—and mine—with people all over the country. But the Nashville part..." She shook her head. "I'm still figuring out how to run this place. Regular travel feels overwhelming, and I have no desire to live part-time in the city."

"And Gabe?" Joyce asked.

"Gabe's important to me. But can I really make a decision this big based on a relationship that's still so new? I'm falling in love with him. What if I take this opportunity and regret it for the rest of my life? I feel like I'm being pulled in two completely different directions."

Joyce regarded her with kind, knowing eyes. "Honey, it sounds like you need time to figure out what matters most to you—not what looks best on paper."

The office door eased open, and Melanie peeked inside. "Sorry to interrupt, but Mrs. Sorenson is here for her Christmas cookie consultation, and she specifically asked for you. Something about custom designs for her Christmas Eve party."

"Go take care of your customer, honey. We'll finish this later if you need to," Joyce said.

The afternoon unfolded in its familiar rhythm of customers, coffee service, and the warm bustle that made Sugarplum Bakery feel like Mistletoe Falls' living room. But throughout the familiar activities, Claire found herself paying attention to details she'd taken for granted—the way Mrs. Henderson always ordered an apple turnover and shared photos of her grandchildren, how the Martin siblings argued good-naturedly about cookie selection while their mother smiled with patient affection, and the way visitors from neighboring towns commented on the bakery's atmosphere and authentic charm.

Each interaction felt precious, yet Claire couldn't ignore the thought that a television show could introduce her bakery to thousands of families who might never set foot in Mistletoe Falls. Was keeping things small and local truly honoring her grandmother's legacy—or was it limiting her own potential?

By closing time, the questions weighed heavier than ever. The life she'd been building here was wonderful, but was she being naïve to turn down financial security and national recognition? And how much of her hesitation was about the opportunity itself... versus fear of disrupting what was quietly growing between her and Gabe?

"You look like someone who's been wrestling with big decisions all day," Hannah said as she swept through the bakery door just as Claire flipped the sign to Closed. Her best friend carried a bottle of wine in one hand, a bag from the local Chinese restaurant in the other, and wore a determined expression.

"Perfect timing," Claire said, leaning in for her friend's warm hug. "Want to come upstairs? I need to talk something through with someone who'll be brutally honest."

"Brutal honesty is my specialty," Hannah replied with a grin.

Twenty minutes later, they were curled up in Claire's cozy living room, glasses of wine in hand and cartons of Chinese food spread out between them. Outside the front windows, the Christmas tree in the town square twinkled against the early winter night, casting a warm glow into the room.

"Okay," Hannah said, settling into her usual corner of the sectional, "what's going on? You sounded stressed when you called earlier."

Claire drew in a steadying breath and told her everything—the television offer, the generous financial package, the production requirements, and the growing knot of uncertainty over what she truly wanted.

"And then there's Gabe," she added quietly, swirling the wine in her glass. "Hannah, I'm falling in love with him. Really falling—not just infatuation or some silly schoolgirl crush. And I'm terrified that taking this opportunity could ruin something that feels... special. Life-changing."

"But you're also terrified of passing it up," Hannah said knowingly.

Claire nodded. "The money would change everything for the bakery. I could replace all the equipment that's barely holding together with prayers and duct tape. I could renovate the kitchen properly. I'd have real financial security."

"And the show itself?"

"That's what's so confusing," Claire admitted. "Part of me is genuinely excited. Having my own show, sharing recipes with people across the country—that's huge. But the Nashville travel requirement... I don't want any part of it."

Hannah was quiet for a moment. "Claire, can I ask you something without you getting defensive?"

"Sure."

"How much of your hesitation about Nashville is really about the practical challenges—and how much is about not wanting things to change between you and Gabe?"

Claire sighed. "Both, honestly. I left Atlanta for this bakery and because I was miserable there. The thought of traveling to another big city on a regular basis doesn't exactly thrill me. But yeah... the idea of not seeing Gabe every day, of having to schedule time together...

it bothers me." She hesitated, then added, "Is that ridiculous? We've only been dating for a little over a month."

"It's not ridiculous if what you have with him feels right," Hannah said gently. "But, Claire... what if you're looking at this the wrong way?"

"What do you mean?"

"I mean, look at what Heartland's offering you—it's just that, an offer," Hannah said. "Offers don't have to be accepted exactly as they're proposed. I'd bet they're expecting you to come back with ideas or changes."

"Go on."

"Here's how I see it," Hannah continued. "Heartland sought you out. They spent good money while they were here—learning about you, this bakery, this town. They see something in you they want, and from what you've told me... they want it badly. Claire, you're one of the most creative people I know. So instead of just saying yes or no to their version, what if you figure out what you actually want—and then find a way to make that happen?"

As the conversation stretched late into the evening, they tossed around possibilities Claire had never considered. Maybe the real question wasn't whether to accept Heartland Cooking Network's vision of her future—but whether she was brave enough to create her own.

By the time Hannah left, Claire's mind was buzzing with ideas that felt equal parts exciting and terrifying. She had three days to make a decision that could shape the rest of her life.

Chapter 31

The cinnamon rolls emerged from the oven with perfectly golden tops, their rich, buttery scent filling the kitchen—but Claire barely registered their beauty. She moved with practiced precision, sliding the steaming pans onto cooling racks, every motion efficient despite the exhaustion dragging at her limbs. She'd managed maybe two hours of restless sleep, most of the night spent tossing in bed or hunched over her kitchen table with her laptop, a pot of coffee, and a growing sense of clarity—like sunrise breaking through a bank of storm clouds.

"Claire, honey, you look like you've been wrestling with angels all night," Joyce said as she stepped inside for her morning shift. "And losing."

"Not losing," Claire replied, her voice surprisingly steady despite the caffeine humming through her veins. "Winning, actually. I think I finally figured out what I want."

Carol and Melanie followed Joyce through the back door, their usual morning chatter tapering off as they took in the sheer volume of baking already done.

"Did you sleep here?" Melanie asked, unwinding her scarf and eyeing the impressive array of pastries covering every inch of cooling space. "Because it looks like you've been baking since midnight."

"Close," Claire admitted, pulling a tray of snickerdoodles from the second oven. "I've been awake since midnight, but most of the night I was at my kitchen table, working on something important."

She hesitated, suddenly aware that only Joyce knew about the Heartland offer. "I need to tell you all something. Something big."

Joyce headed straight for the coffee station, pouring two steaming cups. "Sit," she instructed firmly.

"I'm fine," Claire protested—though she still found herself wrapping her hands around the mug Joyce pressed into them.

"You're running on fumes and stubbornness," Carol observed with gentle precision, leaning against the prep counter while Melanie claimed a stool near the decorating station. "What's going on?"

Claire took a steadying breath. "The Heartland Cooking Network offered me my own television show. They want to call it Claire's Country Kitchen and focus on family recipes and small-town traditions."

"Oh my stars," Carol breathed, her coffee mug frozen halfway to her lips. "Claire, that's incredible—national television!"

"That's amazing!" Melanie exclaimed, bouncing on her stool with barely contained delight.

"And," Joyce prompted, her tone inviting the rest of the story.

"The production would be based in Nashville," Claire explained. "It would mean regular travel and time away from the bakery. Plus monthly filming here, with camera crews and equipment disrupting our normal routine."

The excitement in the room dimmed as the reality set in.

"Nashville's three hours away," Carol said slowly. "That's not exactly a commute you could manage while keeping things running here."

"Exactly," Claire said. "That's what kept me awake most of the night—trying to figure out if there's a way to make this work for me, the bakery, and this town."

Claire moved to the prep area where Gabe's morning order waited to be finalized, double-checking that everything was neatly packed. Her hands worked on instinct, even as her mind replayed the decision that had felt impossible yesterday but crystal clear at four o'clock this morning.

"So, what did you decide?" Joyce asked.

"I'm going to make them a counter-offer," Claire said, feeling a steady current of strength in her voice as she spoke the words that had taken shape during a long night of research and soul-searching. "Instead of a regular series filmed in Nashville, I'm proposing a special Christmas program filmed right here in Mistletoe Falls."

"Here?" Joyce echoed, setting down her coffee with interest. "How would that work?"

Claire's exhaustion began to lift as she shared the vision born from her midnight brainstorming. "A Christmas in July special—seasonal baking, holiday traditions—filmed entirely in the bakery and around town. And if that goes well, an actual Christmas special next December that showcases not just my recipes and the bakery, but the whole community: the tree farm, the holiday celebrations, everything that makes Mistletoe Falls magical."

"That's brilliant," Carol said, her enthusiasm growing. "You'd get the professional recognition and cookbook opportunities without having to leave home."

"Plus," Melanie added, her artistic mind clearly alight with ideas, "imagine how gorgeous the bakery would look on television with all our Christmas decorations and those vintage display cases. And filming here in July? They'd get to capture what Christmas all year round in the mountains really feels like."

"It would be amazing publicity for the whole town," Joyce said with pride. "Think about tour buses full of people who saw Mistletoe Falls on television and decided they had to see it for themselves."

Warmth spread through Claire's chest—born not from caffeine, but from the realization that her plan didn't just protect her own dreams and desires; it celebrated the community that had welcomed her back home so completely.

"The best part," she continued, "is that it would be a special project, not an ongoing commitment. A few days of filming for the Christmas in July program, potential Christmas special filming here in December, cookbook deals featuring both my recipes and Mae's—but no constant Nashville travel and no major disruption to our daily operations outside those filming periods."

As they fine-tuned the details of her counterproposal, Claire felt the last threads of uncertainty dissolve into confident resolve. This was right. It honored Mae's legacy while building her own future, created opportunities without uprooting the life she'd built here, and—most importantly—kept her exactly where she wanted to be: in Mistletoe Falls.

"Joyce," she said, sealing Gabe's delivery boxes and glancing at the clock, "would you mind making the delivery to the farm this morning?

I need to send some emails and make a few calls while my courage is still running high."

"Of course, honey," Joyce replied, already reaching for her coat.

Claire pulled a sheet of bakery stationery from the counter and began to write, the words flowing almost without thought:

Gabe

Sorry I couldn't make the delivery myself this morning. I have some important calls to make regarding Heartland. I've made my decision and would love to share it with you this afternoon if you have time.

Claire

She folded the note and handed it to Joyce along with the delivery boxes. "Could you give this to Gabe?"

"Will do," Joyce said with a reassuring smile. "Now go handle your business—we'll keep things running here."

After helping her load the van and waving her off, Claire gathered her laptop, phone, and a fresh cup of coffee. Determination carried her to her office, her steps light with purpose.

The proposal she'd drafted earlier looked even better in the light of day—professional, creative, mutually beneficial, and most importantly, true to who she was and what she wanted.

Claire refined the language, weaving in specific details about Mistletoe Falls' tourism appeal and deep-rooted Christmas heritage. She attached supporting materials highlighting the town's festival calendar and visitor statistics before taking one last steadying breath and clicking send on the email to Katherine McPherson. As the message whooshed away, something in her chest settled—an unease she'd carried since Thursday morning's unexpected visit from Heartland finally giving way to calm resolve.

Later, the phone call made proved easier than she'd imagined. Katherine's initial surprise at the counter-proposal quickly shifted into clear interest as Claire outlined her community-focused alternative.

"Ms. Whitfield, this is quite different from what we originally discussed," Katherine said, her tone thoughtful rather than dismissive. "You're suggesting a special programming format instead of a regular series."

"I'm proposing authentic storytelling," Claire replied, surprised by the confidence in her own voice. "Instead of recreating small-town life in a Nashville studio, you'd be filming the real thing—in a community that embodies everything your network celebrates. And a Christmas-themed special filmed in July would give you programming no other network could duplicate."

"The tourism angle is intriguing," Katherine admitted.

After thirty minutes of detailed discussion, they scheduled a late-afternoon video conference to present the proposal to the full Heartland team. When Claire ended the call, she felt cautiously optimistic instead of desperately nervous.

Her phone buzzed with a text from Gabe: *Free all afternoon. Come to the cabin when you're ready. Missed seeing you this morning.*

Those last five words stirred something in Claire's chest that had nothing to do with professional anxiety and everything to do with the quiet joy of knowing someone noticed her absence—and cared.

She typed back quickly: *Meeting with the network at 4, then I'll head your way. Have news to share.*

His reply came almost instantly: *Good news, I hope?*

Claire smiled at the screen, then typed the truth that had taken her all night to uncover: *Maybe. I'll know more later.*

As she turned back to refining her presentation and gathering materials for the meeting, a sense of deep satisfaction settled over her—the contentment of someone who had stopped trying to choose between competing dreams and had instead found a way to honor them all.

Chapter 32

Claire adjusted her laptop one last time, positioning it on the bakery's front counter so the afternoon light spilling through the wide front windows would illuminate her perfectly. Behind her, the magnificent Christmas tree she and Gabe had decorated together gleamed in the winter sun, its ornaments scattering tiny rainbows across the room—exactly the backdrop she wanted the Heartland Cooking Network to see.

At 3:58 PM, she smoothed the front of her cream-colored sweater and checked her reflection in the laptop camera. The woman staring back looked calm, professional, and—most importantly—genuinely excited rather than desperately nervous.

Right on the hour, her laptop chimed. The screen flickered to life, revealing a boardroom filled with Heartland executives seated around a gleaming mahogany table, their faces framed like a jury preparing to deliberate her future.

"Ms. Whitfield," came Katherine McPherson's familiar voice, warm yet polished. She leaned forward, a professional smile that put people at ease brightening her features. "Thank you for joining us this afternoon. I'd like you to meet our programming team."

One by one, Katherine introduced five executives—Programming Director Marcus Webb, Content Development Manager Sophia Cortland, Production Supervisor David Rupert, Marketing Director Jennifer Hayes, and Senior VP of Development Adam Sullivan. The weight of their titles alone told Claire this proposal had climbed to the highest levels of consideration.

"Ms. Whitfield," Marcus began, glancing at the notes on his tablet, "Katherine's shared your counter-proposal with our team, and I have to say—it's quite different from our standard programming model. Could you walk us through your vision?"

Claire took a steady breath, drawing confidence from the familiar comfort of her bakery and the certainty that she was fighting for something worth protecting. "Instead of recreating small-town Christmas in a Nashville studio, you'd be filming the real thing—an authentic small-town Christmas in a community that lives and breathes holiday traditions all year long."

She gestured toward the surrounding bakery, knowing the camera was capturing the vintage charm and genuine atmosphere. "Mistletoe Falls isn't just decorated for Christmas—it is Christmas, year-round. We have a family-operated Christmas tree farm that's been running since 1924, restaurants serving holiday recipes passed down for generations, and community celebrations that draw visitors from across the region."

"The location is certainly picturesque," Sophia said, making a note on her tablet. "But help us understand the audience appeal. Our research shows viewers lean toward aspirational content—celebrity chefs, high-end techniques, sophisticated presentations."

Claire felt the first flutter of challenge and met it head-on. "With respect, I think your research is showing you what networks assume people want. What they're craving is authenticity. They're tired of manufactured perfection. Two weeks ago, at our tree lighting ceremony, I served refreshments to families from right here in town and from as far away as Georgia and Michigan—and every single one of them experienced what a real community Christmas feels like."

She reached for the folder she'd prepared, sliding out neatly organized printouts of the town's tourism statistics. "Mistletoe Falls welcomes over 400,000 visitors each Christmas season, with sixty percent traveling more than two hours specifically for our authentic mountain holiday experience. These aren't people looking for celebrity chefs—they're families seeking traditions that feel real."

"Tourism numbers are impressive," Jennifer Hayes admitted, glancing at the figures, "but how does that translate into television ratings?"

"Because television audiences want the same thing, those families are willing to drive hours to find," Claire said, her confidence growing as she found her rhythm. "They want to discover the cinnamon roll recipe that's been served at our bakery counter for years. They want to see how a Christmas tree farm creates the perfect holiday centerpiece. They want to watch community celebrations where neighbors greet each other by name."

Marcus Webb leaned back in his chair, studying her through the camera. "You're proposing we film in July for a Christmas special. Explain the logic behind that timing."

"Christmas in July celebrates the reality of living Christmas year-round," Claire explained, her voice warming with enthusiasm for one of her favorite parts of the proposal. "Your viewers would experience a genuine year-round Christmas town—content you can weave into your own programming and compete directly with other networks that lean heavily into Christmas in July. We could film me testing holiday recipes, showcase local chefs creating seasonal dishes in our restaurants, tour the town, and feature segments highlighting everything this community offers. The possibilities are endless."

She gestured toward the Christmas tree glowing in the background. "And filming Christmas content in July gives you something no other network can replicate. Instead of competing with everyone else's December specials that are only repeats originally shown the previous winter, you could own the summer Christmas market entirely—with a fresh, unique twist."

David Rupert spoke up, his tone edged with skepticism. "Ms. Whitfield, I appreciate your enthusiasm, but summer filming in Tennessee poses significant logistical challenges. Weather, transporting equipment to a rural location, and housing for crew—production costs could climb quickly."

"Mr. Rupert, Mistletoe Falls already hosts multiple large-scale festivals and conventions each year, including a major music festival that brings in touring production crews. We have established relationships with equipment rental companies in Knoxville and Nashville, plus a range of lodging options—from the historic Mistletoe Lodge to vacation rentals specifically designed for visiting professionals."

She reached for another folder and slid it into view. "I've also researched comparable location shoots for networks similar to Heartland. When you factor in authentic set design, props, and the background talent needed to recreate a genuine community atmosphere, the cost difference between filming in rural Tennessee and a studio is actually minimal."

Adam Sullivan, who had been quiet until now, leaned forward, genuine interest sparking in his eyes. "Ms. Whitfield, what about cookbook opportunities? How do you see that component fitting with community-focused programming?"

Claire felt her excitement rise as she turned to the part of her proposal she loved most. "Instead of only my recipes, you'd have access to treasured family recipes from across the community. My grandmother Mae's traditional and authentic mountain recipes. Seasonal menu items from The Fireside Diner—dishes that have anchored our celebrations for decades. And there are multiple restaurants here that I'm confident would want to participate."

She paused, meeting the eyes of each executive through the camera. "A comprehensive cookbook that represents an entire community's Christmas heritage—not just one baker's repertoire. Every recipe paired with its story, family photographs, the kind of authentic content that creates an emotional connection rather than offering just instructions."

"The marketing possibilities are significant," Jennifer Hayes observed, jotting notes as her expression warmed. "Community cookbook, location-based tourism, even potential product lines featuring authentic mountain Christmas goods."

Sophia Cortland looked up from her tablet. "What about ongoing programming potential? If the specials are successful, how could the concept expand?"

"Seasonal specials showcasing different aspects of mountain life," Claire replied, pleased they were already thinking beyond Christmas. "Spring could feature traditional gardening and preservation techniques. Summer might highlight the music festival and outdoor cooking, and celebrations... or another Christmas in July special. Fall could explore harvest traditions and preparations for winter."

She leaned forward slightly, allowing her genuine passion to shine. "The Christmas programming would always be the cornerstone—because that's when Mistletoe Falls is at its most magical."

Marcus Webb conferred quietly with his team for several minutes before turning back to her. "Ms. Whitfield, assuming we move forward with your concept, let's talk timeline and financial structure."

Claire's pulse quickened, a cautious optimism threading through her nerves. "I'm listening."

"Summer filming would need to take place in May," Sophia Cortland explained, "to allow time for post-production and marketing. We'd be looking at roughly one week of intensive filming, with the possibility of returning for Christmas programming during your actual holiday season—if audience response warrants expansion."

David Rupert tapped his tablet, pulling up budget figures. "The financial package would be structured for special programming rather than a full series, but it would be comparable to our original offer. That includes the initial filming fee, a cookbook advance, and revenue sharing on any product lines developed from the programming."

"Plus," Jennifer Hayes added, "there's strong potential for marketing partnerships with the town itself—tourism promotion, business features, the kind of authentic location branding that benefits everyone involved."

Warmth spread through Claire's chest as the pieces began falling into place exactly as she'd envisioned during her sleepless night. "That sounds wonderful, but I need to emphasize—community involvement can't just be background atmosphere. These are real people with real businesses, and the programming needs to honor their contributions appropriately."

"Absolutely," Katherine McPherson assured her. "We'd work with you to ensure participating businesses and community members are properly credited and compensated. This concept only works if everyone benefits."

Adam Sullivan leaned forward, his tone carrying the weight of authority. "Ms. Whitfield, before we can finalize anything, we'd need to present this concept to our full board and coordinate with Mistletoe Falls' city government for filming permits and community approval."

"Of course," Claire said, her excitement building with each positive response. "Mayor Hayes and our city council are very supportive of projects that showcase our community in a positive light."

"We'd also need to visit Mistletoe Falls again with additional associates," Marcus Webb added. "We'd want to see the broader filming possibilities firsthand, meet with local business owners, and confirm that the logistics match your presentation."

"I'd be happy to coordinate those site visits," Claire offered. "Gabe Mills at the Christmas tree farm, the owners of Mistletoe Lodge, our mayor—everyone will be eager to discuss the possibilities with you."

The executives spent several minutes conferring over technical details while Claire waited, her excitement building with every passing moment. Everything was falling into place exactly as she'd hoped—professional recognition without sacrificing personal happiness, financial security without giving up the life she'd built, and opportunities that honored Mae's legacy while allowing her to create her own.

"Ms. Whitfield," Katherine said at last, "I think I speak for our entire team when I say this proposal captures exactly what Heartland viewers are seeking—authentic content, community connection, and programming that celebrates traditions worth preserving."

Sophia Cortland nodded enthusiastically. "The Christmas in July concept alone gives us a unique position in the summer programming market. Paired with potential holiday specials, you're offering content no other network can match."

"We'd like to move forward with preliminary development," Adam Sullivan announced, his voice carrying executive finality. "Site visit within the next two weeks, community meetings in January, and target filming dates in early May if all goes according to plan."

Claire's heart soared with relief and excitement. "That timeline sounds perfect."

"We'll have contracts drafted to reflect the special programming structure we've discussed," Marcus Webb added. "Financial terms comparable to our original offer, but structured for project-based work rather than an ongoing series commitment."

"And Ms. Whitfield," Katherine said with clear satisfaction, "congratulations. You've presented innovative programming that sets Heartland apart from the competition. We're excited to work with you."

After another ten minutes spent ironing out logistics and agreeing to follow up within forty-eight hours, the video conference ended. Claire stood staring at her laptop in amazed joy. Not only had they accepted her counter-proposal—they'd embraced it with the same enthusiasm she'd felt in the quiet hours of her midnight inspiration.

More than anything, Claire felt at peace with what she'd negotiated—professional recognition without personal sacrifice, financial security without abandoning her community, and opportunities that honored both Mae's legacy and her own dreams.

She gathered her materials, but instead of immediately closing her laptop, she let her gaze wander across the space where she'd just shaped her future. The vintage display cases had showcased family recipes for three generations. The Christmas tree—a symbol of community celebration and shared joy. The warm, inviting atmosphere that made Sugarplum Bakery feel like Mistletoe Falls' living room.

This was exactly right. All of it.

Pulling out her phone, she typed a quick message to Gabe: *Meeting went better than I dreamed. Have the most amazing news to share. On my way to you.*

His reply came almost instantly: *Can't wait to hear everything. Drive safely.*

As Claire closed her laptop and gathered her purse, anticipation bubbled up in her chest. She had incredible news to share, but more than that, she had the joy of sharing it with the man who'd helped her discover what home really meant.

Chapter 33

Claire's boots crunched over the light dusting of snow on Gabe's porch steps, her heart thudding with excitement. Before she could knock on the door, it swung open to reveal Gabe's familiar silhouette, backlit by the cozy glow inside.

"Claire," he said, his voice a blend of relief and something that might have been hope.

Baxter bounded past him with unrestrained enthusiasm, nearly launching himself into Claire's arms as though she'd been gone for weeks instead of a single day.

"Hello, sweet boy," Claire laughed, crouching to give him the affection he demanded, her own excitement bubbling like champagne. "Did you miss me?"

"He's not the only one," Gabe murmured, stepping aside to let her into the cabin's warmth.

Straightening, Claire took in the sight of him—dark green flannel, worn jeans, and the quiet strength in his stance—but her gaze lingered on the subtle tension in his shoulders. The protective distance she'd noticed since telling him about Heartland was still there, a careful guard against possible disappointment.

Well, she was about to change that.

"Come here," she said, stepping across the threshold and pausing just inside.

Gabe approached, curiosity in his eyes. Claire pointed upward with a grin she could barely contain. Above them, a fresh sprig of mistletoe hung from the foyer ceiling, its red berries catching the warm light from the living room.

"Well," Claire said, reaching for the front of his flannel shirt and gently pulling him toward her, "we can't ignore tradition."

Before he could respond, she rose on her toes and kissed him—a kiss that tasted of joy, relief, and the certainty of having made exactly the right choice. His initial surprise gave way to warmth as his arms came around her, holding her close while she poured every bit of her happiness into that sweet, lingering moment.

When they finally parted, Gabe rested his forehead against hers, his expression filled with wonder and a spark of renewed hope.

"I like where this is headed," he said softly, the corners of his eyes crinkling.

"Good," Claire replied.

She reached for his hand, their fingers intertwining. "Can we sit? I have so much to tell you."

Gabe closed the front door and followed her toward the living room, where the massive stone fireplace crackled with warmth and golden light that made everything feel magical. Baxter trotted at their heels, clearly pleased to have his two favorite people together in his favorite place.

Claire settled onto the sectional, tucking one leg beneath her so she could face Gabe fully as he claimed the spot beside her.

"So," he said, his gaze intent, "your text mentioned the best news. How did the meeting go?"

Her smile deepened at the memory of the video conference that had changed everything. "Gabe, they said yes. Not just yes—they were excited."

His brow lifted slightly. "Said yes to what, exactly?" His tone carried a careful edge, as if he was afraid to hope for what her answer might mean.

"I didn't accept their original offer," Claire said, watching his expression as she delivered the news. "I made them a counterproposal—and they loved it."

She walked him through the details of her negotiations, explaining the Christmas in July concept, the community-focused filming, and the special programming that would showcase Mistletoe Falls without requiring her to spend time in Nashville. With each point, she saw the guarded distance in his expression dissolve, replaced by something closer to amazement.

"You negotiated a completely different deal," he said slowly, as if testing the words to be sure he'd heard them right.

"I created a deal that works for me, for the bakery, for this community, and..." Claire met his gaze squarely, "...for us."

Baxter had settled on the rug beside the couch, his bright eyes flicking between them as though he understood the weight of the conversation.

"Claire," Gabe said, his voice threaded with awe, "that's incredible. You took a situation that seemed impossible and found a way to honor everything that matters to you."

"Everything that matters to me is here," she said simply. "The bakery. This community. Joyce and the staff who've become family.

The life I've built... you. I wasn't willing to give that up for money or recognition or anything else."

She watched as the last of his protective walls fell away, replaced by relief, pride, and something deeper—something that made her pulse skip.

"But the financial security," Gabe said. "The equipment you need, the recognition you deserve—"

Claire interrupted gently. "The financial package they are proposing now is good. I'll have cookbook deals, marketing partnerships, professional recognition—everything I want, and on my terms."

He was quiet for a moment, processing her words. When he finally spoke, his voice carried the careful honesty she'd come to recognize in their most meaningful conversations.

"Claire, I need to apologize. When you first told me about Heartland's offer, I..." He paused, running a hand through his hair in that familiar gesture that meant he was weighing each word. "I got scared. Not of your success—never that—but of losing you to something bigger and better."

"I know," Claire said softly, giving his hand a reassuring squeeze, her heart catching at the vulnerability in his eyes. "And I understand why. But Gabe, I need you to hear something important."

She shifted closer on the couch, close enough to catch the clean scent of his soap and see the gold flecks in his green eyes, made even warmer by the firelight.

"I proposed something entirely different to Heartland because I needed to," she said quietly but with steady conviction. "If they wanted me badly enough, they'd have to accept my terms—what I want for my own life. And you are part of that life. What we have... I don't want it to change. I want it to grow. I want to see what a future with you could look like. I love exactly who you are and the life you've built here."

"Claire—"

"Let me finish," she said gently. "When Heartland offered me that show, I was flattered and excited. At first, I focused too much on the money and what that nice, big check could do for me. But then I started thinking about what accepting would really mean—having two lives. One here, where I'm happy, and one in Nashville... which I want no part of. Spending weeks away, then coming back and turning the bakery into a television set for another week? Not for me. I'd miss you, my family, my friends—and all the little moments that make life worth living."

She reached up, her fingers brushing his cheek in a gesture that felt as natural as breathing.

"Success isn't about how many people know your name or how much money you make. It's about building a life that feels right and surrounding yourself with people who matter. And Gabe, you matter to me more than any television show ever could."

The firelight caught the emotion in his eyes, and when he spoke, his voice was rough with feeling.

"Do you have any idea how much it means to hear you say that?"

"This life we have here—it's beautiful," Claire said with quiet conviction. "It's everything I didn't know I needed."

Baxter chose that moment to stand and rest his head on the couch between them, his soulful eyes shifting from Claire to Gabe as if he wanted to weigh in on the conversation. The sight made them both laugh, easing the emotional intensity while adding the perfect touch of lightness.

"I think someone approves of this discussion," Gabe said, scratching behind Baxter's ears. The dog's tail wagged in obvious agreement.

"He's a smart boy," Claire replied, running her hand along Baxter's head.

"So what happens next?" Gabe asked. "With Heartland, I mean. What's the timeline?"

Claire leaned back against the cushions, still turned toward him, feeling lighter now that the hardest words had been spoken. "They'll meet with city officials and schedule site visits within the next two weeks to talk with business owners and scout filming locations. If all goes well, filming will happen in May for the Christmas in July programming."

"And you're excited about it?" Gabe studied her closely.

"I'm thrilled," Claire said honestly. "This feels right. I'll get to showcase the bakery, share Grandma Mae's recipes alongside mine, highlight our community traditions, create something that celebrates everything I love about this place—and build my career without giving up my life."

For the next hour, they talked through the practical details of potential filming, the opportunities to highlight local businesses, and the ways the program could benefit the entire Mistletoe Falls community. As the conversation flowed, the last traces of tension between them faded, replaced by shared excitement for a future that honored both their individual dreams and desires and the life they were beginning to build together.

"Claire," Gabe said during a comfortable lull in their conversation, "spend Christmas Eve with me."

"I'd love to," Claire answered without hesitation, though the glint in his eyes told her this was more than a simple invitation. "What are you up to?"

"I'll pick you up at seven," Gabe said, his smile carrying a spark of barely contained excitement. "And dress warmly."

She tilted her head, studying him. "Gabe Mills, you have to give me a clue."

"Just trust me," he murmured, reaching over to tuck a strand of hair behind her ear with a touch so gentle it sent her pulse skipping. "I promise it'll be worth it."

Chapter 34

Claire smoothed her emerald-green sweater one last time as she checked her reflection in the bedroom mirror. She'd chosen warm layers as Gabe had suggested—the soft sweater over her favorite jeans, warm boots that could handle whatever outdoor adventure he might have planned, and her cream-colored wool coat hanging ready by the door.

A knock sounded at exactly seven o'clock—punctual, as always—and her pulse quickened. She grabbed her coat and purse, heart thudding in anticipation, and opened the door.

Gabe stood there on her landing, looking devastatingly handsome in his dark wool coat, his breath visible in the frosty night air, his eyes lit with a mix of barely contained excitement and something warmer... something just for her.

"You look like a man with secrets, Gabe Mills," she teased.

His smile—slow, genuine, and laced with affection—made her stomach flutter. "You look beautiful, Claire."

He held her coat for her as she slipped it on.

"So," she teased, accepting his offered arm as they started down the stairs together, "are you going to give me any hints about this mysterious Christmas Eve you have planned?"

"Nope," Gabe replied, his voice light and cheerful as he helped her into his truck. "But I promise—you're going to love it."

As they drove through downtown Mistletoe Falls, Claire's breath caught at the sight before her. Every window glowed with a welcoming light, the town's magnificent Christmas tree rising in the square like a beacon of joy.

She turned to study his profile in the soft glow of the dashboard. "Should I be worried?" She asked, "or excited about whatever you've planned?"

"Excited," Gabe said, his grip on her hand tightening ever so slightly. "Definitely excited."

When he turned onto the road leading to his farm, anticipation fizzed through her like champagne bubbles. But instead of heading toward his cabin, he steered toward the main entrance of the Mistletoe Magic Christmas Tree Farm—where something immediately caught her eye.

"Gabe," she breathed, leaning forward as her heart gave a quick, surprised flutter. "What did you do?"

The entrance to Mistletoe Christmas Tree Farm had been transformed into something out of a winter fairy tale. Thousands of twinkle lights wove through the trees along the drive, creating a tunnel of golden radiance that beckoned them forward. From the branches hung battery-powered lanterns, their gentle glow casting playful shadows on the snow-dusted ground.

He parked near the North Pole Trading Post, and before Claire's boots even hit the ground, Baxter came bounding toward them, his red bandana bobbing merrily against his golden fur.

"There's my favorite farm ambassador," Claire laughed, crouching to scratch behind his ears. "Did you help Daddy plan this surprise?"

"He supervised," Gabe replied with affection, reaching for her hand as Baxter fell into step beside them. "Come on. There's something I want you to see."

Inside, the Trading Post had been transformed into an intimate, magical haven. A small table near the crackling fireplace was set with an array of cookies artfully arranged on vintage plates. Twinkle lights and the gentle flicker of battery-operated candles bathed the rustic room in a warm, romantic glow, making it feel like they'd stepped into the heart of a Christmas dream.

But it was the hand-lettered sign above the fireplace that made Claire's breath catch and her chest tighten: Our First Real Conversation—November 2025.

"Gabe..." Her voice softened, wonder etched across her features as she turned toward him. "You recreated our business meeting."

His hands came to rest gently at her waist, his eyes holding that rare, unguarded honesty that told her something important was coming. "Claire, there's something I need to tell you about that day. About why I was so nervous."

"You were very nervous," she agreed with a small, knowing smile.

"That's because I was already completely head over heels for you," Gabe admitted, the words spilling out with a raw sincerity that made her pulse skip. "Had been for months. Every Saturday morning at the bakery, I'd find some excuse to linger, trying to work up the courage to ask you out. That business partnership?" His lips curved faintly. "It was me finally finding a way to spend time with you without stuttering through some pathetic attempt at asking for a date."

Claire's smile widened as long-pondered pieces clicked into place. "I did wonder. You always lingered at the counter, and Joyce kept telling me how nervous you seemed around me. But I wasn't sure if I was imagining it."

"You weren't imagining a thing," Gabe said, his thumbs brushing slow, tender circles along her waist. "I was just terrified you'd say no."

"Gabe Mills," Claire said softly, lifting her hand to cup his cheek, "if you had asked me out, I would have said yes. I was attracted to you too."

"We're both terrible at reading signals. Good thing Baxter here decided to help things along."

Baxter sat beside them with his tennis ball, looking hopeful for playtime. Claire laughed and scratched behind his ears while Gabe fished a treat from his coat pocket and offered it to him.

"Ready for the next part of our story?" Gabe asked, his voice warm with promise.

Hand in hand, they stepped outside, passing beneath the canopy of illuminated trees. A pathway lined with softly glowing lanterns guided them forward, each pool of golden light casting a gentle warmth against the cool December night. Baxter trotted a few steps ahead like a furry tour guide, stopping now and then to make sure they stayed on his approved route.

"This is absolutely magical," Claire murmured, giving Gabe's hand a tender squeeze as they wandered through a grove of Fraser firs that seemed to shimmer with their own inner light. "How long did this take you to set up?

"Two very busy days—with the help of my crew," Gabe admitted, satisfaction in his tone. "Derrick thought I'd lost my mind, but he stayed until midnight last night to help me get everything perfect."

"It is perfect," Claire assured him, pausing to take in the way the lights glimmered off the snow-dusted branches, casting playful shadows along the path. "Completely, absolutely perfect."

Their second stop brought them to the exact spot where they'd chosen the community Christmas tree—now marked with a simple wooden sign that read Our Perfect Tree—December 2025. The area had been transformed with string lights woven through the surrounding Fraser firs and a small warming station complete with thermoses of hot drinks and two comfortable chairs set to face the view toward town.

"Look," Gabe said, pointing through the trees to the soft glow in the distance. "You can see it from here—that glow in the center of town? That's our tree."

Claire followed his gesture to where their magnificent Fraser fir rose above the town square, its thousands of lights shimmering against the night sky.

"Claire, that day we picked that tree together..." Gabe's voice gentled, carrying a truth he'd been holding close. "I knew I was falling for you. Not just attracted, not just interested—but genuinely falling in love with someone who sees the same magic in simple things that I do."

"That was when I started falling too," she admitted, her voice threaded with the honest vulnerability that had become second nature between them. "Watching you explain the science behind growing the perfect Christmas tree, seeing how deeply you cared about creating magical experiences for families... That's when I realized you weren't just attractive. You were extraordinary."

"Ready for the grand finale?" Gabe asked at last, his voice threaded with barely contained excitement—and just a hint of nervous anticipation.

"Lead the way," Claire replied, noting the way his eyes sparkled with whatever surprise awaited at their final stop.

The path wound deeper through the trees toward the back of the property, where a warm, golden glow shimmered ahead. As they stepped from the grove, Claire stopped in her tracks, breath catching at the sight before her.

Gabe's pond had been transformed into the most romantic setting she had ever seen. String lights traced the entire perimeter, their warm radiance reflecting off the glassy ice like a thousand tiny stars. The pavilion glittered under a canopy of twinkle lights draped beneath the tin roof, casting a soft, enchanting glow over the space. Nearby, a fire pit blazed, surrounded by inviting chairs draped with plush blankets, each positioned for both the fire's warmth and the sweeping view across the farm to the twinkling lights of Mistletoe Falls in the distance.

But it was the music—drifting softly from hidden speakers in the pavilion—that brought happy tears to her eyes: the gentle instrumental version of one of the songs they had danced to at the Mistletoe Ball, the night Gabe had first kissed her.

"Gabe," she whispered, her voice thick with emotion. "How did you do all this?"

"Mom and Dad helped... a lot," he said with a smile. "They got everything ready, tended the fire, and had strict instructions to head home when they saw us coming."

He led her into the pavilion, where she looked up to find what had to be hundreds of mistletoe sprigs suspended among the twinkle lights.

"This is the most beautiful thing I've ever seen."

"Dance with me," he said.

Claire placed her palm against his without a moment's hesitation, letting him draw her close. They began to sway beneath the twinkling lights; the firelight flickering nearby and casting a golden shimmer across the ice, while the string lights above formed a canopy of stars. The peaceful hush of the December night mingled with the music—a song woven through their history—wrapping the moment in magic.

"Claire," Gabe said softly, and something in his voice made her look up, meeting his gaze head-on. "I love you."

"I love you too," she replied instantly, rising onto her toes as he bent toward her. Their lips met in a kiss unlike any before—deeper, more certain, carrying the weight of their mutual confession and the promise of everything it meant for the future. When they drew apart, both were smiling, joy radiating from within.

"I have something for you," Gabe said, reaching into his coat pocket and pulling out a small wrapped box that made Claire's heart give a quick, excited flutter.

"Gabe," she began as he placed it in her hands, "you didn't need to—"

"Open it," he urged gently, his eyes bright with nervous anticipation.

Claire unwrapped the small box, then gasped. Nestled inside was the most beautiful ring she had ever seen—a rich, glowing ruby encircled by diamonds that caught the firelight and seemed to hold their own inner flame.

"It's beautiful," she breathed, her voice barely above a whisper. "Gabe, it's absolutely beautiful."

"It might be a little big," he admitted, a flicker of nervousness crossing his features. "I didn't know your size... or even if you liked rubies—"

Claire silenced him by cupping his face with her free hand. "It's perfect. You're perfect. This whole evening is perfect."

"This is only the beginning, Claire," Gabe said softly, taking the ring from its box and sliding it onto her left hand. It fit almost perfectly, just slightly loose in a way that could easily be adjusted.

Claire looked down at the ruby glittering on her finger, the diamonds catching the firelight, then lifted her gaze back to Gabe's face—where love, hope, and absolute certainty shone in equal measure.

"You know something, Gabe Mills," she said, her voice ringing with confident joy, "I'm gonna marry you someday."

Gabe's grin broke wide and unrestrained, the kind of smile that could light the whole farm. It made her laugh out loud, the sound pure happiness.

"Is that a promise?" he asked.

"That's a guarantee," Claire replied, pulling him into a kiss that tasted of joy, certainty, and the kind of love meant to last a lifetime.

They danced for another hour beneath the mistletoe and twinkling lights, speaking of their future with the easy certainty of two people who knew exactly what they wanted in life. As the evening deepened and the fire settled into a bed of glowing embers, they wrapped themselves in warm blankets, watching the stars reflect on the still water while Baxter dozed contentedly at their feet.

"Thank you," Claire murmured, her head resting on Gabe's shoulder. "For tonight. For trusting me with your heart."

"Thank you," Gabe replied, pressing a gentle kiss to the crown of her head, "for choosing us."

Christmas Eve wrapped around them in perfect peace, and Claire felt the deep, quiet satisfaction of knowing exactly where she belonged—in Mistletoe Falls, in the community that had embraced her so completely, and in the arms of the man who made everything better simply by being himself.

Tomorrow was Christmas, and she would spend it with Gabe's family at his home, both families gathered together as one. In just a few weeks, the Heartland Cooking Network would arrive for their site visit, marking the beginning of the next chapter in her professional dreams.

But for now, it was enough to sit beside the man she loved, surrounded by the magical beauty he had created just for her, knowing this was only the beginning of their story.

"Merry Christmas, Gabe," she whispered into the peaceful December night.

"Merry Christmas, Claire," he said, holding her closer. "The first of many."

As the stars shimmered on the icy pond and the music played softly on, Claire knew with absolute certainty that every choice—both personal and professional—had led her to this perfect moment.

She was exactly where she belonged, with exactly the right person.

And this was only the beginning.

Leave A Review

I f you enjoyed this book, please consider leaving an honest review on Amazon

Visit Our Website:

www.tarabaisden.com

Visit Our Amazon Author Page HERE

Find Us On Social Media:

Facebook

Facebook Author Page

Instagram

Also by Tara Baisden

<u>Riverbend Valley Series</u>

#1 A Cowboy's Second Chance

#2 Wanderlust & Wild Horses

#3 Heartstrings on the Horizon

#4 Runaway in Riverbend Valley

#5 Mended Hearts

#6 Healing Hearts

#7 Home to Lost Creek

<u>Mistletoe Falls Series</u>

#1 Whisk Me Under the Mistletoe

#2 Once Upon a Christmas

#3 The Mistletoe Express

#4 Candy Canes & Sweet Dreams

#5 Wrapped Up in Christmas

#6 Jingle All the Way Home

About The Author

Tara Baisden is a Contemporary Christian Inspirational Romance author who proudly calls the beautiful state of West Virginia her home. Nestled on a sprawling mountainous property, she is surrounded by the peace and serenity of nature. Her days are happily spent in the quiet of country life, writing heartwarming stories of love, faith, and second chances. Tara also enjoys quilting, working in her garden, tending to her beloved pets, and soaking in the beauty of her surroundings.

With deep roots in West Virginia, family is everything to Tara. One of her favorite pastimes is gathering on the front porch with loved ones, sharing stories, laughter, and enjoying the simple, meaningful moments that life offers. When she's not crafting her novels, Tara can often be found exploring the rich history of her home state, visiting local historical sites, and, of course, stopping by every bookstore she passes! Her passion for reading and discovery always fuels her next adventure.

Tara is the author of the Laurel Ridges series of novels, as well as the Riverbend Valley series of novels, of which have been beloved by fans of inspirational romance. Her novels reflect her love for faith, family, and the timeless beauty of the world we live in.

Known for her sweet and clean romances, she creates characters that feel like family and settings that make readers want to visit again and again.

You can find out more about Tara and her latest releases at www.tarabaisden.com or follow her on social media for updates and behind-the-scenes glimpses of her writing process. Stay connected—you won't want to miss the heartfelt stories of love and family she has in store!

About Mistletoe Falls

Welcome to the fictional town of Mistletoe Falls, Tennessee!

Where Christmas Magic Lives Year-Round

*H*igh *in the Tennessee mountains, where winter lingers longer and Christmas spirit fills the air year-round, lies a town that feels almost too perfect to be real and looks like it stepped straight out of a holiday postcard.*

The winding mountain road to Mistletoe Falls tells you this isn't just any destination. Scenic Route 265 climbs higher into the Smoky Mountains with each breathtaking curve, past ancient trees heavy with snow that arch over the road like nature's own cathedral. But it's the final approach that steals your breath—crossing the enchanting Snowbell Covered Bridge, draped in evergreen garland and twinkling lights, as it spans the crystal waters of Mistletoe Creek below.

Beyond the bridge, the Welcome Pavilion greets every arrival with a hand-carved wooden sign: *"Welcome to Mistletoe Falls—Home of the Christmas Spirit."* The cheerful red pavilion, complete with candy cane striping and an archway of year-round twinkle lights, promises that something wonderful awaits just around the bend.

Mistletoe Falls (population 6,200) nestles in a perfect valley where the musical sound of cascading waterfalls mingles with church bells and children's laughter. The town spreads gracefully along Mistletoe Creek, whose series of waterfalls create the melodic backdrop to daily life.

This is Tennessee's beloved Christmas Town—because Christmas simply lives here. From the gas lamp streetlights wrapped in evergreen garland to the horse-drawn carriages clip-clopping down brick streets, every detail whispers of simpler times and sweeter moments.

The town square draws everyone like a magnet, centered around a Victorian gazebo where carols drift through the air and community life unfolds. Ancient oak trees frame the square, their branches creating natural shelter for the wooden benches below—each dedicated to a beloved neighbor who helped shape this special place. Thousands of lights transform the square into pure magic.

Mistletoe Lane curves gently around the town square before branching into charming side streets lined with century-old brick buildings. Each storefront tells a story through hand-carved details and cheerful striped awnings in hunter green, burgundy, and cream. Wide brick sidewalks invite leisurely strolls, while cozy benches appear just when you need them most.

The architecture whispers of careful love—original stonework preserved alongside modern conveniences, ensuring comfort while honoring the past. Three-story buildings house everything from the town bakery to the bookshop, with apartments above where business owners live.

From November through February, Mistletoe Falls transforms into a living snow globe. The special mountain microclimate ensures gentle snowfall that blankets everything in pristine white, while temperatures hover between 15 and 45 degrees—perfect for outdoor adventures and cozy indoor moments.

The partially frozen waterfalls become nature's chandeliers, catching winter light like thousands of diamonds. Snow-covered trails wind through frosted forests where the only sounds are your footsteps and the distant laughter from the town below. Long winter evenings mean crackling fireplaces, hot cider, and the kind of conversations that matter.

The Mistletoe Lodge stands as the town's crown jewel—a century-old mountain lodge with wraparound porches and stone fireplaces where love stories begin over morning coffee and evening wine. Its guest rooms blend historic charm with modern comfort, creating the perfect retreat for visitors who never quite want to leave.

The Snowbell Covered Bridge serves as more than transportation; it's where proposals happen and first kisses are shared, sheltered from mountain weather while framing perfect views of the approaching town.

The Mistletoe Christmas Tree Farm spreads across rolling hills on the town's outskirts, where families create memories among rows of Fraser firs and the air smells like pine and possibility.

What makes Mistletoe Falls magical isn't just its picture-perfect setting—it's the people who call it home. Three generations often work side by side in family businesses, while newcomers quickly discover they're not visitors but neighbors-in-waiting.

Local business owners coordinate holiday decorations and community events with the kind of collaboration that creates the seamless magic visitors remember long after they've returned home. This isn't performed charm—it's the real thing, preserved and protected by people who understand what they have.

In Mistletoe Falls, Christmas isn't a season—it's a way of life. The town square's gazebo hosts summer concerts alongside winter caroling. Local shops maintain touches of holiday magic through every season, because visitors quickly learn that any time is the right time to discover this special place.

The waterfalls provide cooling mists in summer and ice sculptures in winter. Mountain trails offer wildflower walks in spring and dramatic vistas in fall. But somehow, every season here feels like it's building toward December's grand celebration.

www.ingramcontent.com/pod-product-compliance
Lightning Source LLC
Chambersburg PA
CBHW011850300726
48970CB00009B/2721